Tales
of the
New World

Tales of the New World

Sabina Murray

Black Cat
New York

Portions of this book have appeared in slightly different form in the
following publications: "Translation" in *The Yale Review*; "Paradise"
in *The New York Tyrant*; "Full Circle Thrice" in *The Common*;
"The Solace of Monsters" (as "Monsters") in *The Hartford Courant*;
"Balboa" in *Southwest Review*; "His Actual Mark" in *Southwest Review*;
"Periplus" in *Massachusetts Review*; and "Last Days" in *Drunken Boat*.

FIRST EDITION

Printed in the United States of America
Published simultaneously in Canada

ISBN: 978-0-8021-7083-5

Black Cat
a paperback original imprint of Grove/Atlantic, Inc.
841 Broadway
New York, NY 10003

Distributed by Publishers Group West

www.groveatlantic.com

11 12 13 14   10 9 8 7 6 5 4 3 2 1

For Valerie Martin

Contents

Tales
of the
New World

Fish

I.

The light filters through the window into the still, dark air. In the whirling dust, Mary can make out the fairies, winking, disappearing, toes pointed and wings tensed. She hears them whispering her name, tormenting her. "Mary, Mary," they say, and then are gone. There is nothing left to break the silence but the sluggish tick from the thick hall clock, its pendulum swung in lethargy, like a fat man swinging his pocket watch: and both pass time. Mother has bricked all the windows over but this one and the house presents its sleeping face to the street, where heels click by and dogs raise their legs to the rusted wrought-iron fence. Women's rustling skirts drag on the uneven paving stones and thieves, or so Mother says, stand in shadow stropping their knives, sucking on their yellow teeth, waiting and waiting for something worthwhile to come within arm's reach.

   When Mary was just a baby, she pitched into the river, her small body dragged to the bottom by her thick woolen clothes. She was not afraid. She stared upward through the icy, sluicing water and could make out the sun—a chilled orb of splintering white—shining beyond the surface. She remembers lifting up her hand to better sense herself falling away. Then there was the dirty young man, fishing her out. Back on land, he gasped in the cold, and the nurse wailed and wailed while the small crowd of people endeavored to remind her that all was well now. Look. There's the baby, wrapped in a coat. Take her home. Dry her off. Give the gasping, dirty young man (dirt like that takes more than a plunge in the river to rinse off) a coin.

"Mary," Mother has said, "even a sharp little thing like you can't remember so far back." But she does.

Light gives Mother headaches, aggravates the neurasthenia, but even Mother acknowledges the need to see. In the hallway, the unbricked window spills the last of the afternoon sun into the gloom and Mary reaches to it. If she puts the backs of her hands together, knuckles pressing, and swims her arms around, she can pretend she is beneath the water. She strokes her way through the air in the vestibule. The fairies, nasty things, are laughing now. "Look at her," she hears a sharp, little voice. "That's not swimming. This is air. This is air, and for air you need wings."

"Stupid fairy," says Mary. "What do you know?" She swims up the first two steps and swims down. "Stupid fairies," she says again. "I'm no little girl. I am a fish."

"Mary," comes her mother's voice, like a ghost floating through the hallway, down the stairs. "Mary."

Mother's voice is always weak, weak and urgent. Mary's heels clunk on the stairs, her vital footsteps sound on the bare boards as she walks quickly up the hall. She pauses at her mother's door, pale eyes wide and curious.

"Mary."

"Mother, I'm here."

"Why didn't you say? Come sit on my bed."

Mary sits at the foot of the bed, careful to avoid Mother's feet, careful not to make the covers pull too hard on her legs since they are always in pain, a pain that courses over them, like heat. Remember when you have the flu and everything feels tender, as if every tiny pain feeler in your body is waiting, alert, awake, ready to stick you? Remember that? Mother feels that way always. She's ill and hasn't left the house in years. She's ill and has bricked up the windows. She's ill and Father doesn't like to spend time in this house, with its sluggish ticking clocks and dust-filled air, with fairies sneering at you behind the moldering, threadbare curtains, and Mother all afire with her tiny pain-people who hide where no one can see them. Father has been gone for three years, since 1867, when Mary was five. He is traveling in the South Seas as the Earl of Pembroke's personal physician.

"Mary," says Mother, "fix the curtain. The light is coming in."

In the South Seas, the women walk about naked, their shining black skins right there for all to see. Father writes that the South Sea women are beautiful with big, white teeth, that the sun loves their black skin. If Mary were to walk about in the sun like that, she would sizzle up. The clean, cold air outside the house lays one bare. How could she show her arms to the sun?

"Mary, the curtain," says Mother. She groans softly as the pain-people do their work beneath her skin.

Mary fixes the curtain. She can hear Helen's footsteps up the stairs. It must be time for Mother's lunch. Hers will be waiting in the kitchen. Helen appears at the door with the tray, another weak broth that could not fortify anything. Mary can tell, just by smelling it, that this soup would not fill her up. Nothing will. She will not be satisfied today in this house where there is no noise unless she makes it, where there is no one to talk to, except for Helen, who has taken to enlisting her in the housework and is best avoided. Two of the fairies are sitting on the curtain rod, smirking at Mother and her soup.

"Ma'am," says Helen, "I must make an order with the butcher. What do you think? A nice beef roast, or leg of lamb?"

At the thought of real food, Mother blanches. "You decide, Helen. You know what the master likes." She struggles to sitting.

"So Father is coming home?" says Mary, her excitement carefully disguised. Mary arranges cushions at the small of her mother's back, which is how she likes it when she eats.

"Yes," says Mother, "and I suppose that means you will be spending all your time in the study, listening to his stories."

The fairies listen, their pointed ears picking up all the things that aren't quite said.

"And not here with you?" says Mary, her voice quavering slightly.

Helen fixes Mary with a frank, sympathetic look. "Cold ham for you, Miss, in the kitchen. And there's bread. And some of that cheese you liked so much yesterday."

"The same as yesterday," whispers one of the fairies. "And it didn't fill you up. You're hungry, always hungry, even when you sleep."

Father will be coming soon and Mary has volunteered to dust the banister. Poor Helen is doing her best with the potatoes and carrots, the mystifying asparagus, which she has chopped to the size of peas and means to stir about in eggs—a recipe given to her by Gladys-up-the-street, whose employers order such fancy fare. The leg of lamb is set on the counter—pink, vulnerable—not roasting yet because Father likes it rare and fresh from the oven. Mary knows Father would prefer rabbit, and that the asparagus were just boiled, but she doesn't want to hurt Helen's feelings. In the South Seas, sometimes he eats nothing but seeds and fruit. Sometimes he eats stringy mashed roots that taste like rubber, might even be rubber, he said once, and chicken and pork cooked with so much pepper that you have to eat it in your shirtsleeves, beads of sweat rolling past your ears.

"Mary," comes her mother's voice. "Mary."

"Mary, Mary," mimic the fairies, their voices tinny and malicious. "Mary."

She flicks her cloth at a fairy sitting Indian style on the newel post, and the fairy sneezes.

Mary makes the journey to her mother's room. "I'm here," she says.

"Do you hear that noise?" Mother asks.

There is a rhythmic thunk and thunk, and then it stops. Mary smiles at her mother, her eyebrows raised cheerfully. Then the thunk and thunk starts again.

"What is that?" says Mother, squinting, shuddering, as the pain-people dance along the muscle, along the bone.

"It's Charley. Helen sent him out because he was underfoot in the kitchen. I think he's throwing his India rubber ball against the side of the house."

Charley is home from school to see Father. Charley hates school. He finds it boring. Mary, of course, would love to go, but she is needed to take care of Mother, to walk up the stairs every half hour, to present her pale and cheerful face at the door.

"You must . . ." and Mother's eyes shut and she inhales sharply, so clearly in agony that it makes Mary wince.

"I'll make him stop," she says.

Mary rushes down the stairs. She doesn't want to hear the chorus of voices singing at her in evil glee, their flickering wings stirring the air. In the kitchen, Helen's broad back is hunched over the stove. At the sound of Mary's boots on the flagstones, she turns. Helen's face is flushed, shiny with sweat and steam. She's holding a spoon and her face is anguished.

"Oh, Mary," says Helen. "Come taste this."

It's the asparagus with egg. Mary dutifully takes the spoon in her mouth.

"Is it right?" asks Helen.

"I'm not sure. What's it supposed to taste like?"

Helen laughs. "Well, you didn't spit it out!" she says.

Mary pats Helen's arm. "I have to go and stop Charley. He's bothering Mother."

"Bothering Mother," Helen says, now back at the pots and stove, and quietly—to herself—but Mary hears. She knows that Helen will go on to tell the boiling potatoes and thickening gravy that this is no way for children to grow up. All this tiptoeing about. And the dark! Not good, not good at all.

"In the South Seas?" says Father. "In the South Seas? There are birds as big as you, Mary, with jeweled feathers, et cetera, et cetera, and people with bones in their noses, people who stick needles in their skin because it's how they pray, people tattooed from head to toe," Father dodges to one side to let Helen serve the soup, "from head to toe, Helen. Aren't you going to ask me how I know?"

"No, sir," she says, but her eyes are twinkling, "and I'll warn you that if you wish me to keep topping up your wineglass, you should say no more of it."

"Why don't the natives wear clothes?" asks Mary.

"Because it's hot."

"But you wear clothes."

"Of course."

"But don't you get hot?"

"Don't be stupid, Mary," says Charley. "Englishmen don't get hot."

"I should like to go see it myself." Mary knows the fairies can hear her, although they're quiet now, with Father sitting there and Charley stuffing his pointed face, but she doesn't care.

"What would you like to see?" asks Father.

Charley smiles maliciously, although he's not sure why. He can sense Mary's need and knows it is the stuff of humor.

"I should like," she says, straightening her shoulders, "I should very much like," she says, "to travel to Samoa."

"Oh, Mary," says Father, "Samoa's no place for a girl—"

"But you said, Father, that there are already girls—"

"Those aren't girls," says Charley, "they're natives." He sniggers. "They're natives, and you're an idiot."

Mary sets down her fork. She takes her linen napkin and carefully touches the corner of her mouth. "If Samoa is no place for girls," she says, "then I shall go to Africa."

"Africa?" says Father.

"Yes," she says, "like Burton."

She's past crying, never been one for tears, even though she can see pity in her father's eyes, thinks of it—that pathetic sympathy—welling into the room and drowning her. Father knows that she's lucky to make it out the front gate, and wonders—he's told her as much—if all this time without the company of girls her age, of anyone but Mother and Mother's pain, has made her eccentric. And dinner passes in this way, with the fairies beneath the table, tugging at her skirt and pinching her legs, but Mary does not let her discomfort show. She sits straight as ever, a pleasant smile (being pleasant is one form of defiance) on her narrow face.

"Is there any dessert?" says Charley.

"Helen's made a pudding," says Mary.

"Pudding? It'll be tough as leather. I wanted cake . . ."

And then Charley's mouth moving and moving, little beads of sweat appearing on his head, his middle part looking like a great tributary through the thin, brown, Kingsley curls, as if one could sail up it, past the crest of his head, or maybe paddle in a canoe. She would like to sail up rivers, back and back to the beginning of things.

"Mary," says Charley. "Mary!"

And Mary comes back to the present.

"Can't you hear Mother calling you?"

Helen, serving the pudding, jerks her chin up toward the ceiling. Directly above is Mother's room. "I'll go, Miss," she says.

"No, no," says Mary, "she's asking for me."

"Then I'll bring up your pudding."

Mother looks quite lovely sitting there, her skin pale as ivory, her hair spread out across the pillow. Her eyes are watery and icy blue.

"Here's Mary," Mother says.

Mary knows better than to ask her what she needs. Mother simply needs her. "Shall I read to you?" she says.

"Oh, I don't think so," says Mother. "Unless you really want to. What's on the shelf?"

Mary sees a few dusty books, two by Uncle Charles: *Westward Ho!* and *The Water-Babies*. "Let's read this," she says, holding up *Water-Babies*.

"Isn't that a bit young for you?" asks Mother.

"Nonsense!" says Mary. She's read it many times and each time finds something a little different: maybe it's her that's different, and the words on the page shift around, like leaves floating on the surface of water, to accommodate it. "It will be your bedtime story," says Mary.

Helen appears at the door with the pudding and some tea and sets the tray on the bedside table. "Anything for you, ma'am?" And Mother shakes her head.

"Sit here beside me," says Mother.

"I'll take off my boots," says Mary. "I'll get under the covers, and keep you warm."

The pudding isn't tough at all. It's heavenly, buttery, and the sauce is so rich with rum that Mary can feel her bones warming up. She flips through the first couple of pages and, after a swallow of tea, starts to read: "Once upon a time there was a little chimney-sweep, and his name was Tom. That is a short name, and you have heard it before, so you will not have much trouble in remembering it." Mary reads in a pleasant, animated way. Mother laughs here and there, even though the book is by Uncle Charles, who never approved of Mother, who married up and never visits. Mary reads past the bit about the mysterious Irishwoman, who turns out to be a fairy, and to the part where Tom gets lost in the interminable maze of flues and pops out of the fireplace to see the beautiful little girl asleep in her snowy sheets, her golden hair spread out on the pillow. "And looking round, he suddenly saw, standing close to him, a little, ugly, black, ragged figure, with bleared eyes and grinning white teeth. He turned on it angrily. What did such a little black ape want in that sweet young lady's room? And behold, it was—"

"It's him," cuts in a fairy.

Mary looks to Mother, and sure enough, her eyes are shut, her breathing slow, although she never sleeps deeply: the fairies wouldn't speak if she were awake. And there they all are, sitting in a neat little row on the brass bed rail, their wings twitching restlessly.

"He's dirty," the fairy continues, "and he's never noticed it before, and he's all ashamed and bursts into tears." There's some mean-hearted laughter.

Mary closes the book, although she keeps her place with her right index finger. "Keep reading," says another fairy.

"You've heard it so many times. Surely you don't need to hear more?"

"Spiteful Mary," say the fairies, because they *do* want to hear more, especially about the water fairies, who live in the rivers and travel far and wide, who aren't trapped like Mary in the dusty, somnolent house, where the only fresh air is blown in with Father on his rare visits. "Read more."

"Say 'please,'" says Mary.

The fairies shift on their little buttocks, point their toes. They hate saying "please," especially to Mary, but there's nothing else to be done, because fairies cannot read.

"Please Mary," they say, in a screechy little chorus. "Please read more."

Mary looks over to Mother, who shifts a little in her sleep, but seems peaceful.

"All right then," she says, "but you mustn't interrupt."

II.

It happens quite suddenly. First Father, in bed, because of what the rheumatic fever had wrought on his heart. And then, two and a half months later, Mother, although the stroke had done half death's work at that point. Sometimes, it was as if the stroke had wound Mother back to childhood, as if Mother were returning to her past instead of moving on. And then one day she was asleep not to wake up and the cycle was over—discomfortingly undramatic, a stingy, unfair end.

Mother's death should be easy for Mary. Everyone else seems relieved on her behalf, but her life's work—twenty-nine years of constant caretaking—is now ended and Mary, who has done little but look after Mother and concoct fantasies, finds herself with nothing but a few thwarted desires, all of them absurd. This amuses her, but she is also unsure of how to proceed.

Father's death is sad, but the house did not know him so well, and Mary has to remind herself that he is actually dead, not off with General Custer in America, not in Bora-Bora, not in New Zealand.

What is there to do but fold Mother's seldom-worn dresses for charity? There is a woman who runs some sort of mission in Calabar who, apparently, is always looking for clothing. But what Africans wear dresses like these, buttoned up to the chin, mutton-sleeved, and made of such tightly woven wool?

"Mary," say the fairies, "Mother's dead and you can go anywhere you want."

"She did not hold me prisoner," says Mary. "She loved me."

"What's the difference?" says a fairy, and the others laugh heartily.

"Stupid, stupid fairies!" says Mary.

"Stupid, stupid Mary!" they mimic. "Open the curtains! Let in the light!"

And Mary does just that, sending the fairies scrambling to the shadowy corners, their eyes squinting.

There is a great deal of packing to be done. Charley wants to make the move from the Cambridge house—so much better than the one in Kensington where Mary grew up—to London. Charley wants it and so Mary wants it, although she knows she'll miss her friends, hard-won friends that she earned with her unconventional learning—German, natural sciences in general, fish in particular, Latin, history. Anthropology. Plumbing. She is quite handy when armed with a wrench and confronted with a leak. All this awkwardness of a life spent alone with books and dark rooms and imagination has made her quite singular. This, and her cockney accent, inherited from Mother (who else was there to speak to but Mother and Helen?), make forays out of the house painful and uncomfortable, the shock of contact almost painful too. But refreshing. She does not really know how to converse, finds herself lecturing and telling jokes, and then realizing the other faces around her, smiling and unfamiliar. Face, face, face. The only face she's accustomed to is her own—in the mirror—and there's certainly no point wasting time meditating on that. When she's uncomfortable, she blushes and smiles. Her teeth are fine and even if the way she smiles—sincere and fast—seems a bit immature, it serves her well when it comes to making friends. But now they'll have to visit her in London.

The box of papers has a layer of dust on it, and when she disturbs the lid the dust rises up, making her sneeze and the fairies, sneeze, sneeze, sneeze, one after the other. What is this box? Is it Mother's? Father's? There are some papers inside. Father's birth certificate. Did one keep that? And if so, why? She has his death certificate, too. Not important, but still to be kept, although a life is what happens in between. And thinking of that, where are the crates and crates of Father's papers—his "books"— going to fit in the little apartment four flights up that Charley has chosen for their home? She rifles through the box's rustling, whispering contents. Father bought a horse at one point. And he sold it. Two sets of papers prove this. Here's a contract for *South Sea Bubbles* with Macmillan. The advance is almost embarrassingly low. Father never did make much money and Mary will have to be careful. But what would she do otherwise? Buy fashionable hats? Eat at fancy restaurants? This mourning black suits her fine. And here is Charley's birth certificate, January 12, 1866. And here is Mary's, October 13, 1862. And her parents' marriage certificate. Unlike Uncle Charles, Father had married down, to the daughter of a publican who rented rooms, whose rooms he rented. And here they are, bachelor George Kingsley, spinster Mary Bailey, October 9, 1862. What's this?

She reads the date again.

Married, October 9, 1862.

Yes. Between the two certificates a mere four days—evidence of little time and much import. Mary, not often stunned, is stunned. The fairies, sensing this, flit over. They hover around her ears, the high pitch of their wings buzzing.

"What, Mary?" they ask. "What, what, what?"

One of them steals the paper and flies up to the high corner of the room. The others follow. All the fairies snicker and giggle, because they know they've got something. But fairies cannot read.

"Keep it," says Mary.

"What does it say?" they ask, and then, in clear, tortured desperation, "Please Mary. What does it say?"

"It says," she replies, "that I belong nowhere, that I never have, and now that Mother and Father are gone, there's really nothing for me to do."

"It says all that?" asks a fairy, the clever one. She wrinkles her nose, unconvinced.

"Yes, yes it does. And you can keep it. It's of no use to me."

This might be the lowest time of Mary's life: alone, orphaned, and spinstered. She is an accident and her parents' marriage is not a bold, class-violating, romantic statement, but an accident as well—an attempt to remedy with poison. And this strange yet fiercely accurate truth: Mother did not give birth to her, but rather she birthed her mother: created that cradled, coddled, frightened thing by destroying what might have been love, what was surely impulsive, and that evidenced a different mother than Mary had ever known.

Mary, who excels at equations, wonders how many years she and Mother have paid each other for these acts of violation, but of course it is the same amount: twenty-nine years, Mary's first and her mother's final.

The fairies are lined up on the edge of the desk. They've grown bored of the birth certificate, as has Mary, and it's on the floor curled back into a tube, which makes it easy for Mary to kick it across the room.

"Who cares?" she says.

The fairies aren't sure how to respond. Which would bother Mary: if they cared or if they didn't? "It doesn't matter anyway, because I'm leaving."

The fairies mass and splinter off.

"I'm going on a boat," Mary says, now with conviction. "I'll be gone a long time."

"You'll never do it," say the fairies, challenging.

"Let me finish packing."

"We won't let you pack, wicked Mary, going off on a boat, when you should be cooking for Charley," says the clever fairy. "You should be home where people get sick and need you to hold their hand—"

"And change the sheets when they mess themselves!" says another, and they all giggle.

"Who's sick?" says Mary. "I'll tell you. I am. And Charley's off to China, gathering material to write a book."

"You know he won't," says the clever one, "he's even stupider than you are. He can't do anything."

"Nothing, nothing at all," chant the fairies.

"You're going to have to stay in England to cook and clean and fix his clothes and hold sick people's hands and listen to Charley complain and complain and complain—"

"What is this beautiful thing!" says Mary, standing at the closet door. "I think it's a piece of gold, the way it glitters."

The fairies come over immediately. "We don't see it," they say.

"Look, on the floor, beside my galoshes!"

And the fairies are in and Mary slams the door shut.

She can hear them flying around, trying to get out. Stupid fairies. They're not strong enough. Their wings sound like moths hitting a lampshade.

Why the Canary Islands? Because Mary needs a reason to travel and the only one that works for someone in her position— spinster—is that of tonic recuperation. And the Canary Islands are as close to West Africa as Mary can get without the possibilities for her health being reversed. And when Charley finally packed off for the Far East and no longer needed her to keep house for him, this was the easiest trip to plan. The quickest. The recuperative advantages are already being felt by Mary, who now strides across the deck, her mourning black as trim and functional as an umbrella, and who occasionally—with a "Good day, sir!"—will initiate conversation. On board this merchant steamer in all its industrial, dirt-generating practicality, Mary feels oddly herself. She has never felt this way before. What is this new ease?

She wonders who that creature is whose life she's been inhabiting for the last twenty-nine years.

James Batty, who trades along the Gold Coast, has been her friend on this journey. He's told her stories that have chilled her bones, told her stories that have made her laugh, just stopped short of finishing others off, which has made her curious. He thinks he's being charming, falls into charm easily, as some men do, but Mary's being provoked by a much larger spell, perhaps the spell cast by his spell. She will go to Africa. She will because she has nothing to lose. For one brief second she's euphoric—literally dizzied—by this: her intoxicating life of value to no one. Worthless translates quite narrowly as freedom.

"And there you are, blown about by the wind and not caring at all, Miss Kingsley," says Batty.

"Let it blow harder," she says. "I've never felt better in all my life!"

"What will you do when you reach the Canaries?" he pursues.

"Take a look around," she says. "Maybe go on to Africa. See what that's like."

"So it's a holiday, is it? You seem rather determined for one so—"

"Undetermined?" asks Mary. She laughs and juts out her chin, smiles fast and strong. "It had better be a holiday. I've no profession. If it's not a holiday, then it's nothing."

They stare out at the waves. If Mary were a different sort of person, this might be romantic: the two side by side, dark continent before her, stuffy England behind, thud of drums before her, rustling silk behind . . . and so on. But this is Mary and she does not care for that tender cage, nor any cage.

"Tell me about Africa," she says.

"The native songs and wild beasts, the fear and beauty—"

"Don't be silly," she says. "How can I equip myself to travel?"

"Alone?"

"There's no one else."

"Well then you can't, short of becoming a man."

"And if you were more liberal, what would be just short of becoming a man?"

"You're serious?"

"Don't doubt it."

"Well, then I'd have to say spirits."

"Spirits?"

"Alcohol."

Mary ponders this. "I don't understand how my drinking would solve anything, unless, so addled," here she has a twinkle in her eye, "I would be unable to make the journey."

"Should it cure this desire to travel alone, such intemperance would be beneficial. However, should you find yourself wandering about Africa unaccompanied, it would make sense to have a role, perhaps as trader." Batty takes a moment with some matches—it's windy, but he's skilled—and lights his pipe.

"I'll peddle anything but God," says Mary.

"Spirits and tobacco will open every door, where there are doors that open." Batty puffs efficiently, like a steamboat. "The missionaries will most certainly disapprove. But they will give you a good Christian burial."

"When I succumb to malaria."

"Or some unnamed fever."

"Or get eaten by a leopard."

"Or hostile natives."

There's an awkward silence because this joke flies parallel with the truth. Where does one laugh? Mary sets her boots upon the railing, looks out at the water. She nods with satisfaction. "Well then, spirits it will be."

Mary returns to her cabin. The door shuts with a loud creak and slam behind her. She holds her head firmly with one hand and pulls out the hat pin with the other. Her headache immediately subsides, but one must pin one's hat tightly in such wind, even if it does pull at the scalp.

She can now indulge in some private moments with Albert Günther's *Introduction to the Study of Fishes*. Even though she could not bring herself to share it with Batty, she has ambitions, an embarrassing thing for any woman, but particularly for her, who has a magpie's education from the College of Whatever Happened to Be on Father's Bookshelf: consisting of a whole lot of exploration, some antiquated naturalism, bully novels, introductory mechanics, and, the one thing that had actually involved a teacher, German—German to help Father in his writing, because he couldn't be bothered to learn it himself. She knows that French would be more helpful because it is what the natives speak. But surely French is not as useful as a native dialect, Fang, or some other, but who could teach her that? Fish it is. She'll learn about fish and maybe one day become a collector, take a river deep into the heart of it, on a canoe—her barque to sail into a new life. Just Mary and a number of naked natives and jars to fill with fish that people back in England have never seen. Preposterous. Impossible. Essential.

How is she to accomplish anything? This trip ticks to its end as she eagerly consumes it and then back to England, back to Charley, back to that other self as if she is a playing card—let's be frivolous, let's say the queen of spades—and this vivid woman will soon be flipped over to present only the tile pattern that is accepted and does not disturb. Think ahead. Plan. She feels England reeling her back: the shepherd's hook on the Vauxhall stage. She would stop herself from dreaming, from entertaining these ambitions, but she cannot stop. She is too far gone.

Mary wonders if she has recuperated, although—back in England—her lungs already feel half-collapsed. She's frank about her condition to herself and no one else is concerned. Then she remembers that she was supposedly recovering from grief, although she feels that she has walked back into that as one walks into a cold room. The air is dry and the dust heavy on all the surfaces. Good. English. Dust. In the apartment on Addison Road, everything has been shut tight for months. Mary wonders where dust comes from, what generates it. Charley has returned and no matter how Mary reminds herself of duty, reminds herself that she has a responsibility to keep house for him, reminds herself that he will leave again to leave her to leave, reminds herself that she does not mind, reminds herself that all this endless reminding is exhausting, useless activity, she has a hard time watching him sit.

"You hate him," whispers a fairy. Mary can feel the pressure of the tiny feet on her collar. "Admit it," they all chime in, "you wish he were dead."

"Nonsense," says Mary. The response comes fast and chipper with no thought, a rote response for a rote life. "I wish for no such thing."

Although sometimes she wishes she were dead. She feels herself to be an animated corpse performing the actions of her days, while her mind replays her voyage. Her forays to the African mainland return more vivid than the present rotation of gas-lit rooms and long faces and sun-starved mornings. She plays through one evening when, having spent four uneventful days strolling through the crooked streets and haphazard dwellings of Freetown, she boarded the boat for the Canaries and found her cabin occupied by four dead men. When she finally tracked down the captain, he was shaking from lack of alcohol, his face flushed and sweaty, his demeanor broadly macabre, comic even.

"How may I be of assistance, Miss Kingsley?" he asked.

"It's my cabin. It's occupied by four men."

"Are they bothering you?"

"Not exactly. Well yes, I mean, no." She felt herself smile and then repressed it. "They're all dead."

"West Africa," said the captain, philosophically, "White Man's Grave."

Mary, sensing the discussion over, returned to the deck and eventually fell asleep sitting down, her back against some wall, hoping all the while that she was truly shielded from scrutiny by a grouping of barrels. This was not her first night asleep with the elements: she'd been stranded overnight on a small volcanic island off Grand Canary and spent the night exposed to wind and pelting rain. All these things, these intolerables, are to her quite tolerable. Better the White Man's Grave than whatever twilit life London provides.

III.

Mary is journeying back to Africa aboard the *Lagos,* a trade steamer loaded up with bales of whatnot and boxes of such and such. Captain Murray likes to talk and talk and it seems he's never met such a good listener as Mary, who knows nothing of interest and draws all the information from him as if her inexperience causes a vacuum. Captain Murray has taught her that in Africa, everything comes out, nothing goes in, except "some rubbishy bolts of cloth, a few things necessary to keep the missions going, the stuff we need to build empire—rivets, tools, that sort of thing. Iron and irons, both to be born by the natives." An uncomfortable chuckle here, but a chuckle nonetheless. "Also, the stuff to draw its betters out: tobacco, whiskey, beads, which come back ivory, rubber, diamonds."

Mary is steering the boat, which Captain Murray has let her do of late, after some instruction. "Sounds like magic," she says.

"Magic?"

Mary nods, keeping her eyes on the horizon. "Goes in a glass bead, comes back a diamond."

"Well observed, Miss Kingsley," says Captain Murray. "You should see what Africa does to men."

Through the soles of her boots, Mary can feel the efforts of the engine, a shiver running up the length of her legs into her hands where she grips the wheel.

What has Africa done to her? Lured her with emptiness, promised nothing. What will she call forth from this dark continent? What will it call forth from her? She is armed with jars for collecting fish, bottles of whiskey and packages of tobacco for trading with the natives. She is light-headed with awareness of her lunacy. Mary, self-styled trader, has decided to penetrate the interior on foot. This comes to her in an inspired moment, while doing her accounting. There's enough to send a boat up the river, but nothing for the return. So leasing a boat is out, unless she wants to start rallying investors, and one look in the mirror is enough to discourage that.

She keeps her cards close to her chest. She has a hard time defending herself against accusations of foolishness and ignorance. Her only defense is that no information exists— nothing: no European has been into the interior, or if he has, is yet to reemerge—therefore there is nothing negative. This does not sound like a defense, rather an admission. The whole ordeal of defending herself to strangers is demeaning, yet her endless articulating of her rather vague mission, "to explore the interior," has given her a collateral resolve. And why shouldn't she be foolish? She's spent her time thus far being useful to others. Why not expire in the jungle? It would at least be a comic ending to one whose life has been in dire need of levity.

Monsieur Gotard, whose mission is two days in from Libreville, does not see the levity of a single woman blundering into the jungle. And the stock of liquor and tobacco, although quite good at explaining one's purpose with the natives, only adds to his dismay, as if, as he desperately tries to save the savage soul, Mary is out there, skirts dragging, bottles clinking, an odd emissary of corruption.

He fiddles with his waistcoat, a missing button recalled by a tassel of thread. "I do not think you will be able to afford your entourage, even if it is composed solely of natives," says Monsieur Gotard.

"Really?" says Mary. "How many do I need?"

"Well, for your trading stock, I would say four porters. And a guide, who must speak something of use—some French, for you have none—"

Mary takes the insult.

"—and Fang, if you wish to trade with the Fang, many of whom have never seen a white person, less a woman." He throws his hands up in despair.

"But if they've never seen any white people, how can I be more remarkable by virtue of my being a woman? I'll just be a very strange-looking trader."

"It is still impossible."

"Why? Surely I can afford five natives for a couple of weeks."

"Seven."

"Seven?"

"The hammock bearers. How do you propose to travel from one place to another? There are no rickshaws there, no carriages, no trains."

"I propose to go on my own two feet," says Mary, stifling laughter. She's been in a hammock, rocked to and fro like a baby. It was something she could have lived without experiencing. "And I'll trade for ivory and rubber, and if I run out of money, I'll come back."

"On your own two feet?" says Monsieur Gotard, each word inflected.

What does this man know, he who has never been into the interior? How can he possibly help, sitting there on the edge of the continent, with his hurricane lamps and quinine, with his well-meaning wife teaching the native women the best way to iron and starch when these people don't even wear clothes? And the native men, all taught the basics of mechanics, when there is very little machinery to be found and that, when it succumbs, as it often does to rust, mildew, rot, whatever, a general wasting away (much like the European population), can't be repaired anyway. And all of this sanctioned by Jesus Christ of the Middle East, by way of France.

But finally Monsieur Gotard does give her the porters and the guide, whose linguistic skills are comprised of a smattering of French, no English, and a lot of woolly, clapping native tongue that Mary soon begins to learn.

Into the liquid jungle she goes. The tree trunks rise smooth like bones and atop them rests the vegetation; beneath her feet is nothing but dirt and the sky is a distant, abstract thing—to look up is to see green—a thing one's memory situates in the past, like snow, and traffic, and miles of pavement giving way to more and smoke and industry and the whole clatter of Victorian, Regency, Tudor, medieval, Norman, Roman, Gaelic, English history that somehow has come to a point with her and her two leather boot tips edging into the West African forest. Absurd describes it quite well. Ripe with event does too. So does utterly stupid. So does magnificently brave. So does pleasantly pointless.

"Here village!" says her guide.

"Right," says Mary. She sees a narrow muddied track, a brightening at the edge of the trees. "So what do you think?"

"Talk," says her guide.

"Talk, with the chief?" Mary says. "I wonder what he has to trade? Or if he'd prefer liquor to tobacco? Do you know if he's friendly?"

"Talk," says her guide.

And Mary laughs because she talks all the time and to little purpose. "Thanks for the encouragement," she says.

The chief is happy that Mary has a few words of dialect, although she's not sure which one, but the words find their mark with him and soon she is sitting on a tree stump, her stash of tobacco at her feet. She does three hand-pumping gestures to indicate a good amount and waits for the chief to wave over his kinsmen, who will show her the equivalent in rubber. After the transactions have been completed to everyone's satisfaction, her hosts provide a meal: native "chop" of snails, some cassava, a palm oil stew that is so curious she wonders how and why the natives manage to produce the same taste over and over. And over. And over. For she has brought little of her own food, and of that she has only one tin of sardines, a precious four biscuits carried in a linen napkin like relics, and a bottle of Madeira, which she thinks keeps her blood hot and healthy. The village women stand and sit close by, and then even closer, and then are riffling through her hair, amazed at the spectacle of hairpins.

"I wish you wouldn't take those," Mary says.

A woman puts the hairpin in her mouth, bites it, bends it a little. She pokes it into her hair, making her friends laugh.

"But of course you will," says Mary. "And that's fine in the end. I'm a mess, always was. At least now there's no one to see me."

This last bit strikes Mary as ironic because, in truth, she's never been around so many people in all her life. Day in and day out she marches through the jungle with her companions. She falls in mud up to her knees and they laugh and she laughs too. And now she's the center of attention. "Do you ever cook with salt?" she asks.

And the chief responds with something that is translated into something that has the word *mange* or something like it thrown in, and Mary is at least pleased with the fact that they are both talking about food. Then someone says something, and someone says something else, and everyone bursts out laughing. Mary does too, and her usual dark joke, "Is this when they eat me?" flickers across her mind.

But they don't eat her. The chief gives Mary his hut to sleep in, which, when a heaving downpour begins about the village, is almost a hundred percent waterproof. The thunderous rain is a relief: it washes away the insects, discourages the villagers who were eagerly peering through the gaps in the hut walls, generously widening them with sticks to accommodate all the others who wished to see Mary: this gin-wielding, skirt-wearing apparition. She begins unlacing her boots, thinking the relentless pounding of the rain is its own kind of silence. But what is that smell? Not like anything she's ever experienced, and, apprehensively, she begins to follow it about and to its origins with hesitant little sniffs. There's something hanging from the rafters, a flat basket suspended in a triangulation of twisted fibers. It's too high for her to see into: there's no furniture to speak of, just the cot, and she knows it won't support her weight. She reaches for her hat and her walking stick. "This should do it," Mary says. With a resolute jab, she upsets the basket, knocking its contents into her hat.

Mary will write about this incident in *Travels in West Africa,* how she peered into her hat and saw a series of little bags, each tied with string. The smell was formidable. She jerked her head back, nearly upsetting what the hat contained. Bravely, she untied each little bag and found—with more wonder than dismay—human fingers, toes, and an ear. She will stand before crowds of a hundred people, more than that, learned men, and tell them how she put each object back in each bag and returned it to its proper place. She will fill letters with stories: one time she entered a village where human livers and lungs were on spikes at its perimeter, believed to be "witches" existing within now deceased witch doctors: fishing in a canoe, she pulled in an enormous catfish, and as she and her companions struggled to remove it—it was nearly as big as her!—she found herself pitched out of the canoe and sinking quickly, her long skirts and woolens and other things pulling her down: she tells of how a witch doctor came knocking in the middle of the night and how she followed him to a distant village and of the woman that she cured with European medicine, her juju, at which she is now a skilled practitioner, an able nurse. She holds court in the tiny Addison Road flat, now bursting with artifacts and relics, Mvungu!—a three-foot statue that greets visitors at the door, frightening with his fearful visage, his repulsive smell that Mary was told is the result of his having been daubed in human blood.

To be truthful, Mary finds London frightening. Through the icy rain spattering against her window, she can make out the specter-like hansom cabs, the beleaguered horses, a grimy coal worker shoveling away, hacking up bacterial phlegm with his ruined lungs. The cold depresses her, and Charley, in his moth-eaten sweater and carpet slippers, padding around all day, pronouncing various important things: snobberies, opinions, needs, and the like—Charley who will not leave her alone!—who sees no need to get a job or bother himself with bills and when he feels like it, regardless of expense, will go to visit friends in other places, spilling coins around with no thought to where they come from. But Mary puts up with this because she wants him gone. She's writing a book, *The Bights of Benin,* to finance her next trip to Africa, which she plans to make as soon as Charley does whatever it is that attracts him, whenever he decides to, whenever the pull of the unknown and purpose and embarrassment overpower the ennui that keeps him close by, that occasionally manifests itself in a bad cold, but usually achieves form in Charley's endless peering over Mary's shoulder.

What could be so important as to take all her time? Charley is relieved when relatives fall ill and Mary has to go nurse them. That's what she should be doing, after all. He cannot bear Mary being in Africa even when he's overseas. He cannot bear her being out of the house. Sometimes Mary wonders if he returns home from his trips abroad to recall her, to remind her that her first duty is to care for him and that all her books and lectures and argumentative friends magically disappear in a puff of smoke if he but desires a cup of tea.

Arthur, the teaboy from downstairs, has agreed to help Mary carry the jars, which have been cluttering her apartment ever since her return. It's Arthur's day off, but he's taken some care with his appearance. The fierce cowlick that usually springs up right at the back of his head has been tamed with something like lard, and he's smiling at her and at the adventure of taking off to the British Museum. Arthur sees Mary smoking at her back window when he takes out the garbage. He knows he's not supposed to look, but how could he not notice the spectacle of Miss Kingsley puffing into the chill Victorian air—Miss Kingsley who went off to Africa alone. Miss Kingsley who ate a man!

"Coach is out front, Miss Kingsley," he says.

"Thanks for fetching it," Mary replies. "Now the real work begins."

There are four crates and even though, as expressly instructed, Arthur has gotten a coach rather than a hansom, it's still going to be a bit of a squeeze, even with Arthur sitting up top with the driver. And then she's carrying the crates down the narrow stairs, tilted in her heeled boots, fairly toppling down upon the crate and the boy, who is cheerfully going backward and taking the majority of the weight. Jars of fish in chemicals are not light.

"Miss Kingsley," says Arthur, "can't Mr. Kingsley help you with this?"

"What? Charley?" says Mary, her cockney accent achieving a comfortable flair with the teaboy. "You're better off with me. Besides, he's in Oxford or Dover or some place."

As Arthur unpacks the last of the crates, which he has to do if Mary is to fit in the coach, she takes a minute to smooth her hair in the window's reflection. And to fix her hat, an odd little hair in the window's reflection. And to fix her hat, an odd little thing with antennae springing from it—her friend Violet Roy thought it fetching—but Mary now thinks it makes her look like an insect. She has to laugh. But it's too late to do anything about it. Albert Günther, the preeminent fish expert, has agreed to look at her collection. His book *Study of Fishes* has been her bible, and Uncle Charles has set up this meeting at the insistence of cousin Rose.

Mary squeezes herself onto the seat between some neatly balanced jars. Arthur hands her a particularly large one in which a snake floats, with diminished menace, in brine.

"Are you all right in there?" asks Arthur.

"I'll be fine," she says. "Let's go!"

The trip is bumpy and long, thankfully without event, but standing in front of the British Museum, its columns and marble evoking millennia of civilization that starts in Greece yet ends in England, Mary has a desire to flee back to her jungle. Günther. What is she thinking? She'd do anything right now to be back where she's comfortable, marching through the mud with her naked cannibals.

"Miss Kingsley," says Arthur, "this is Mr. Günther's secretary."

She sees a thin young man, no taller than she, peering at her through some wire spectacles. "Miss Kingsley, I am Mister Ogilvie. Pleased," he says, although he looks anything but, "to meet you."

"Right," says Mary. She gets out of the cab and, her arms embraced around the snake, begins to follow the secretary up the front steps and into the building.

"Yes, yes of course I do," says Mary.

"It's just that you're carrying a snake."

"I'm aware of that," she says, now flustered. "I caught this snake myself," she says, "with a forked stick." Is she bragging now? She feels the blood rise into her face. "It's a poisonous snake and the natives said it was quite rare."

"I see," says the secretary. He opens the door to an office—tidy and silent—and points her in the direction of an uncomfortable-looking chair. "Please wait here, Miss Kingsley. I'll find some people to help your boy bring in the rest of your . . . collection."

"I appreciate that," says Mary.

She sits in the stiff chair with the snake in her lap hearing muffled voices from down the hallway, a laugh that is quickly silenced. The ceiling is high, and in the upper windows Mary sees the pigeons crowding outside, hears their soothing burble and croo. She taps her boots on the floor in an anxious little drumbeat. The dust circles through the light. Mary wonders if this is what most people feel in church: small, frightened, awed.

"He's left you out here, has he?" comes a voice.

"Mr. Günther!" says Mary, struggling out of her seat, which is hard, for the seat has no arms and her jar weighs over twenty pounds.

"Let me help you with your snake."

Günther looks at the snake. "Miss Kingsley, what is this?"

"I have no idea," says Mary.

"Neither do I." Günther has a twinkle in his eye. Not knowing might mean she's found something new. Not knowing, to Günther, is a good thing.

Later, Arthur and the others bring in the rest of the jars, unpack crates, and set each specimen upon the long table.

"You go with guides?" asks Günther, arranging a jar into a different grouping.

"I do when I need to, but I'm good at handling a canoe." Why does she sound like a child? "As good as any African at this point. Of course, it took me a while to get the hang of it. I got fished out half-drowned, natives had a good laugh, that sort of thing." Why does she keep prattling on? "My favorite thing is to paddle around in the middle of the night when the moon is full." Nerves, is it? Or maybe she's just happy.

"Alone?" asks Günther.

"Well, no one else wants to go, not at that time. Besides, everyone's asleep."

"It must be very quiet."

"No, not with the frogs," says Mary. "The frogs are almost deafening, but it is peaceful."

Günther smiles at her. "You need better equipment." He holds up an old gin bottle with a curious-looking tadpole in it as evidence of this. "I will provide it for you the next time you go."

Mary finds herself suddenly speechless and, horrified, thinks she might start to cry.

"That's very kind of you," says Mary, "to do that for me."

"Not for you," says Günther. "For science."

The jumper goes into the trunk and then she takes it out and then she puts it in again. It's the kind sailors wear to keep out the damp and cold, a tight-knit wool thing that you pull over your head. Mary hasn't had a garment quite like it since she was small—encouraged to wear the jumpers that Charley had worn out in the elbows, since he couldn't wear such things at school and there was no one to care, should she.

"You'll look stupid in that," say the fairies. "Mary, hairy Mary, hairy Mary," they sing.

It's been two days since she's seen them. Mary thinks they're avoiding her, worried about the upcoming trip.

"Might come in handy," says Mary. "And what looks more stupid than being unprepared?"

"Smart Mary," says the clever fairy. "Spinster Mary," she says, lisping it out in the nastiest way. "Spinster Mary says things like that, clever things like," and here in falsetto, "'What looks more stupid than being unprepared?'"

There's a chorus of giggles and snickers and more richly insulting laughter.

Mary wonders where the fairies learned such a word. From Charley, no doubt. Charley, with his false sympathy, who said, just yesterday, as the last of Günther's jars arrived— threatened, he was, by Mary's sense of purpose—"Don't worry, Mary. It's not easy being a spinster, but whatever happens, you'll always have a place with me." And Mary read the "whatever happens" to include the following possibilities: Charley's never leaving the house, Charley's marrying some incompetent woman who needs Mary as her servant, Charley's falling ill, paralyzed, incontinent, or bored. This need on Charley's part will always justify her existence, as does an aunt developing the flu, as does anything that needs doing that no one else wants to do. London runs on an army of spinsters administering to everyone's needs: silent, solicitous, free of charge, and bitter.

"Are you finished?" she says, addressing the top of the wardrobe, where the fairies crowd a corner, sitting like gargoyles.

"Spinster," says the clever one.

"You don't even know what a spinster is," says Mary. They can stay if they want. She doesn't need them, not in Africa, where the land is alive and the air so full with the clack-song of frogs, crash and howl of monkeys, high-pitched whining insects, the succulent drip and drip of the jungle moving upward, outward, tearing at whatever England or Europe or Christianity tries to put there. "Stay then," says Mary, and she slams the trunk lid shut.

IV.

"The poor man arrives at the settlement and of course he expects to be met by the agent, who is the only other white man for a hundred miles. He waits at the pier for some time, and then finds a native with a little French to take him up to the agent's house. When he gets there, the servants are milling about in the most awkward way. And the subagent doesn't know what to make of it. His first time to Africa." Lady MacDonald takes her parasol and, with one well-delivered smack, kills a cockroach crawling on the wall. "He waits on the verandah for almost an hour and no one so much as offers him a glass of water—"

"Probably a good thing, Lady MacDonald," says Cowper.

"Might have been," she says. "All the while, there's this horrible smell coming from somewhere in the agent's house." Here Lady MacDonald raises an eyebrow and sets her chin in a knowing way. "He manages to get one of the servants to take him in, following the smell and a curious buzzing sound through the corridors, further and further, and all the while terrified of what he might find. He reaches the bedroom." Here Lady MacDonald pauses. She rests one gloved hand upon the other, leaning onto her parasol, now balanced on the deck.

"And there is the agent, or what's left of him, menaced by several rats and black with flies. Lord knows how long he'd been lying there. And the poor subagent, well, it takes him a while to recover."

"I heard he killed himself," says Cowper, a subagent himself.

"Nonsense," says Lady MacDonald. "Back to England he went, back to the countryside, but his mind was never right."

"I heard," says Cowper, "he'd never even been to London before that trip out to the Bights."

"That may be true, sir," says Lady MacDonald.

"Horrible place, that, Miss Kingsley," says Cowper. "The Bights of Benin. I'd stay away."

"Too late for that," says Mary. "I've already been there."

"And written a book about it," adds Lady MacDonald.

"Quite accomplished, aren't you?" says Cowper.

It sounds like an insult.

Cowper gets up to light his pipe, leaning casually on the rail. "There's Calabar, ladies," he says.

"Really?" says Lady MacDonald. "I can't make it out at all."

"But can't you feel it?" says Mary. "I can feel the land. It's as if the sea is giving up on you." There's an awkward silence.

Cowper lifts his hat in some sort of farewell gesture, as if he's given up on them.

"Right you are, Miss," he says. "I'll see you at the pier."

Lady MacDonald smiles. Mary can tell she's waiting for Cowper to leave. "We won't see him at the pier," she whispers. "He'll be off with some native girls before we've even found porters."

Lady MacDonald has been Mary's traveling companion ever since she boarded the *Batanga* in Liverpool several weeks ago. Sir Claude MacDonald is governing the Niger Coast Protectorate and as such is an important ally for Mary, not only in this part of the world but back in London. And Mary and Lady MacDonald have become great friends.

"I don't mean to alarm you, Mary. I know how you feel about parties, but there will be some sort of to-do when we arrive."

"Oh, I hope I'm not so fragile as all that," says Mary, the nervousness plain in her voice.

"Gird yourself, Mary," says Lady MacDonald. "You might find a couple people of interest."

Mary takes particular care with her appearance. She makes sure that her hair is as severely parted as possible, that her dress has the highest collar, the plainest wool, although she's heard from friends—her friends know everything—that there are certain elements who find such a strident appearance appealing, as if her conservative dress might be stripped off to reveal a tender center. As if she were a nut. Yes, she was innocent once, but no more. She has heard men with women, seen their naked bodies, smelled an occasional earthy odor—animal scent, but human nonetheless—that must exist in England, although well hidden. Not like in fleshy Africa, where abomination abounds, or is accepted: where abomination is not even abomination. She knows the men who end up in Calabar: agents, subagents, missionaries, traders, and criminals. She knows that there are women even less appealing than she: older, uglier, fatter, more religious, less humorous, eager. She must not indulge in any immoral behavior—not that she cares at all, she doesn't even have Christianity to blame for her blamelessness—to avoid attracting negative attention to herself that might limit her freedom. Although the prospect of meeting some handsome trader or sea captain does have an unmistakable attractiveness, however unlikely.

"Straight to the wine, Mary," she advises herself in the mirror, "then off to a corner with some dull lady who won't notice if you're talking nonsense."

That is her intention, but instead of the dull lady, she finds herself seated next to an Irishman of civil nature, formerly of Stanley's Volunteers, and Sir Claude MacDonald's trusted employee whom, to use Sir Claude's wording, he is "devastated to lose to some odd sort of consular appointment in Lourenço Marques."

The Irishman is appreciative of this display of admiration, but withholding.

Sir Claude says, "Roddie, I still don't know why you're going."

To which the man, who was introduced to Mary as Mr. Casement, replies, "It is government business, the precise nature of which will be determined when I arrive in Portuguese West Africa."

Mary raises an eyebrow. Holds his cards close to his chest, this one does. She wonders what Mr. Casement is hiding. His manners, unlike many at Sir Claude's table, are impeccable. Although she's not sure where the conversation's gone: agents, sub-agents, traders, King Leopold, Niger to the north, Cape Town to the south, and Rhodes all over the place, making some very rich, and others—like Mr. Casement and Sir Claude—uneasy. But she's lost at this point and hopes no one asks her opinion. After four glasses of wine, Mary is feeling somewhat foggy. She sits in a cloud of addled self-consciousness wishing to be invisible, or miraculously transported up to her room.

"You're very quiet, Mary," says Lady MacDonald.

"Tired is all," she says. "Bit of fresh air would perk me right up."

Dinner has, thankfully, ended, and people are drifting out onto the wide verandahs where a stiff, heart-lifting wind comes off the sea. For a moment Mary stands there alone. She has some ideas of how she will spend her time, going where no one else has been, she thinks, up the Ogowé, across Fang lands, down the Rembwe. Of course people, even natives, are telling her that it can't be done, but failing in the attempt, won't that be worthy knowledge? She imagines her obituary. "They said it couldn't be done and they were right!"

"The intrepid explorer," says Mr. Casement. He stands a polite distance away and lights a cigarette.

"Well, I don't know if I've earned the title." Mary smiles. "I'm lost half the time."

"That's what explorers do," says Mr. Casement.

Mary finds herself staring at the cigarette burning seductively in his hand.

"Is this bothering you?" he says, holding the cigarette up.

Mary shakes her head vigorously.

"Or perhaps . . ." He fishes into his pocket for his case. "You want one yourself."

"I do," says Mary, "but I don't think I should."

"Nonsense." He extends his cigarette case.

Mary takes the cigarette, holding it gingerly. "Keep an eye out for me," she says. She takes a light. "I have to keep my nose clean, steer clear of suffragettes and trousers and the like."

"Yet you seek the company of cannibals?" says Mr. Casement, amused.

"Girl's got to have some fun." A servant comes by with a tray of drinks and Mary takes one, as does Mr. Casement.

"Cheers, sir, to us and to Africa."

"Cheers!" he says, and they clink glasses and drink.

Mary regards him obliquely. "Mr. Casement."

"Miss Kingsley."

"Do you ever wonder how long you'll live? I mean, how long do you think either of us will survive?"

"Survive?" Mr. Casement thinks, shrugs. "Who knows? After all, shouldn't both of us be dead already?"

Mary is on a boat journeying to the island of Fernando Po with Lady MacDonald and Sir Claude, along with an unfortunate retinue of servants in stiff white linen, who appear at her elbow at odd junctures, startling her with their presence.

"Lovely man, that Roger Casement," says Lady MacDonald. "What were you talking about for so long?"

"Books mostly," says Mary. She's lying, but any in-depth talk of native culture, Mary's so-called fetish, makes Lady MacDonald's eyes glaze over. "Although I haven't read anything next to him. He likes modern people."

"Who does he read?"

"He likes Conrad, he says he met him a couple of years back. I think the book has 'folly' in the title. Do you know it?"

"No, can't say I do."

"And he reads a whole lot of poetry, about which I know even less—if one can know less than nothing."

"Reserved, isn't he?" poses Lady MacDonald. "Reserved, and rather handsome, don't you think?"

Mary hears a weird voice echo in her head. It says, "Handsome is as handsome does." She does not know where she's heard this and suppresses it, keeping the odd sentiment to herself, thinking of it as spoken by her inner spinster, another clever thing—an adage to keep real life at bay—just dying to come out and taint her with its worn and charmless wit.

Months later, in the throws of a hallucination, she will hear this refrain echoing in her head. *Handsome is as handsome does.* Only now it is in the voice of the clever fairy, although the fairy is back in England, with all those other voices chorusing in her head—Charley's, cousin Rose's, Violet Roy's, Arthur from downstairs, Günther, even Helen, who has been dead from tuberculosis these last ten years. And all of them are singing it together, their faces rising at the side of the canoe, then floating off, and coming back. Is she on the water? No. Then why is she rocking? She remembers in a shock of clarity that her fever's back—malaria, no doubt—and that she's being born upon the shoulders of her men. The jungle roof lies dense above her, the light splintering through: she remembers her near-drowning as a child, the surface receding, her hand reaching up, and so she reaches her hand up again. For one moment it is the hand of a baby, then a woman's, and the difference between the two causes an ache of nostalgia—and what is she longing for? Perhaps she is a fish, swimming and swimming through the air that is not quite air, more liquid. She remembers her father talking of Venice—of all places—which he'd visited on the way back from somewhere more typical. And he's speaking to her now, although he's young—Mary's age. ". . . as if the air was watery rather than gaseous and the swallows swooping and dipping seemed more minnows of the sky than birds. If I let my thoughts wander, it was possible to imagine the earth turned upside down, the water the air, the air the water, as if the act of diving into a canal would stun me into wakefulness, dispel the dreamy reality of being under the liquid spell of where I stood, feet placed upon a marble bridge. You could hypnotize yourself, Mary, into believing the opposite of what was true, and the shock that it had all been just a construct of your mind was sadness itself." Then there is Helen kneading the bread, pushing her hair off her forehead, leaving flour on her nose. "You were four at the time, and your Uncle Henry asked you what you wanted to be when you grew up. First he asked your cousin Rose, and she said a lady. And then he asked you. And you know what you said? You said you wanted to be a fish!" Helen laughs and laughs—all that is left of her, as if she's wasted in stages, from her original plumpness down to the tubercular wraith that Mary visited in the public hospital, and now to this: a sound. And then Lady MacDonald is there, as she was on the terrace of the house in Fernando Po. "Don't mind me if I don't join you, although a walk would do me good. Not that fear is something *you* know, Mary, but the natives *here* are absolutely harmless, not through some sort of *virtue,* because there's little of that to be found on the island. But we Europeans benefit from a sort of disregard. The natives think we're fish. That's why we're pale. That's why we cover up. Fish, all of us, and *queer* fish at that." Mary wants to swim and struggles to reach the water. Suddenly there's a chorus of native tongue, too natural, almost unnatural. A pair of strong black hands pushes her back into the canoe and she feels her bier being lowered.

"Take me back to the water," she says. And then, "*L'eau. L'eau.*" They give her a flask, not comprehending her wish.

"Take me!" she says to one black face. Who is he? How does she know that his name is M'bo? "Go! Go!"

M'bo consults with the others. "This place," he says, which Mary knows to mean he intends for her to stay. His face gets a distracted look, as if someone is talking about him some distance off and he is trying to eavesdrop. This is politeness from these Igalwa natives. They would like to accommodate, but if that is not the order, they make it seem as though the discourtesy were an absentminded mistake. On the ground, Mary no longer wishes to swim in the water. She has remembered who she is, where she is. She must rest before the journey up the Ogowé continues. The natives all sit down, as if sensing this sudden harmony that now exists among them.

In the night, her dreams are thick and tainted with reality. She remembers Monsieur Gacon's warning: "Of course, we can find no Fang men to go with you into Fang territory. These are *lower* river Fang, and they know better than anyone that the *upper* river Fang would as soon make dinner of you as call you cousin. I have a couple of Igalwa men who don't know any better, who know a few words of English, although more French, of course. And do not doubt that it is a great sacrifice, my sending them with you, because I'll probably never get them back."

As M. Gacon stood by the edge of the river, the sending-off a protracted affair since the current was strong and progress slow, even with all four men struggling against it, she remembered the words of her old friend Captain Murray. "To know the mind of the African? Miss Kingsley, I think such a thing impossible. They are not only a mystery to the European, but to themselves. I have known an African to be laughing of an afternoon, and that evening to have hanged himself. Life means little to them, and the best advice that I can give to you is not to throw in your lot with a bunch of Africans. This too is suicide." And M. Gacon's concerned face still visible on the riverbank, as if her crew were rowing not only upriver, but against time itself, causing it to stall. It's not too late to turn back, you silly woman, she told herself, and then, as if by miracle, they were past the current, and M. Gacon and the dregs of Europe were lost behind the bend as Mary was freed to the wilderness.

The fever retreats, leaving Mary jittery, shocked at the constant stimulus of life—the ferocity of sensation. There is no reason to turn back. Her intention is to canoe up the Ogowé, traverse through Fang land that has never before been penetrated, and catch the current back down the Rembwe and into Gabon. She has told her supporters and detractors (these more numerous and vocal than the former) that it is all about fish: better fish here, rarer fish, than in other places. Such passionate adherence to the study of fish is almost stranger than having no purpose for her journey. Once this filled her with gloom—to be thought a fool—but now the glorious stupidity of it all has set in. She means to write a memoir, *Log of a Light-Hearted Lunatic,* about this trip, should she make it back. The very frogs seem to question her fate, pounding "she did, she didn't, she did, she didn't" into the night air; above it all the leaves, stirred by wind, whisper "suicide, suicide." She was assured, farther downriver, that the inhabitants of this Fang village would doubtless eat them all. And again, she has survived, waving some tobacco in front of her as a talisman to ward off evil. Now, she is guarding the stores while her men, who have long outlived their life expectancy in Fang land, get some food, palm oil stew, which she can identify by smell. Tonight she will treat herself to a biscuit and a belt of Madeira to offset the discomfort of having to sleep in her boots. The day's marching has caused her feet to swell and she knows, from experience, that should she remove her boots now, the effort of returning them to her feet tomorrow will be extreme and painful.

M'bo is walking up to her, smiling. She smiles back. "So how are these Fang? What do they have?"

"Rubber," he says. He shrugs. "A little ivory."

"What do they want?"

"Tobacco," he says. "A little gin." M'bo has maybe thirty words in English, but in this conversation, oft-repeated, he achieves an almost casual fluency.

"You know the drill," says Mary. "We hold back on the gin and push the tobacco."

"The gin is heavy, sar," he says.

"Yes, but the tobacco gets moldy, and if we have it much longer, I might smoke it all myself."

M'bo laughs. "Very good."

"I'll go," says Mary. "You wait with the things. How's the food?"

"Oh, delicious," he says. "Many flavors, all fine."

"I can tell you're lying," Mary says. "I can tell, and I don't care."

She's happy here, among the Fang. She finds them beautiful, their bodies hairless, smooth and muscled. She knows her appearance here is anomalous in the extreme. Once, with Helen, she attended a traveling magic show. At some point there was an explosion onstage—an effect of gunpowder laced over with red dust—and from it stepped a man in a wizard costume, Merlin himself, he claimed. Of course, Mary believed it. For all she knows, it was Merlin. Stranger things have happened, are happening, and she's taken to entering the various villages by stating, "Here's Mary," something her mother would say when she appeared at the bedroom door, and Helen, when she showed up hungry in the kitchen. Here's Mary! Here I am! Don't go to any bother on my account. Oh, horribly funny. She likes the Fang villagers' startled faces, the blind grasping for a spear that won't, as is soon revealed, be necessary. Here she's looked at all the time, unlike in London, where she disappears into sofas, wallpaper, wainscoting, drapery, like some sort of spinster chameleon. Here's Mary, she thinks, here I am, as if she has been waiting for herself in the jungle all these years—waiting to be found, her spirit flitting through the endless twilight of the forest, the pounding rain, here and there through the mangrove swamps where the trees look like so many women lifting their skirts from the water (head cocked to the left) or the arched fingers of a skilled pianist about to run the length of the keys (head cocked to the right), darting back and forth across the water, watching the crocodiles break the surface—their musky smell rising first. Here I am, she thinks. Pleased to make my acquaintance.

Falling asleep in her hut of bark and dried vines, the tiny embers of the bush lights gleaming like fiery eyes at the perimeter and the whole washed over in a gauzy haze by the chintz curtain of her mosquito bar, anything seems possible, everything impossible, nothing the same at all. The rattling rage of the jungle night sounds loud, louder still; it's like being trapped in a witch doctor's drum. Yet she's peaceful. Mary finds the constant threat of death a comfort, the comfort of life waiting for her in England a torment. Time for the belt of Madeira. Time to break into the stores of tobacco. Take time while it's still yours.

V.

Tell it funny, she reminds herself, although it wasn't funny at all at the time. The swamp stretched out as far as she could see and the hopelessness that engulfed her—nothing romantic about it—can still produce a chill. She writes, "It stretched away in all directions, a great sheet of filthy water . . ." But the plants were pretty, prettier still for insisting themselves into this great sewer—"out of which sprang gorgeous marsh plants, in islands, great banks of screw pine . . . with their lovely fronds reflected back by the still, mirror-like water." There's something for the English public. Never mind that the screw pine looses its spiked tendrils beneath the surface, ready to snare you as you pass. She knows the women will gasp at her "courage," which they "admire." Hah, she says, remembering the reaction of one dowager. Not yet in print, the story was extracted from her at a gathering for women of a certain class, where she'd been trotted out, a novelty, for entertainment. And of course they wanted to know what she wore. Was this their one question? One goes to the opera: What did you wear? One goes to the jungle: What did you wear?

"I see no reason to dress differently in Africa than I would here. Indeed, I was once saved by my dress."

"Saved?" asked the chorus of powdery, lavender faces, the rose-water reek wafting over the smell of perspiration smothered in wool.

"Yes. We had marched up the Ogowé and were crossing uncharted lands before reaching the Rembwe. I was leading my men through the jungle and there was a clearing, and I stepped into it, and all of a sudden the earth gives out beneath me. And I'm stuck in a hunting pit, stretched out over nine ebony spears. The only thing that saved me was my skirt. Had I been dressed like a man, I would not have fared so well. One of my men asked, 'You kill?' and I said, 'Not much.' And that, as far as I'm concerned, ends the discussion of my attire."

Oh, it was a good story and gave rise to much laughter and surprise, but also questions. Who, after all, had fished her out of the pit? Black hands are always rescuing her, dragging her from the water, righting her as she navigates a native two-trunk bridge. Black bodies are always falling against her in canoes, heaving in sleep beside the fire (beside Mary!) when the day's march has ended. She wonders how they're faring now, freed from her service, M'bo, and the other Igalwa, and the Fang who joined them, whose names she never learned: Flannel Shirt, Pagan, Silent. As long as they stay in the Congo Française, they should be fine, but the traditional rubber-collecting paths all pass through the Belgian Congo, a place to which she swears she will never return because of the treatment of the natives. Although she was there for two days, she cannot remember the look of Leopoldville, just the smell of blood and refuse coming from a column of workers, chained, who were sitting in the blazing heat when it would have been just as easy to give them shade. There were flies crawling over the lips of one man, who, although alive, did not seem to notice.

In the Congo Française, her men might be picked off by a leopard or crocodile, flattened by a hippo or elephant. One man says he witnessed his uncle's brains bashed out by a gorilla that was swinging him by the ankles into a tree. A parasite might swim into some tender orifice and eat its way out. Her natives might be stolen by a neighboring tribe while out gathering rubber, have their rubber taken, and then be eaten in retribution for some cousin who was eaten in retribution for some uncle who was eaten in retribution for someone's father, all picked off while gathering rubber. Despite all that—minor, traditional dangers—the Congo Française is safety itself compared to what King Leopold of the Belgians has to offer: a little "civilization" just to the south.

But enough procrastination.

Mary looks back to the page. How to tell of the swamp and make it funny?

It's not one of those times when she thought she might die: those at least get the pulse going and blood hot. The swamp had overwhelmed with enervation. The sheer stillness and gloom infected her, reduced her will, made her forget why she wanted to get across and what had driven her there in the first place. Already exhausted, Mary stood at the edge of the slick surface of the swamp. The vegetal smell was enough to lay low one's spirits. "Like something out of Dante, this," she said. And there was, "Yes, sar," all around. They may not have read the *Divine Comedy,* but they knew what she was talking about, and they felt it too.

In went one of her men, just to see how deep it was. There were his head and shoulders—then he vanished. Then he was dragging himself out. Was it possible to cross? The plants themselves seemed to cling to the surface of the water, wandering in the currents. Mary wondered what sort of things lived in the sludge at the bottom, what creatures moved beneath on powerful legs, scenting through the muck for the weak and foolish. Looking at it, the swamp itself offered only Mary back, although an aged version. She almost felt sorry for her companions for having to look at her. There, she thought, a little humor. Maybe she hadn't given up.

"Does anyone have any ideas?" she said. She poked M'bo a couple of times and gave him an encouraging nod so that he knew to translate.

M'bo translated. There was a moment of silence, followed by a deluge of native clack-clack, as she thought of it. She understood, "return to village," and "crocodile," and, a few times, "other side," before she realized Flannel Shirt wanted to know "what is on the other side" that was so important that they reach. It was a valid question.

"What we do?" asked M'bo.

"I don't know," said Mary.

"What you like, sar?"

"You really want to know? I want you to lead for a while. I got us into this mess and I'd like for you to get us out of it."

Mary sank onto her ankles and rested her elbows on her knees, her fingers intertwined. Perhaps she should have felt grandly despairing, but she didn't. She knew she was tired, and ill-prepared, and itching in places where it was impolite—and therefore impossible—to scratch. She squatted like that, hoping she looked deep in thought, when in truth she was napping with her eyes open. Perhaps they should all turn into fish and swim across. She imagined this transformation—her legs lost, her pale eyes swiveling at the sides of her rapidly flattening head, the soothing liquid murk—until finally stirred by a minor commotion: Flannel Shirt and Pagan had seen something. She looked in the direction that had so animated them and saw nothing, just the swamp asserting itself into forever, much like the night sky. Then, in the distance, Mary saw some sort of bobbing creature making its way across the surface of the water: a crocodile, maybe, or a snake.

"M'bo, what is that?"

"That rubber, sar."

Rubber? Sure enough, he was telling the truth. The bobbing creature was a file of rubber workers, their loads balanced on their heads, making their way through the water on some sort of subterranean bridge. All members, men and women, were submerged from the neck down.

"Blimey," said Mary. She watched their rhythmic progress, their shared grace. But this was no time for spectating. She set her hand on M'bo's shoulder. "Go to them. Bring 'em back here. There's gin in it for them if they get us across."

M'bo said something to Flannel Shirt, who ran out along the muddied edge and called out. The column stopped. He called out again, a pleading in his voice that she hoped these people—maybe kinsmen—would not refuse. They listened and the snaking procession began to loop around. Words flew back and forth. The rubber workers stared at her nervously and then with concern. Finally, one of the men smiled at her. Mary stood up. "Pleased to make your acquaintance, each and every one of you." And then, in Fang, "You and I are friends. You are welcome in my village."

The rubber workers were all naked, their clothes carried in bundles on their heads. Her little band started to remove their clothes, everyone except for Mary, that is, who entered the water in her woolen skirts, every undergarment, stay, and stocking another weight to bear. She marched like this for two hours. Once, she faltered—her boots did not grip like feet, did not sense the sliding, subaqueous stuff that the path was made of—and she was under! No sense of what was up and what not, the world suddenly awash and blurred in deep green. Then those hands again, pulling her up, setting her straight.

M'bo: "You kill?"

Mary: "Not much."

She fell twice more before they made it to the opposite side, which meant the bank of the Rembwe was not far off and was even reachable that evening, but she was so dizzied by loss of blood—the swamp was thick with leeches—that she could not quite appreciate her accomplishment. Out came the stock of trade salt and they shook it liberally on each other. The leeches slowly loosed their hold.

Mary wonders if this is funny. Is a black man shaking salt upon your skin humorous or scandalous? How can she make the nightmare of that swamp an invigorating, appropriate story?

She writes: "One and all, we got horribly infested with leeches, having a frill of them round our necks like astrachan collars . . ."

"What does it say?" ask the fairies. "Please, Mary."

"You're bothering me. I'll lose my train of thought."

"If you tell us," says the clever one, "we'll go away."

So Mary reads to them about the swamp and the leeches.

"That's a horrible story, Mary," they all say. "Write a better one."

"Thanks for your support," she says. "But I think I'll go for a walk."

As she's locking the front door behind her, she hears the fairies' gossip drift from the parlor. "She's lying, it's all lies, no one will believe her, and if they do, they'll know she's lost her mind."

The dinner invitation arrives and Mary is inclined to beg off, to say she's feeling poorly, or has to be somewhere else, but at the last moment decides she wants to see this Montagu's house. She has a fascination with Jews and their appreciation of beautiful things. But she feels the pang that comes from lying to herself: it's not their love of beautiful things, nor their "dreamy minds," but rather an otherness that reminds her of Africa. Being in a Jew's house is sort of like being overseas. Also, Jews and Arabs are very much alike, Mary's read *Tancred,* and she's also always had a fascination for anything Arab. Maybe she should just stay at home. She lacks worldliness and people expect it of her. An African jungle that has never known a European, other than herself, is possibly the least worldly place on earth. She is so terrible at drawing rooms, dining rooms, arranging hair, arranging conversation. She still moves like a ten-year-old and this charms and repulses at the same time. She imagines herself on one side of the dining table, her host on the other, their conversation a sort of chess game: Montagu's is white and cosmopolitan, Mary's black and exotic. Which piece should enter the board first—a pawn (what it's like to live off native chop) or a knight (her ascent of Mount Cameroon) or something else all together?

Or she could just sit through the chitchat in her normal, awkward way. The man who brought her into dinner is Lieutenant Colonel Matthew Nathan, the secretary of the Colonial Defense Committee. He's handsome, Jewish, like her host, and has an easy gaze. He makes her nervous, as does her dress, some low-cut muslin thing deemed appropriate, although she can't understand why: she feels half-naked, cold, and ridiculous wearing gloves inside, when fabric would make more sense elsewhere.

She's been silent through the soup (cream of asparagus) and fish (salmon asphyxiated in hollandaise), but at some point during the game (Pheasant Mandarin), she seems to have found her voice. She's telling a story—although from the high pitch and strain of her speech it feels like lecturing—about the ascent of Mount Cameroon, spectacularly impressive on the page and fresh in her mind for having just committed it there. Mary's climbed the slope in skirt and boots, lost her men, found them, been soaked to the bone, run into a singing witch doctor, slept exposed to the elements, although poorly, et cetera, et cetera, wild animal, weird native, perseverance, humor, a few unexpected turns, some minor injuries, and now finds herself in the Montagus' dining room.

"What was the biggest challenge for you?" asks Lieutenant Colonel Nathan. He bends his head toward her, ostensibly the better to hear, but also to accommodate the removal of the game plate and the introduction of the meat: it looks like veal with mushrooms.

"One of two things," says Mary. She looks at the remaining forks and grabs one that looks like it will do the job. "First, Mount Cameroon was completely bathed in mist so deep you couldn't see a thing, and I had to keep reminding myself that I was on top of a mountain, because, truly, I could have been in this dining room for all I could see—nothing—so a challenging factor was the lack of visibility." Which had demoralized her so. Was this what she had risked her life for—the life of her men? To stand bathed in this cold mist so thick that one's hand disappeared into it. The mist had swallowed everything—the air, her companions, whatever view the mountain might have offered, her sense of purpose and accomplishment, the last of her money.

"And the second challenge?" asks the Lieutenant Colonel.

"Oh," Mary smiles. "I had this jumper of the variety worn by sailors and while trying to pull it over my head I nearly pitched off the side of the mountain. I felt challenged! But I did win that one."

And everyone laughs, but Mary has not been invited to this dinner merely to add a female or some color. Lieutenant Colonel Nathan's questions are coming quickly now, as are the dessert courses. Once manageable, Sierra Leone has become a hotbed of rebellion and unrest. This situation is due to the hut tax, and now her views on the hut tax are to be displayed, awkwardly, like her chest. She's stuffed to the gills and feels the mousse au chocolat somewhere in her throat, the veal asserting itself against her stays. She has heard the rumors that Sir Frederick Cardew, governor of Sierra Leone, could well be recalled. And now she sees that Lieutenant Colonel Nathan could well be his successor.

"The tax is not an unreasonable amount," says Lieutenant Colonel Nathan. "I've seen the native persevere through far more difficult circumstances—"

"By persevere you mean put up with, knuckle under. But you haven't learned any native law. These people don't understand the concept of tax. To them it means that their hut has been stolen from them: their hut, their land, their inheritance, their ability to gain a wife, and wives for their sons. This tax means they have lost it all, and that you are not a governing force but an invader, a pillager, cause for resistance at whatever cost."

"But that's hardly true," says the Right Honorable Joseph Chamberlain, who happens to be the colonial secretary.

"Nor is it false. Why don't you raise the taxes on goods—salt and tobacco. Leave the native his hut. Do we really need to tax that? The very term 'hut tax' has a predatory ring to it, as if we colonizers were capable of no human compassion nor kindness—"

"But the tax is a civilizing influence," says Chamberlain.

"How is it civilizing?"

"Civilized countries have taxes," says her host with a chuckle. He seems to think that this is helping Mary, a little sand to put out an awkward fire.

"So we're some sort of missionaries—missionaries for profit. We take their money and in return for being taxed they're civilized?"

"Surely order is a good thing," says Chamberlain.

Mary knows that now they are attributing her obstinacy to female lack of understanding. She is reminded of that nasty drawing-room suffragette (what was her name?) from last Saturday and wishes she were here to see what happens when women and their intellects come together with men. "The hut tax is a mistake. There are better and more peaceful ways to raise money—more money—and your adherence to this foolish policy shows your complete blindness to the reality of the situation."

"And I suppose that's all you have to say on the matter!" says Lieutenant Colonel Nathan.

"There you're wrong, sir," says Mary. "I have much to say around tables like this, in drawing rooms, across fancy desks in government offices, and I've been known to put pen to paper."

"I've seen your views in the *Spectator,*" says the previously silent Lady Enfield. She stuffs an oyster into her mouth. "You think we should bring liquor to the native."

"As a trader of liquor in Africa, I see its value. I have not introduced liquor to the Africans. They have their own. And I've seen more drunks in one hour on the Vauxhall Road than in all the time I spent in West Africa."

"And," says Lady Enfield, "you also support polygamy."

"It comes as a result of a village wanting to be responsible for all its people, all the children, all the women who lose their husbands at an appalling rate. The African woman is never lonely; she never wonders who will feed her children should something happen to her." Mary's voice is quavering. "And all these blessings are vilified by the notion of one man having many wives. This—let's call it the polygamy aspect—overshadows all the goodness, and generosity, and love that exist within the native village." She'd be happy to be back with those savages and not explaining the wrong-mindedness of the hut tax to people who define wrong-mindedness as that which they do not think.

"You have very strong feelings, Miss Kingsley," says Lieutenant Colonel Nathan.

"They're actually thoughts—not feelings—just like you have." She smiles bravely, but she thinks herself an idiot. She is attracted to this man—such a rare sensation that at first she had not identified it, but thought herself frightened of him—and now she has rolled out all the old eccentric beliefs in her usual inelegant manner. Her face—splotched red with emotion—is reflected back to her in the lens of Lady Enfield's lorgnette.

Mary decides to walk the four miles to Alice Stopford Green's house. She knows that this will make her late, and she's fine with it. Alice, widowed for some time, writes books on English history. She likes to have people over to talk about "things," people like Winston Churchill (a young war correspondent), John St Loe Strachey (the editor of the *Spectator*), Henry James (an American author), and others even more famous than that. Sometimes Florence Nightingale makes an appearance and that's good with Mary: she and Mary can talk nursing and, if nothing else, Mary is an accomplished nurse.

      Mary has seriously considered begging off from this salon because her mind is in such disorder. Matthew Nathan's latest letter is in her pocket, already disintegrating at the seams: she's memorized it. She can play it in her head, dictated by Matthew Nathan's voice, and this fact both embarrasses her and makes her giddy. He's written, "It was your personality rather than your work that engaged my attention," in his fine, although somewhat cramped handwriting. He's written that he wants to understand her. No one has ever wanted to understand Mary. She would have been happy enough to stay in her apartment composing her reply to Matthew Nathan, a letter that is now over twenty pages long, but Alice has insisted that she come. Roddie Casement is back from Africa, but not for long, and has asked after her. Edward Morel, a Welsh journalist who has been very positive about both her books, *Travels in West Africa* and now *West African Studies,* has indicated that he might show up. All these people whom she now knows and who know her! She likes the lecturing well enough and the lecture fees in particular, but being a celebrity puts you in the same circle as other well-known people, and what could be more inconvenient? But she'll be happy to see Alice, who has just finished another book. And she missed the last gathering at Alice's because she was nursing an aunt back from a cold: all these people falling ill, invaliding themselves, and seldom dying. Duty. Duty. Duty. Sounds like a death march to Mary and she's happy to be escaping it—not to be needed—for a few hours. Alice has indicated that the conversation should be lively and of the variety where Mary's views are valued and entertaining. And hadn't Mary said for Alice to invite her when Casement returned to London?

So the walk is a compromise and she hopes that by the time she reaches Alice's house, her long trudge through the streets of London will account for the disorder in her appearance and manner, her general flightiness, her difficulty in stringing an argument—a sentence!—together.

Mary hands her hat and coat to the maid and notices the maid's dismissive look at her poor garments, the mud on her boots.

"Here's Mary," says Alice, appearing in the hallway.

"Am I late?" Mary asks, hopefully.

"Not at all. It's just Roddie and me. Come have a smoke before the proper folk show up."

"How many proper folk are coming?"

"Don't sound so terrified," says Alice.

"Anyone but Sarah Bernhardt," says Mary.

Casement is standing by the drawing room window. He looks thin and aged, and Mary wonders how his health has been. "There you are, Mr. Casement. Pleased to make your acquaintance again."

"As am I. And call me Roddie. May I call you Mary?"

"Why not?"

"What have you been up to, Mary?" Casement asks. "I hear you're causing all kinds of trouble with the hut tax."

"All you need to do is ask and you get my opinion. There's a rumor that Governor Cardew is going to be recalled from Sierra Leone, and I hope he'll take his foolish hut tax with him."

"But if they recall Cardew," says Casement, "they will install Nathan. And he supports the hut tax."

"No he doesn't," says Mary.

"Yes he does," says Casement.

"Who'd you hear that from?" asks Mary.

"The Right Honorable Joseph Chamberlain, colonial secretary," says Casement.

"Well, you can't trust everything *he* says," says Alice. She's being facetious.

"I think Lieutenant Colonel Nathan is still gathering information," says Mary.

"Has he consulted you?" asks Casement.

"As a matter of fact—"

"If he wasn't a Jew, he'd be one of the most eligible bachelors in London," says Alice.

"I sense our fine conversation descending into gossip!" Casement waggles his eyebrows dramatically.

Mary, holding tightly to her cigarette, watches Alice cast about for the matches.

"Are you all right, Mary?" Alice asks. "You've gone red all of a sudden."

"I'm quite well," Mary responds, tight-lipped. "It's just the warm air after my walk."

"Well, the hut tax will be forgotten soon," says Casement.

"What do you know, Roddie?" asks Alice. The match flares—a light for Mary.

"Just rumors. But if you really want to be au courant, you should start looking at Natal."

"Natal, Transvaal, that's hardly news," says Alice.

"What do you think, Mary?" asks Casement.

"About what?"

"About the Boers!" says Alice. She is about to light Mary's cigarette but holds back. She gives Mary a frank and searching look. "Are you sure you're feeling all right?"

Mary is not feeling all right. She has sent her letter off to Matthew Nathan and now wonders if she has lost her mind. If she has, is it important? Is there anyone to notice and really care? Probably. All these dizzying dinner eaters going from one fancy trough to another, making "conversation," making it out of her! And who cares about any of them? What do they know? What have they accomplished in their lives, other than to make money, have children, cheat and lie and destroy?

"Who, Mary," say the fairies, "who cheats and lies and destroys?"

Has Mary been speaking? She must have been muttering out loud in her fevered state. She'll crawl back into bed, realize an hour later that she hasn't moved—hasn't noticed the passing of time—but her jaw has fallen open and her mouth is dry.

"Still in bed?" says Charley.

"Still feeling poorly?" says Charley.

"You know what? I've decided that the next time you go digging around Africa, I'm going with you," says Charley.

"Why should you have all the fun?" says Charley.

And then one day, "Matthew Nathan left his calling card. You should pull yourself together. He's visiting this afternoon."

Has Matthew Nathan relented? Does he now wish to understand her? Does he find her personality engaging once more? The fairies sit at the end of her bed, chattering away.

"Turned into her mother, this one has."

"But her mother had Mary."

"And Mary has no one."

No one. No one. She should take a draft of something. What kills people? Arsenic? That would entail making her way to the chemist. Her mirror announces that although she's thirty-six, she looks ten years older. Would powder help? A hairbrush? Hairpins?

But Matthew Nathan never shows up. He sends his regrets on another cream-colored card.

The bell is ringing downstairs. Where's the girl? Surely she's back from the shopping. And would it kill Charley to check it himself? Doesn't Mary have enough to handle with the packing? Problem is, it's a small trunk and has proven quite stubborn, refusing half her things.

The bell rings again.

Mary is down to deciding between books and clothes. She has a hard time believing that there will be no time to read; the three-week journey alone makes books a necessity, and surely they have clothes in Cape Town. Besides, she'll have to wear a nurse uniform the vast majority of the time, regardless. And if she leaves all these ridiculous letters of introduction behind, no one will invite her to dinner anyway and she can leave the topless muslin thing here in London, where it belongs.

And there's the bell again.

"Get the door, Mary," say the fairies. "Get it. Get it. Get it."

"Shut up, you lot!" says Mary. And she adds, "I'll be rid of you soon enough."

The bell rings and rings.

Mary turns to the trunk, then to the door, beyond which are the stairs, the street, the world. Who would be so persistent to be ringing all this time? Then she hears a key in the lock and she knows the girl's back from the market, bringing the mysterious bell ringer (whom Mary's already nicknamed Quasimodo) into her house.

"I've been out there five minutes at least," comes the voice. It's Alice and she's angry. "Has everyone gone mad?"

"Absolutely," says Mary, allowing herself to appear at the top of the stairs.

"There you are," says Alice. "Why have you been hiding?"

"For the precise reason you've been looking for me," says Mary.

"I've been looking for you because you need a voice of reason. There's no point in acting like a jilted—"

"Rather you didn't announce such sentiments up the stairs." Mary jerks her head toward her room in invitation.

Alice looks at the trunk, looks at the emptying closet, looks at the stack of books.

"Now, what did you need to say to me?" asks Mary.

"You're acting like a jilted schoolgirl."

"Is this what schoolgirls do? Because I've never heard of any schoolgirl, jilted or otherwise, leaving for South Africa. I'm an able nurse and an expert in African infectious diseases. I can be most useful in one of the field hospitals."

"Did Matthew Nathan make any promises?"

"You're more fixated on him than I am." Mary smiles, coaxing a smile out of Alice in the process. "No one made any promises." Mary shrugs. "*I* might have said a couple of things, and I won't lie to you. There are other scenarios I would have accepted into my life, but I do want to be in Africa—"

"But as a scholar! A naturalist and anthropologist!"

Mary lowers her voice. "These are my choices, Alice. Either I go to South Africa as a nurse and go alone, or I return to West Africa and take Charley with me."

"You need different choices," says Alice.

"Well, I could add to that staying in London and nursing every hypochondriac my family can throw at me, doing the occasional lecture—"

"Seeing me whenever you want to."

"Alice," Mary says. "Don't think you're not important to me. But you have to see it my way: South Africa brings me closer to the Congo. I'll work my way up north eventually."

Alice spins the globe on Mary's desk. She stops it in her hands. "Are you sure Cape Town is actually closer? It doesn't really look much nearer than London."

"Stay, Alice," says Mary. "Stay for lunch. Take the train with me to Southampton tomorrow. See me off. It might be a while before we get a chance to chat."

VI.

Hard to believe that here she's actually heeding the call of duty. How could there be anything noble at all in walking through this pleasant park, the sun shining generously, the grass trimmed back to an unnatural flatness, the paths laid out neat as lines on a chessboard, that cake-like mountain thrown up against the shock of blue sky with a frill of cloud spilling down from it. And then Lion's Head with its paws pulled coyly in, looking out over the ocean to the south and the Antarctic.

There's a guinea hen ducking in and out of the roses, no doubt lost, as is Mary.

Where is the war? Mary orients herself to Table Mountain. Natal and Pretoria are over to her right, somewhere to the north. That's where Mary's going, where everything converges: Boers, English, Rhodes, Kruger, soldiers, farmers, cholera, gangrene, enteric fever, bayonets, and, of course, gold. The guinea hen pecks and pecks, full of purpose in the dirt, accomplishing, to Mary's untrained eye, nothing. Sometimes—in states of abstracted simplicity that feel like enlightenment—Mary finds it absurd that the English should have a war in Africa, and with the Dutch. Something about it reeks of drawing-room blueprints and false bravado: a sort of heavily armed and highly dangerous picnic. A good game for men to play at, located in a place where it can't offend the women with its outrageous stench. But of course, in her moments of reason, she knows that these Europeans want to be in Africa and there's nothing for them to do once here but to kill every African who wanders into their sights, and, on occasion, each other.

Hard to think about all that death in this bath of sunshine, where, if she moves her head a little to the left so as not to see the drunken black passed out facedown beside the hedge, all is lovely: the best of England (roses) joined together with the best of Africa (light), although she's caught herself doing it again: abstracted simplicity doesn't enlighten—it just makes you simple. Any fool knows that the bastard child of this union is the war.

At the other side of the rose garden, she sees a couple of nurses hurrying along in their little white caps and capes. Mary breaks into a run to catch up with them, because they're walking, in the manner of nurses, very quickly.

"Hello," says Mary, struggling to catch her breath. "Could you point me in the direction of the Nursing Administration?"

"That building there," says the older one, pointing with a clean and cracked-looking hand, the knuckles rubbed red and tender. "Go to the third floor. And quick. The office closes in a half hour for lunch."

The younger nurse, bobbing her head like the guinea hen, gives an eager nod of agreement and encouragement. And Mary's off—up the pathway, up the stairs. These practical nurses are her kind of women: short on conversation, big on action, functional, plain, and tidy. She raps at the door with an efficient, nurse-like knock.

"In," says the voice.

Mary enters. She sees a very small man sitting behind an enormous desk. Two tall stacks of papers rise on either side of him with an architectural intensity. He sits there: a man framed by his work.

"Sit," he says.

Mary obeys.

"Volunteer?" he asks.

"Yes, that's right," she says.

"Papers?"

"I have my passport."

"No," says the man. He's been forced to use a word that, apparently, he was saving for some other, more worthy occasion. "Assignment papers, from London."

"No." Now she's started hoarding her words. There's a standoff. Mary looks at him, blinking.

"Anyone know you were coming?"

"Yes."

"And?"

"They said not to."

"Why?"

"They didn't give me a good reason, which is why I'm here."

"What reason was given?"

"They said I wasn't needed. But I'm able-bodied and an experienced nurse, also an expert in infectious African diseases."

There's silence again.

"Name?" he says.

"Mary Kingsley."

He writes the name down. There's a moment of recognition, some paper shuffling. He reads through a letter, peering up at Mary every couple of lines. He's developed a nervous twitch in his right eyebrow. He puts the letter down and laces his fingers together. There's a surge of thought happening now, some intense deliberation.

He says, "You are not needed. Sorry for your trouble."

"This is ridiculous," she says. "Nurses are needed. People are dying. And I've just spent the last three weeks on a boat."

"Nurses are needed," he says. "Not authors. Not celebrities."

"I'm not leaving," says Mary. "Not until you give me an assignment."

The man searches about for some response. Mary thinks of M'bo, who could converse in English in certain situations, and not at all in others. M'bo could do this man's job as effectively as is being done.

"Madame—"

"It's Miss, and I hope you like company." Mary digs around in her bag and pulls out the knitting—socks for soldiers, what every nurse is knitting right now—and starts looping and clicking, swinging her foot in time.

"Come back after lu—"

"No."

"Miss—"

"No." Mary refuses to look up from her knitting. "If you find me a job, I will go do it. Otherwise, you had better get used to me."

How does it go? That line from Horace? Of course Mary has the obvious ringing in her ears—*Dulce et decorum est pro patria mori*—although, after the third hour of carting bedpans and chasing hallucinating men down the aisles of the hospital ward, she knows that it is neither "dulce" nor "decorum" to "mori" "pro patria." There are better lines from Horace. There are probably better lines *than* Horace, and why she chose that book of Roman poetry to take her through the jungle (was she seeking to improve herself?) seems like an odd choice now, an odd choice then, another reason to look at all the choices she's made and have a good laugh about it.

Ellen comes up behind her with the lunch cart.

"*Vitae summa brevis spem nos vetat incohare longam,*" says Mary.

"What was that, Mary?" says Ellen.

"And translated, 'Life's brief total forbids us cling to long-off hope.'"

"Does it?" says Ellen. "Maybe it does."

"It's Horace," says Mary.

Ellen nods, and Mary, done—for the moment—with the bedpans, done scrubbing her knuckles, her eyes watering from the carbolic reek, makes her narrow way between the narrow beds. "You should take a break, Mary," says Ellen. "Didn't your shift start at five?"

"I came on at three," says Mary. "Ruth had an attack of—"

"She had an attack of being Ruth," says Ellen. "I want you to try and sleep, just a couple of hours. I'll get you up. No worries."

"I'll sleep with my boots on."

But Mary is too tired to nap. Here, in Simon's Town, her patients don't sleep unless they're never waking up. She knows the officials thought she would turn down this position— nursing prisoners of war—as if the shameful thing was not the war itself. At least now, her German is nominally useful. She can cough up a word or two to ease some suffering. Earlier that day (or is it the previous night when it's three in the morning?), she had the oddest sensation as she held the hand of a farm boy, bayoneted through the intestines, who was quickly dying. She could feel herself draining through her hand into his. She could feel him taking some vital thing from her, although it did him no good. His eyes were round like saucers and an unnatural cornflower blue. His hands were coarse—already a life of hard work completed, although he was only fifteen—and for a long moment they sat there, Mary feeling quickly depleted, his eyes lighting up like an electric bulb. Then he died, falling a little deeper into the pillow, and as the spirit left, there was the usual chill. Mary made her little prayer to Allah, just a few seconds of respectful mourning for this terrible waste of life, but then there was a man showing himself at the end of the bed. Mary could see him between the two screens—patients died when they saw others dying, as if the sight of it were enough to create a contagion—his eyes wide and hysterical.

He was a huge man. In his cot, Mary had noticed his feet sticking out the end, his arms hanging down so that his knuckles rested on the floor. Upright, Mary wasn't sure she could handle him. The giant was twisting his standard-issue nightshirt in his hands, wrinkling the coarse cotton, nervous, like a child.

"Where have you hidden my pants?" he asked, in the odd Germanish gibberish, but she could understand.

"Let me take you there," she responded in German. She reached out her hand.

And then she's walking this giant through Fang land. Hand in hand, like Hansel and Gretel, two lost people wandering around Africa.

"Mary! Mary, wake up!"

"Hello!" says Mary, startled. Ellen and Ruth are standing at the foot of her bed, giggling away.

"How long was I out?" The window's already flattened out with darkness.

"Four hours? Five?" says Ellen.

"Bloody hell. Why didn't you wake me up?"

"Good day to you too, my lady!" says Ruth. She's hiding something behind her back, which she reveals with great ceremony. It's a bottle of wine. "And I've got two more."

"Did those come from the butcher?" asks Mary.

Ruth nods.

"You know he's married," says Mary.

"I thought," says Ruth, who's too clever by half, "you said that men should have lots of wives."

"Not that," says Mary, "but something like it."

Ellen has already wrenched the cork out of one bottle and is pouring it into tumblers.

"Is this really a good idea?" says Mary.

"I think it's a great idea," says Ellen.

Mary takes the glass, has a good mouthful. "But what about the patients?"

There's a moment of silence, during which some poor soul's groaning can be heard from the ward.

"The patients?" says Ruth. "But we've only got the three glasses."

And who wouldn't laugh at that?

Besides, how else would these women survive without their smoking and their wine and their endless gallows humor? It's not as if they can stop the men from dying. Typhoid's the problem, and what can you do for that? The work done by bayonets and shot—a second's work—can't be undone by her, or even a doctor most of the time. The body needs to heal itself and that's where she comes in, clearing bedpans, keeping skin clean, responding to questions, being able-bodied almost as an example for the indisposed: remember you used to walk around like this, arms swinging, shoes clicking on the tile floor.

"You're not going to tell the doctor, are you, Mary?" asks Ruth. She means her love affair with the butcher.

"Tell him," asks Mary, her glass extended for more wine, "about what?"

Simon's Town is not a bad place, once you leave the hospital. Mary likes to get up early in the morning and go walking on the beach. There's a spot just offshore where monstrous boulders are worn to sculpture, imposing, glorious. Allah's work. Something to balance against all the smells and clotting, fly-flecked blood back in the ward. One morning she'd woken weeping and couldn't remember her dream; whether the dream had made her cry, or if it was being returned to her life that had so upset her. She'd walked to the beach and unlaced her boots, waded through the frigid water, and in the day's cold first light scrambled onto a boulder (some effort here) to sit and watch the world grow bright. At first she didn't know what they were, but someone had mentioned the whales to her. She could see them playing, unmolested, powerful. There were just a pair of them exploding out of the water, falling onto their backs. The spray shot up, flashing bright white with sunlight. The whales were gone, then back again, floating calmly. She knew they were going to leave. She knew she was going to lace her feet back into her boots, spend her day walking the ward, facing all that death, which meant accepting her whole life, her life alone. Alive. What did it feel like to live in the water unexposed, cradled, unlike the nakedness one felt in air? She used to think this all the time, a girl who wanted to be a fish. "But now I'm a nurse, who was once an explorer." She'd broken the spell by speaking out loud. The whales, as if sensing this, descended, leaving oily circles on the surface of the sea. And Mary? The tide had shifted and she knew she'd have to swim back to shore, that the water was ice cold, and that she'd do it—just as always—in her skirts.

Mary's sluggish today. And clumsy. She gets up off her knees, having mopped up another spill—bedpans. No matter how close to death these people are, they still manage to fill the bedpans.

"I think you need a break," says Ellen. "Go have a cigarette. Things can wait a few minutes."

"I'm all right," says Mary.

"I really don't think you are," says Ellen. She puts her hand on Mary's forehead. "You're warm. Go see the doctor."

"I'm fine."

"Remember, I'm a nurse."

Mary puts her own hand on her forehead. "Remember, I am too. And I'm fine." But Ellen is right. It's not just the wine from last night. Mary tells herself, *let's pretend it is*. Is it really possible to lie to oneself in this way? And since she's doing this, is something really wrong? Must be. Keep going, Mary. You're strong and always come through in the end. The war will end soon. They're running out of Boers to slaughter and Australians to slaughter them. And when it's over, you can pack up your belongings, your Horace, your fish-collecting jars, your notebook, your cache of gin and tobacco to swap for fetish and ivory, and you'll go wandering again, where Charley can't find you, where you won't have exchanged one bedside for another.

"Mary! Mary!"

Mary's lying on the floor. When did that happen? And there's the doctor and Ruth. Why is Ruth crying? Must be something to do with the butcher.

"I'll take a little nap," says Mary. "Leave my boots on."

She can hear the doctor whispering to Ellen outside the door. "She's adamant that we leave her alone in the final stages. There are two things she insisted upon—that, and she wants to be buried at sea."

Finally, the doctor had heard her. He hadn't wanted to hear anything about final wishes, since it was inconsiderate to admit that someone was dying—such a perversity of politeness. But in the end, he saw that Mary knew, and knew what she wanted. She was articulate through the exhaustion, despite the enteric fever sucking at her, wracking her with chills and abdominal pain.

Although "pain" is a small word to throw at what's actually happening. She closes her eyes, desperate to have it stop, then flings them open worried that this thought—such a small weak thought—might be her last. What did M'bo used to say to her? He'd say, *You kill?* And Mary would answer, *Not much.* For a moment she thinks he's somewhere close. But it's just a memory, and memories exist without the primary players making actual appearances. She's calling ghosts, the ghost of M'bo and Flannel Shirt and Pagan and all her guides. Who will guide her now?

Something's at the foot of her bed—moving there on the chipped iron rail. Maybe a cockroach, and then there's another, and then there are four of them, and then five.

"Hello, Mary," says a fairy.

Mary feels awake now, nervous somehow.

"Mary looks awful," says the clever one. "Doesn't she? Awful, awful!" And all the fairies giggle, then stop themselves.

She feels the pressure of tiny feet as the clever one begins to make her way across the bed covers, wings folded neatly and hidden. "Oh, Mary looks terrible! Even Mother never looked so bad."

"Never! Never," agree the other fairies. They take to the air, flitting close to Mary's face. She can feel the air stirred by their wings.

"Why are you here?" Mary can hear the thick sluggishness in her speech.

"To help you," says the clever one, now by her ear.

"To help me?"

"You've no one else. Mother's dead. Father's dead. Mary's dead—" says the clever one.

"Not yet, not yet," say the fairies.

"Matthew Nathan doesn't care. Alice only cares from far away—only cares about anything when she can write it down. Ellen and Ruth only care because it's their job. No one to love you."

"No one. No one. No one at all," sing the fairies, mournfully now.

"I don't care," says Mary, waving them off of her. But they're back quickly. Mary can hear the doctor in the hallway arguing with Ellen, who wants to go to her.

"You're going to the sea, aren't you, Mary? And we're going with you."

"Yes, I suppose I am."

"Don't be frightened, Mary. Don't you remember? You've always wanted to be a fish," says the clever fairy.

"And you're so dirty now," say the others. "You smell awful. But soon you'll be clean."

"When they throw me in the ocean?" asks Mary. She can hear Ellen sobbing by the door.

"Yes, yes, they're going to throw you in the ocean," say the fairies.

"You'll be happy there," says the clever one.

The fairies start chanting. "Those that wish to be clean, clean they will be; and those that wish to be foul, foul they will be." They chant it over and over. They won't stop.

Where does that line come from? Mary remembers now. It's from Uncle Charles's book *The Water-Babies*. What happens to Tom? She can't remember. Is he a water-baby at the end? Does he marry that little girl, Ellie, the one he discovers asleep in her bed? Is his wicked master, Grimes, punished? Are the wicked ever? What happens in the end?

Translation

... for no other had had so much natural talent nor the boldness to learn how to circumnavigate the world, as he had almost done.
  —Antonio Pigafetta, *The First Voyage Around the World*

1. Wind

At first were the endless stretches of water, weeks of static horizon, circumvolving heavens. And after that the tempests that tossed the ships like cats toss mice, and waves that towered then collapsed, shattering both timber and spirit. One might laugh when the storm was over, a short laugh, one of relief, because few things were funny. When one had tired of the sea and sky and their shared inconstancy, land was welcome: a beach of pale sand or maybe arching cliffs. And if you made it past the reefs, one still had to contend with natives—first a sparking on the cliff top, a quivering mass of darkness, then a rain of spears.

"Still, you say you're not afraid?"

"Since you phrase it that way, I would be a fool not to be afraid. So yes, I am afraid. And possibly a yet bigger fool because I still want to go."

"Do you know why I speak to you of natives?"

"I can guess," said Pigafetta. "Everyone else speaks of a giant squid, which is impossible to fear. A cliff with no bottom. All these unknowns of the natural world invented to disturb the sleep of children, but natives—man—impossible to deny."

The financier chucked his head quickly to one side. "Man is, by definition, the only one capable of perverting nature—his presence instantly corrupts the natural world." He didn't mind playing a little at philosophy if it did not take much time. "So this native is not natural because it is man. But primitive people—are they people? Are they sufficiently removed from nature to be called as such, when they have not yet learned—" And here the financier gestured at the roof beam, load bearer of civilization, and, unintentionally, a rat scuttling across. But his tolerance for philosophical discussion was spent. "I like the fact that you have money!" He laughed and Pigafetta trusted this: frank exploitation. "I need money," he continued. "But I am not a wet nurse and what will you be doing on the ship?"

"I'm a scholar," said Pigafetta.

"Is everything here learned?" and the financier waved into the street, where a steaming pile of horse dung was, in two strokes, delivered by two separate wagons' wheels—one traveling north and one east—beatified.

"Yes," said Pigafetta. "No." Pigafetta thought to himself. "Are you waiting for me to beg you? Because I will. I have no pride. It makes my father angry, and my mother is sweet and fat and has never had reason to prostrate herself, but given one, her big behind would rise in the air very quickly. And I am more like her than him, only thin."

The financier had a twinkle in his eye, so Pigafetta knew he had already earned passage, but he wanted to prove himself as useful. Being decadent and slothful required wealth, but wealth did not require decadence and sloth, and although money, in general, bought respect, after months and months on a ship it probably bought some derision too. "You're going to need a translator," said Pigafetta. "I can translate for you."

"Translate what?" said the financier. "No one's ever been there. That has defined the trip. To go where one cannot. If Pliny's one-footed man who rolls about for ambulation exists, you will meet him. And do you speak his language?"

"If he has a mouth," said Pigafetta, "I will learn."

Twinkle, twinkle. "You will turn his language into my language. Sounds more like—" and there was a contemplative belch.

"Alchemy," said Pigafetta.

He was back on the street, several thick and signed papers rolled into his hand. Had he purchased his own annihilation? He looked over his shoulder, at the man who had managed—through a certain kind of genius—to put a price on this process.

"God save us from the dreamers!" he heard the financier bellow, and this was followed by the pleasant clink of coin hitting coin: the wind behind dreamers' sails.

2. Provision

The commander of the ship was the infamous Ferdinand Magellan—Portuguese and pragmatic—who, after failing to obtain backing from his own king, had turned to Spain.

Magellan had spent years in India, up and down the west coast of that land, securing and protecting the area from other invaders—in this case, Arabs—seeking to do the same. Magellan was successful, although his time as a soldier had left him with a shattered knee and the attendant limp, and when Pigafetta first saw him sawing his way down the quay, he looked as though he were tacking into the wind, a wind that was blowing furiously and auspiciously, ruffling the explorer's beard, threatening to displace his hat, which—possibly because God ordained it, for how else was it achieved?—remained stubbornly upon his head, a large loaf of a hat bearing down on Magellan's round eyes, soft nose, and inflated, cherubic lips; Pigafetta recalled hearing that Magellan's mother had been a Jewess and that others attributed his piety—a frightening and passionate embracing of Jesus Christ—to his maternal origins. Pigafetta saw the power in this man and it awed him. He felt charged with a strange, invisible light and knew, as Magellan approached, that his journey to reach the earth's end would be made to follow this man, rather than the inverse. When the explorer was close enough to hail, Pigafetta called out:

"God keep you, Sir Captain General and Master and good ship's company."

"God keep you!" responded Magellan. "Whoever you are."

"My name," said Pigafetta, and he bowed politely, "is Antonio Pigafetta."

"How nice for you. Are you going on the ship?"

"Yes."

"You're a Venetian?"

"Yes, from Vicenza."

"Ah. You're that rich guy who bought his way onto the boat!"

Pigafetta, who had lived as "that rich guy" for most of his life, found nothing shocking or even offensive in this. He smiled. "I'm a scholar and a translator," he said.

"I have a translator!" said Magellan. "My slave, Enrique, over there."

Magellan gestured down the pier and Pigafetta saw a young and oily-looking Indian with glossy hair and—Pigafetta was surprised to note—a look of cunning. He was wearing a loose cotton shirt and wide, cropped pants, and the wind was whipping all his wrappings with such vigor that they snapped like sails.

"Is he truly a translator?" said Pigafetta. "Can he call himself such when he already has the knowledge of these languages? What value is there in that? Let him bring his cannibal king in all his feathered glory to the court of our Charles, and then he can translate because, and I'm presuming here, he knows English."

Magellan looked over at Pigafetta: fine features, droll look. "I can't imagine that face," he said, "at the end of the earth."

And Pigafetta raised his eyebrows in mild surprise.

"Do you know cosmography?" asked Magellan.

"Oh yes," said Pigafetta. "And here I'll be honest with you—I'm a terrible draftsman and the best of my charts look penned by a drunken Franciscan. But for constellations and calculations, I'm quite accomplished, although I'm assuming you have a pilot."

"I do," said Magellan. "I just wanted to make sure we'd have something to talk about."

Magellan began to gimp his way to the gangplank, but thought to stop. "Pigafetta, yes?"

"Antonio Pigafetta, Captain General."

"You will eat with me tonight."

And then he wobbled past a bale of hay, and past the pigs that were also to make the journey. Past the casks of wine, barrels of biscuit and salted meat and millet, bolts of linen, silk robes fashioned by Turks, copious amounts of sparkling beads, jars of quince, and a bewildering stack of red caps. Who wanted to sally forth without some red caps? Cannons and cannonballs were loaded, arrows, bows, and cutlasses. Pigafetta was all right with a cutlass, providing his adversary wasn't fighting back. He looked around at the others, who, on some far-flung and ferocious island, might be called upon to protect him. They were a scrappy lot—Sicilians, Naxians, Genoese, Galicians, Danes, and Bavarians, to name but a few—and Pigafetta was amused, and strangely comforted, to note that every nation had its class of brutes. And then he realized, with less comfort, that he was to commit two years of his life to their company.

3. Abomination

It was the middle of December, 1519, when the five ships of the Armada de Molucca finally sighted the Land of Verzin. Magellan had already faced the predictable challenge to his authority—mutinies were as common on long voyages as head lice—and there had been an intense and confused juggling of power that had landed a relative of his—yet another Portuguese—in command of the *San Antonio*. On this, a Spanish voyage! The Castilians were outraged, and lucky them, for there was little else to keep one occupied. Pigafetta, of course, had tried to apply himself as a scholar; however, all the skies were charted here and—unless he wanted to learn Danish or Greek, which involved mixing with sailors—there was nothing linguistic to do. He considered being a naturalist, but very few birds presented themselves, and those that did were of the most mundane variety.

But finally the horizon had appeared broken and, quickly, with the wind pressing at his back, Pigafetta saw the land approach—the distance dissolve as if it were the land advancing—and he stood still upon the surface of the water. Once in sight of the beach, an enthusiastic cheer rose up from the men, not so much for the surgeless prospect of land, but for the dull-eyed, thick-lipped, bare-breasted women strolling across it. In little time they had dropped anchor in the waters off Rio de Janeiro.

Predictably, as soon as they were ashore, the sailors disappeared into the bristling huts, and although Pigafetta had no desire to join this orgy at the end of the earth, he found it on the whole entertaining: the men were fucking, the sun was shining, he had his journal. Shaded by a palm, with the swish and swish of waves, an occasional buzzing insect, fresh—although strange—food, it was hard to feel despairing. And Pigafetta was not despairing by nature. Every disappointed hope—and in his twenty-eight years of life, there'd been many—had made him accustomed to suffering; he did not avoid good food and company when feeling melancholic, but rather hoped to offset his gloom with liberal doses of both.

He leafed through the first few pages of his book and began rereading his account of the storm that had nearly wiped him and his problems from the earth, of the appearance of Saint Elmo dancing on the railing like a drunken fairy, and the stillness that followed. Pigafetta realized that it was his guilt that kept conjuring the image of the Sicilian Antonio Salamón: Magellan had ordered him strangled after he'd been discovered with the cabin boy, and *that* poor lad, barely more than twelve, had pitched himself over the side of the ship and beyond the reach of shame. They had strangled Salamón on deck for all to see, to act as a warning, but if Magellan insisted on the murder of sodomites—it was Spanish law—surely his crew would be reduced by half: pragmatism dictated that Magellan look the other way, much as it dictated, on long journeys, that you widen your options for companionship.

Pigafetta looked up and saw one of the native women wading in the shallows. She seemed barely more than a child and wore very little to disguise this. Feeling his gaze upon her, she turned and met his eyes, then looked away, recognizing in an instant, and with an animal instinct, that he would not harm her.

Perhaps an hour later, Pigafetta was lunching on some roasted meat when, with a whirling conflux of emotions, he noted Magellan—his distinctive stride—coming up the beach.

"Antonio!" Magellan said when he was close.

"Hail the mighty explorer," responded Pigafetta laconically, and forced a smile.

"You sound sleepy," said Magellan. He looked at the meat and Pigafetta raised the banana-leaf plate so that he might help himself. "It's good. What is it? Or," and here he squinted pointedly, "should I ask, who is it?" *Ha, ha, ha*.

Pigafetta took back the meat and set it on the rock. Together, they looked at the waves, although it might have been more novel to face inward to land. Magellan took Pigafetta's journal from him and looked it over.

"Well?" said Pigafetta.

There was a moment of concerned silence. "Antonio, I know this is your book, but listen." Magellan brought the book close to his eyes, then a half-arm's distance away, and read, "The men gave us one or two of their daughters as slaves for one hatchet or one large knife, but they would not give us their wives for anything at all."

Pigafetta considered. "It's accurate."

Magellan nodded first to one side, then the other. "Yes, but it sounds—"

"Immoral?"

"Yes. It says these things . . ." And here he trailed off because "saying things," after all, was the purpose of writing. "It's suggestive."

"It suggests that you are buying women for your sailors and that they're sleeping with naked cannibals."

"And they are," said Magellan, pondering and fair, "but can't you make it sound better? For me?"

Pigafetta snatched back the book, hastily scribbled something, and passed it back.

Magellan read, "Mass was said twice on the shore, during which those people remained on their knees with so great contrition and with clasped hands raised aloft, that it was an exceeding great pleasure to behold them." Magellan's face broke into a dazzling smile. The sun was shining through his beard, fuzzing the light around him in a reverse chiaroscuro. "Thank you, Antonio! You are a genius, my only friend on this voyage. You are writing our journey of discovery into history." Magellan rested his hand heavily upon Pigafetta's shoulder and Pigafetta enjoyed the weight of it, the manly salty smell hovering so close to his ears.

"'Our journey of discovery' meaning you, Ferdinand." Pigafetta was now familiar with his captain. "I am writing *you* into history."

"You are morose!" accused Magellan.

"Not morose, my friend, fearful."

"But why?" Magellan looked at him, at the sudden inward turning of his eyes. "It is because of the Sicilian."

"Am I that obvious?" said Pigafetta.

"Yes," said Magellan. "Even Father Valderrama is off screwing someone. He had to get it out of the way because he has to hear everyone's confession tomorrow and he thinks it will take at least ten hours." Magellan smiled. "I killed Salamón because I needed to kill someone."

"He was hardly a threat."

"But a law existed. And it was there for me. And I used it."

"Used it for what? To kill a Sicilian?"

"No, to put down the rebellion."

"There is no rebellion."

"Exactly." Magellan smiled broadly. "Feel safe, Antonio. What use would it be for me to kill a Venetian nobleman with an interest in languages, nature, the stars? How would your death affect the sailors? Would they say, 'That could have been me?' No. The closest thing they have in common with you is that they like the occasional arse." And here Magellan laughed. "But I haven't even noticed you with anyone: woman, man, dog." *Ha, ha, ha.* "You must have some object of your desire."

"Always desire with you, Ferdinand," said Pigafetta. "What of affection, if not love?"

There was a moment of silence, and then the two men began laughing, a laughter made all the sweeter for Pigafetta because it was shared and—with relief—earned, and the monkeys chattered on the branches above and in the ocean a fish leaped, a spit of silver, and with a splash was gone.

4. Language

Three months they had been moored off the coast of Patagonia, and why? Because on Magellan's map there had been straits through to the Pacific, and Magellan, like an unskilled lover, was prodding and poking his way down the coast, looking for his opening and finding none. Now they were waiting for winter—in April—to pass. The men were mad or *mad,* or mad and *mad,* and one ship—the *San Antonio*—had disappeared: reeled back quickly like a toy boat with wheels, pushed and drawn at will. Another had dissolved itself upon the rocks with such efficiency that you marveled at its skill in vanishing. And three captains had mutinied: two killed, one left on a shore spitting and swearing until darkness and distance (and possibly a large cat) swallowed him.

And through all this grumbling and discontent, Magellan had remained in charge. There he was, standing at the porthole in his quarters, his pocket knife in his hand, while Pigafetta, slumped with something that would have been despair in a commoner, but in a nobleman was more like ennui, was looking at him with undisguised passion: disguise having gone the way of the Valencia oranges two months previous.

"Ferdinand, what are you doing with that knife?"

"Thinking that I would like to be peeling an orange." Magellan thumbed the knife a half-orange hemisphere.

"And I am thinking of you."

"I have changed my mind," said Magellan. "With this knife, I am contemplating suicide." He pointed the dull blade at his heart. "I can't take it!" Then a pantomimed death: shock, slack. Recovery. "Only I think this might be funny—over wine—later. The translator in love with me, and me with nowhere to go."

"Your friends will drink and laugh and *you,* Ferdinand, who claim to be my friend, will laugh loudest of all."

Magellan smiled crookedly and Pigafetta braced himself for more humor. "You could try harder. You could play a guitar." And Magellan brushed delicately the strings of his imagined instrument. "You could change your stockings—"

Pigafetta was smiling despite himself. "Change my stockings? Give me a reason to remove them."

Magellan laughed. "I already have. They are the only things left to eat!" *Ha, ha, ha.*

Pigafetta pulled himself to his feet. "There is plenty of food," he said. "You put us on half rations out of longing for something dire."

"Antonio, please, where are you going?"

"Oh, the Spice Islands, and you?"

"You know you are my favorite," said Magellan. He wiped his hands on his leather waistcoat, which, coming from him, was almost an apology.

"Your favorite? Such an honor." Pigafetta nodded. "I saw João yesterday. He was eating his own shit."

"He's gone mad." It was a casual remark.

"And the rest of the men eating rats."

"Only the fast men."

A silence hung, and Pigafetta's aching heart acknowledged that this callousness and endless insult was what fed his love.

Of course, Magellan knew this. "I applaud their resourcefulness. They don't have the luxury of escaping their hunger with a broken heart."

Pigafetta resolved to make his escape and turned to the door.

"'Tonio, no. Don't stand there with your heart breaking, your stomach growling, your stockings stinking. You should write something. Come over here. Look with me out the window."

Disguise, Valencia oranges, and pride. Pigafetta went to stand by Magellan, lured by simple nearness. He saw the coast, that same coast, cold, dead. Deadening. "There's nothing there."

"Nothing there? Make it up."

"I'm not a poet," said Pigafetta. "I'm a chronicler. A cartographer. A translator."

"Then translate!"

"Translate what?"

Magellan gestured outward, embracing everything that was not yet anything. "That is your page."

"It's a big page."

"Then fill it with giants."

Pigafetta tried to resist Magellan's suggestion; he could not bear to reward him, but he was hungry in every possible way and needed distraction. He brought his writing table and chair to the place on deck that promised the least interruption and the freshest air. A short distance away, the Naxian, his name never known so as not forgotten, was moaning relentlessly. Pigafetta began to hum a popular tune to drown out the man, and although he could still be heard Pigafetta found that he had incorporated the moaning into his humming; it worked as a sort of accompaniment. He began to write—

For head	her
For eye	other
For nose	or

—and was hard at it when a familiar shadow fell across the page.

"'Tonio, what are you doing?"

"Taking your advice. The giants. Here they are."

"Giants?" Magellan splayed his fingers over the open page.

"It's their language."

"Is this how you make a giant? You give him something to say? And this language of the giants—it sounds like English."

Pigafetta cocked his head at the page. Magellan was right.

For eyebrows   occhechel

"That sounds like Italian. And it's even like *occhi,* the eyes, for the eyebrows."

For eyelids   sechechiel

"How do you pronounce that one?"

"At least you admit it doesn't sound like anything," said Pigafetta. "And I'm not trying to speak it."

"How about the mouth?"

For mouth   xiam

"And the lips?"

For lips   schiahame

"And tongue?"

Pigafetta turned to face him. He said, "For tongue, *schial.*"

"And throat?"

"*Ohumez.*"

"And finger?"

"*Cori.*" Which sounded like heart, since Pigafetta's was pounding mercilessly in his ribs.

"And face?"

"Cogechel."

"And breasts?" Magellan held two large breasts of air before him, as if desire had conjured a pair of his own for him to play with.

Pigafetta managed an exhausted laugh, and took up the pen once more. He wrote:

For Bosom   othen

"Another one, impossible to pronounce." *Ha, ha, ha.* "What about penis? What about testicles? You care about that!"

5. Cartography.

A map can be many things: a sheet of paper, a peppering of stars, a gesturing spear poked with jovial menace toward the hairy wall of virgin jungle, and in this case, an idea of what must lie ahead. Because Magellan knew where they had to go, the possibility that *where they had to go* might not exist made things impracticable.

They were now in the straits, the Straits. THE STRAITS! These shifting, amorphous tributaries and the sparking: fire in suppurating bursts on the bristling grass.

Tierra: land if land this was.

Fuego: fire, an arse-waggling assertion from the natives.

And good enough, this naming: dramatic, enticing, and bold. Here at the end of the earth, fire mixed with ice, ice with sky, land with, well, fire. There was an elemental purity to it.

"Prosaic. Obvious. And corny," said Pigafetta. "You did better with Patagonia."

"You think so?" said Magellan, and laughed. Patagonia, a neologism, came from *patacones*: dogs with large paws, a reference to Pigafetta's giants, who—along with their enormous legs—had sprung enormous feet, consequently enormous shoes to put them in; his image of padding dogs, *this whole mess* of invention and whimsy (an incontinent word) christening the lower wedge of the continent.

"You need to name the straits."

Magellan shrugged and Pigafetta felt a pang of affection, because of course he wished the straits to be named for him. "Everyone calls it what they want. San Martin says it's the Strait of All Saints, because he believes we need every last one to get through. And there's the Victoria Strait, since the *Victoria* entered first. And your favorite: the Patagonian Strait."

"Why hesitate to name it?" asked Pigafetta.

"Who cares? Do I care? Ask the priest."

Father Valderrama did care. After Big-Footed Dog Place and a land that called to mind visions of the inferno (weren't we looking for heaven on earth?), it was time for something religious. He had a few suggestions, and Magellan chose "Cape of Eleven Thousand Virgins," because it sounded—and was—funny.

"How do we know there were eleven thousand?" asked Pigafetta.

Then Magellan: *Ha, ha, ha*. "How do we know they were virgins?"

Great plates of ice rose up from the arctic waters, and chasms of incalculable depth sheltered every undiscovered beast and fear. Pigafetta marveled at the enormous glacial mirrors, the refracted images of the ship moving past. The air had been thick with moisture, one low-slung cloud after the other, confounding and chilling. The pilot was near fits as he attempted to orient himself. He ran this way and that, peering over, and up, and away from, and in this hysteria of compensation made everyone nervous. Where were the stars?

But sometimes the sky would reveal itself, and in its blinding nudity mock them all, because what use were the stars if they were the wrong stars? Or in the wrong place? What was that blazing stripe supposed to implicate when blazing there? And the scales, now tilted, quite provocative, gave forth the following information: you're lost. And what comfort was it that one was *supposed* to be lost, beyond the point of bearings? The constellation hanging, awkward from this angle, underscored disorientation: it was a nose protruding from a cheek, or teeth massing in an ear. Pigafetta remembered the second of these possibilities from his childhood: an infant covered with hair and spitting tiny bones from its skin, like stones from the earth at first frost; the baby, to the relief of all, had perished within a year.

Magellan, after a well-disguised moment of doubt, was once again all bluster and purpose and trajectory: the cross had appeared in the sky, proving that Magellan was not only blessed, but heading in the right direction.

"Your reasoning is off," said Pigafetta. "If we were headed in the opposite direction, those stars would still be shining."

"I say that it's a blessing, that God approves of what we are endeavoring to do."

"And somewhere over there," said Pigafetta, gesturing into the jungle and, to his understanding, the Stone Age, "a pair of Indians are fornicating under the trees, ready to birth more pagans, their activities presided over by that same constellation. And who's not to say that Orion blesses us, because there's his belt, and over there's some other thing—the twins, or the centaur, or whatever—and that we sail because they wish it and guide us."

"'Tonio, I know you're a sodomite. Must you be a heretic?"

"I'm not a heretic. You interpret blindly and justify this through faith. Faith does not exist to prove your actions, but quite the reverse. Of course I believe in God!"

"Do you?"

"Yes." But for the first time Pigafetta felt a small and difficult-to-ignore refluent stirring amid the usual pounding surf of his faith, asserting itself, somehow strengthened by the effort to bury it. He steered his reason elsewhere. "Ferdinand," said Pigafetta, "I don't think that God wields his celestial power like that: like an innkeeper waving a lantern to light the way for drunks."

Like a termination for all this water and unknowing: the Moluccas.

Like a purpose for all this mad zeal and bravery: Magellan's faith.

What conjured what into being?

Later that night, Pigafetta was disturbed from his sleep. There was always activity, twenty-four hours a day: changing watches, pricking positions, mending ropes, raising sails, rotating hourglasses. Pigafetta had grown accustomed to all of these vital functions; they were the lungs and spleen and stomach of the ship—but Magellan was up, and he should have been sleeping. Pigafetta recognized the thump and drag, thump and drag of the explorer's progress across the deck. Concerned, he roused himself and went to see.

"Although it may hurt you to admit it, the ship moves even while you sleep," said Pigafetta.

"If sleep would come, I would take it and hold it as long as it would have me," Magellan replied.

Pigafetta would have asked Magellan what was bothering him, but it would have been a stupid question. There were many things that Magellan would have to answer for upon reaching Spain. First among these was his stranding of Cartagena, the Spaniard and nobleman, back in Patagonia; he'd replaced him with another relative, Mesquita, whose fittedness—beyond blood—was that he hadn't the skill to sail, thus no will to rebel. Magellan was hated for being Portuguese, but once he drew near to the Moluccas, it would be the Portuguese—protecting their stake in the Spice Islands—who would give him the most to fear. And there was the *San Antonio,* presumed back in Spain and slandering. Once again he would be forced to defend himself, and why? Because he was the greatest explorer! He, Ferdinand Magellan, had the whole world: his seas and lands rolled out before him; his march into creation; this track always slouching off to the west and west; the eternal conquering of diminishing distance and unreachable point. The king had only his red carpet and slippered foot upon it. Yes, greatness was something to be feared—his greatness! But to be feared by a king was also something to be feared.

And that was if he managed to bring the ships back: who knew what lay hidden by the wall of horizon, crouching in the shade of the unknown?

The explorer raked through his beard with his fingers, his head tilted, about to say something—even opening his mouth!—but then, thinking better, resorted to a vague nodding and frowning.

"I have something that will cheer you," said Pigafetta.

"You talk with such confidence, Antonio, as if I am looking for cheer, or peace, or happiness—all these things that men want. I am not a man like other men are men. But not like you either."

"Not peace then. Not cheer." Pigafetta went to stand by the explorer and steered him into the night sky. There were two shreds of cloud—star cloud—as if they had torn off the Milky Way and caught upon some distant, galactic bramble. "Do you see the clouds?"

"Yes," said Magellan. "Is that something new?"

"New or old, it does not matter. We are the first to see it," said Pigafetta. "I would have shown you last night, but the mist was all about, and thick." Pigafetta placed his hand on the explorer's shoulder. "They are the Magellanic Clouds."

"The Magellanic Clouds." Magellan looked at his clouds. "Will they stay?"

"Oh yes," said Pigafetta. "We will go everywhere, but they will stay to laugh at us."

"But there are two. Why not take one for yourself?" Magellan smiled now. "The smaller one," he added.

"No, no," said Pigafetta. "They're both yours, but maybe if we're here again together, you might let me have use of one—of course, the smaller."

6. Peace

The land had vanished, slipped into the horizon like a gold coin into a cardinal's coffer, and now there was naught but a reflective and uncommunicative surface. Magellan had joked that if there were a monster, they'd find it here, and although a great fanged and bristled serpent had not risen out of the water, hovered upon its spiked tail, roared and shrieked before staving in the ship's hull and consigning them all to a quick, efficient burial, they had found their monster: scurvy.

Magellan and Pigafetta had remained scurvy-free—even in this unhealthy air—but Pigafetta wondered if it were not so much their noble lungs and the ability to purify the bad humors, but rather the jars of quince, a staple of officers' dinners. Of course, Pigafetta kept this to himself. There was not enough for everyone, and Magellan had an altruistic nature: he would share whatever remained of the quince if he deemed it curative rather than an indulgence, and although Pigafetta was, on occasion, generous, he could not be quite so cavalier with his beloved captain's life.

If scurvy were the only threat, Magellan would have been a successful steward, but they were starving. Even the leather casings on the mast had been soaked and boiled, served and devoured. There was now a price on the rats, one half *ducado,* and that was money well spent; rat meat fended off both hunger and scurvy. Twenty men had died. Pigafetta struggled with a debilitating compulsion to stare at the horizon with a hopeful resolve that left him cross-eyed and ill, cringing. He closed his eyes, a spike-like pressure asserting itself on the left side of his head. The real issue was time: they could last another couple of weeks at most.

Although maps made clear that only a few days' travel separated Chile from the Moluccas, the ships had been at sea for over three months—propelled by a brisk and unrelenting wind, without a single storm—and still nothing.

Pigafetta was sitting collapsed against the side of the ship in a sliver of shade, his eyes shut, a wash of purple dancing outside, when a shadow crossed this shadow.

"Is this sleep?"

He opened his eyes and sure enough Magellan stood there.

"No," said Pigafetta.

"Why close your eyes?"

"There is nothing to see."

Magellan looked out at the horizon, where Pigafetta's point was amply proven. "If it is not too much trouble, leave the eyes open."

Pigafetta arched an eyebrow. "You were concerned?"

"About what?"

"About me. You thought I was dead."

"How can this matter to you? My concern!"

Pigafetta stood up and went to stand by his friend at the railing. "I saw a bird yesterday. It lays its eggs upon the back of its mate. They have no need for land." Magellan said nothing, his eyes continuing to roam the offing. "Are you listening?"

But Magellan was not. "*Mar Pacifico*."

"*Mar Pacifico?*" Pigafetta scoffed. "Peace? A not-too-distant peace. Call this salted, sparkling hell for what it is: a grave to us all."

"What do you know of death and its gifts? Let peace be one of them, but I am not so sure."

"Who's the heretic now?"

"I am a true believer. I don't only believe the good things. With salvation, there's the possibility of damnation, which makes the salvation all the sweeter."

"And the salvation is there—that possibility—which makes the damnation all the worse, and worse still since we choose it. Tempt me back to God, Ferdinand." Pigafetta smiled handsomely. "Bring me into your fold. Remind me of salvation, the saved, how it's savored—its taste. And what does salvation look like anyway?"

"Sails."

"It looks like sails?"

"No," said Magellan, a fierce delight clear on his face. "Sails!"

There was the cry from the lookout, who no doubt had questioned his first sighting, but now committed the figures flying across the water to recognition: sails, manned by people who needed to eat, or could be eaten. He was that hungry.

7. Conversion

A deeper sloth could not be imagined for people still alive. And the indulgence—meat and fish and fruit and liquor—after all that time spent floating in the *Mar Pacifico* (nothing could be worse than such quiet torture), even the air, fragrant and sweet, made one feel a drunkard: a passionate drunkard. Passion. Maybe they weren't so slothful after all. The men had gone from near death to such fervent fucking that Pigafetta had actually thought to pen it in his book, a naturalist's observation, of how prolonged proximity to death left one with the urge to procreate. Then he thought better of it: his urge to take the basic things in man and endow them with explanation—the need to translate licentiousness into the more noble desire to survive.

The Cebuan women were beauties—Pigafetta noticed, although with the same aesthetic astuteness with which he admired horses and weapons—and more akin to Europeans than Patagonians. A subversive and forking thought entered Pigafetta's mind: was it possible that one's European identity was as tainted by the warmer climes as the Cebuans' was refined by contact with the porcelain, silk, and writing, brought to these islands with Arabs and Chinese? And were Arabs and Chinese a civilizing force? Were they capable of such a thing?

As Pigafetta strode down the beach to find his friend, he searched for the right words. He had resolved for the fifth time in as many days to speak frankly to Magellan, to clarify what had caused the grumbling among the men, and why it wasn't the will of God they were opposing, but rather Magellan's. Pigafetta paused among the bananas, a personal favorite, and pulled one, slightly green, but irresistible in its exotic presentation and convenience, to eat. He had only risen from his sleeping mat a half hour ago and the sun was already reaching its zenith. Magellan must have been up for hours. Where would he be? And then Pigafetta saw it: the cross.

There was a rope and pulley struggle unfolding in a clearing a short distance over the lagoon, and a massing of dark and obedient muscle—native and, to Pigafetta, not to be trusted—and then, like the hand of a clock moving to the twelve, the cross was raised. Pigafetta chewed on his banana and heard Magellan's barking as the cross was secured—a large cross that cast a large shadow, larger still in Pigafetta's mind. He took a few moments to compose himself, but his thoughts were scattered; he'd begun to wonder about his future back in Vicenza, a future of print and privilege, and frankly, as he stood in the steamy heat, a future too known. Magellan would go home to his wife, spawn, and return to the sea, like all those flightless birds he'd seen in Patagonia.

But hadn't *the known* itself been rendered obsolete? Hadn't Magellan done that?

By the time Pigafetta reached what would have been the town square, had there been a town, Magellan had accomplished his erection. The cross was standing quite well, looking—despite its shiny newness and inferior material—quite permanent.

"Are you done with baptizing people?" asked Pigafetta. "Are you on to crucifying?"

Magellan waved his finger in Pigafetta's face. "Only you talk to me like this."

"Only I care enough to speak my mind."

Magellan looked frankly at Pigafetta and shook his head. "This is my duty." He began to walk away.

"Ferdinand, I will not be misunderstood. I think it's wonderful that you've baptized everyone, and the men are, no doubt, grateful to be sleeping again with good Christian girls rather than heathens."

"You make fun of me," said Magellan.

"It is not mocking. It is honesty tempered with affection. You are not here to baptize everyone—"

"There is no greater purpose!"

"Perhaps. But it's not your purpose. I must remind you that you have sailed this far to take hold of the Moluccas for our King Charles, to deprive the Portuguese of this prize, to sail back with the miracle of having sailed west and only west, and to return with our holds filled with cloves. This trip has nothing to do with Christian Indians. Christian Indians. The very term is a mockery of itself."

"And what about that man I healed? He was dying— almost dead, and I said to the Cebuans to burn all their idols and that I would make him walk. And I walked into his hut, and—"

"And he walked. And there was no one more surprised than you, excepting him. I commend you for having all their idols burned, ours being much more handsome, but Ferdinand, I would less fear disaster than all of this success."

"Antonio," said Magellan, and he seemed concerned, "have you lost your faith in me?"

"In you, no, and that is what I fear because I—throwing to the wind reason and intellect and every God-given gift—would follow you anywhere. That is faith, that I would still do that. But please don't ask me if I think you lead me well."

Later, with the sun dropping ferociously behind the mountains and the insects swarming like a chorus of the damned, Pigafetta, a mug of distilled coconut juice dwindling in his grasp, felt a foreboding chill. He recalled their arrival on the island of Cebu, the boom of cannons and King Humabon falling to his knees in fear, while Magellan laughed. Magellan had later informed King Humabon that the Spaniards always greeted powerful sovereigns with cannon fire, and perhaps, unintentionally, had told the truth. After the cannons, he'd dressed one of the larger sailors in a suit of armor and had another attack him all about, much to the astonishment of the Cebuans, who did not even wear shirts, so how could they comprehend this? Then Magellan had boasted that one of his men was equal to one hundred Indians, and at that, King Humabon, although feigning an ignorant deference, had fallen into hushed discussion with Magellan's slave, Enrique. Enrique, to the surprise of all, including himself, was fluent in this dialect, even though Magellan had acquired him in Africa. This was Enrique's forgotten home.

When Humabon and Enrique fell to whispering, Pigafetta was filled with dread. And the next day, when masses of the Cebuans embraced Christianity, Pigafetta sensed that Magellan was being manipulated by a skilled adversary.

Pigafetta wanted to be wrong, but the morning brought cold comfort and understanding. Lapu-Lapu, a rival chieftain of the neighboring island of Mactan—to Humabon's horror—had refused to accept Christianity, and now Magellan had declared war upon him. Magellan's sailors were now soldiers, involuntary crusaders, in his planned offensive. They would attack Mactan and all the heathens there, or at least subdue them, and Humabon and his allies would assert their power to keep Mactan good and Christian.

When Pigafetta paddled out to the *Trinidad* early in the morning, he saw a disheartening bustle: cannons and flint being readied, armor being assembled—for how long had it lain neglected, a home for rats and rust? Pigafetta had insisted on seeing Magellan, even though Magellan had wanted solitude: a time for prayer. Piety supplied the words for Magellan, but what informed God's response? And whatever the will of God, if it was not in the financial interests of Spain, it was not to be listened to.

"Surely you see the folly in this," said Pigafetta, but Magellan was kissing his cross and readying himself for armor. "How many are the Mactanese in number, and what do you know of their leader, Lapu-Lapu? The very fact that Humabon wants him dispensed with and has not done so himself—and the Cebuans number many—fills me with a grave and justified concern."

"This is duty."

"This is hubris."

"I knew you would say that. Why are you here to torture me? I need to pray."

"Then pray that God will give you humility."

"What is the great danger? We have guns and cannons and steel blades. It *would* take one hundred of their number to kill one of our soldiers."

"If we had soldiers. We are sailors and cabin boys and pilots. The only soldier is you, an old man with a heavy limp armed with faith, and sorry, but faith makes a dull blade."

Magellan looked serious but had to laugh. "Go back to the island, and tonight I will see you, and you will apologize for calling me an old man."

But Pigafetta had resolved to go with him. There were many who wanted Magellan dead, and stranding him in battle would be a very good way to accomplish this. The armor didn't fit well and Pigafetta looked silly in it, but if Magellan was marching into battle so would he.

8. Engagement

These are the great generals: Julius Caesar with his flanking phalanxes; Alexander with his speed and daring; Miltiades with his plea for boldness; Hannibal, although he lost; that barbarian Chinese flying on the wind to the very gates of Christendom. Later, when careless history lifted her skirts and fled this bloody battle, she would find other commanders: Napoleon, Sherman, Rommel. And they would all have one thing in common: a plan.

Magellan did not have a plan. He did not even have a battle, really: this was not Gaugamela, nor Marathon. He was bringing faith and civilization to Mactan, a tiny island that even savages—Cebuans with their bronze-bolted penises, their hog-toothed idols, their bare-arsed social mores—considered beyond the pale. Magellan, his ships bobbing harmlessly distant, prevented from approach by the low tide, was wading through the water in his armor. The men were following, slowly, while the cannonballs fell around them, the targets leaping and hooting onshore.

Pigafetta was wading too. The armor was heavy and he couldn't keep track of Magellan, whom he'd planned to protect. His terror was transformed into a kind of ferocity paired with cold reason, which, as he raised his musket and fired at a native, presented this: you had less to fear from the fearless than the truly terrified. The native was hopping around—Pigafetta having missed his mark—but after some awkward fumbling (he didn't want to get the wadding wet) he managed another shot, and to the surprise of both, this projectile hit the native's leg. Each took a second to process this. The native shrieked and fell to his knees in the shallows; Pigafetta, now with a moderate understanding of what battle was about, turned to find another target.

There was now a hut ablaze onshore and the smoke poured out, its thatched roof seizing with flames; the smoke from the weaponry, the dry skunk smell of the gunpowder, the pearl-blue water now turned pink with blood, all of this presented itself and all at once, but where was Magellan? Pigafetta reminded himself that he had injured and probably, although death might wait for morning, killed a native—that he was capable of this, that he should find the battle rather than lingering at its fringes. He felt as if he were a marionette, and that God's large hand—that hand pointing the way out of Eden frescoed on the family chapel wall—was now dangling him here and there, as he splashed about pantomiming assault. His eyes scanned the thick of fighting and found their mark—not the enemy, but his beloved captain, who was battling on with a blow-and-blow efficiency, as if he were cutting a trail in the jungle, a small path for a little light to filter in.

And then Magellan fell. What had felled him?

And then the Mactanese were on him like rain or ants or some other force of nature.

And then Pigafetta felt a sharp pain in his leg, and looked, and saw the bamboo spike pushed through his flesh.

He looked up and Magellan was no longer there, only the glossy brown backs and smooth black hair and a hundred limbs pounding and the water turning a dark red, a fragment of armor floating on its surface like a paper boat.

9. Domus

Pigafetta awoke to the sound of sails. He could hear them flapping in the wind—a steady breeze bringing him back to Europe—awakening him to the familiar. But when he opened his eyes he saw the corners of his bedroom, the draping of the bedclothes, the cold stone of the walls, and a small sparrow whose desperate flutter had entered, translated, into his dream.

Pigafetta woke up in the same state of disorientation every day, the stillness of the room unnatural, the size, solidity, and quiet a departure from the normal. He sat up in bed and placed his feet upon the floorboards. The sparrow swooped and flapped, looping in small and ineffective paths of escape. Pigafetta ducked out of its way and reached for his robe; he would trap the bird and set it free.

He had managed to confine the sparrow to the space between the wardrobe and the wall when a servant knocked on the door.

"Come in," said Pigafetta.

The servant stepped inside.

"And for God's sake, close the door behind you. Can't you see what I'm doing?"

But the servant could only see Pigafetta's back, the unenlightening nightshirt, his bandy legs and bare feet, and the raised robe that made him look as if he were bullfighting with the wardrobe. Was this the madness that all the servants had been waiting for since his return from the east? The servant shut the door with a grudging obedience.

"Keep away from the window," Pigafetta said, and the servant stepped to one side.

Pigafetta, having netted the sparrow in his robe, quickly ran to the window to set it free, but the bird was frightened,

aquiver in all directions; it seemed highly likely that upon re-
lease, the sparrow would once more be inside. Seeing no other
option, Pigafetta threw the robe, unfurling it, out the window.
The servant remained by the door, respectfully still.

"Why are you here?" asked Pigafetta.

"Sir," said the servant, bowing his head, "Lady Carlotta
is here to see you."

"Carlotta?" Carlotta was Pigafetta's favorite cousin. "She
was not expected, was she?"

"No, sir. And I feel obliged to add that she is in quite a
state."

"And what state is that?"

"She is very upset and weeping."

"Weeping?"

Pigafetta had made plans to dine with Carlotta at the
end of the week. There was much to talk about, and in the year
since his return from the east she had been the only person
he confided in. She had nursed him back to health when he
returned from Spain, and when his nightmares awoke him in
his convalescence, it was she whose cooling cloth and soothing
voice calmed him and stilled the demons.

He had returned from Spain, having delivered his deposi-
tion to the king, in a condition of extreme fatigue. Shortly after
having reestablished a household, in Venice itself—he could
not bear the landlocked towers of his native Vicenza—he had
collapsed into a state of delirium, and Carlotta—boozy, sweet,
honest Carlotta, with her current fashion and fading looks, her
progressively younger lovers and fatally aging husbands—had
shown tender fortitude and helped him through it. He remembered her gravelly, hypnotic voice as the one thing that had
guided him through the shadows of that time: her hoarse prom-
ise of the present his only compass.

"There is no more Mactan," she had said. "I have erased it. There is no dissembling king of the Moluccas, no more ships sinking beneath the weight of cloves. There are no more Portuguese to imprison you, to pursue you to the Cape of Good Hope, because that is no more: no fierce winds, no jagged rocks, no endless waiting while you starve for the winds to favor you, and the *Victoria*. The Portuguese are not waiting in Santiago to hang you, but are in Portugal, where they can do you no harm. We have all the food you can eat and sweet water and wine. The Land of Verzin lies only in your imagination. We know no cannibals, nor giants. There are no fish with razor teeth that prey on men, no poison darts to poison dreams. You are home, Antonio, home."

Pigafetta turned to the servant. "Go outside and get my robe," he said. "I need it."

Carlotta was in the living room fanning herself with an anxious vigor. Her hair was up, but had been arranged carelessly, and the overall effect was dishevelment and haste. She was no longer weeping, having moved on to anger. Pigafetta noted all.

"Carlotta," he said, "you cannot always believe what you hear."

"That confirms it," she responded. She flared her nostrils and stomped across the room, flinging herself into a chair. "Why?"

"For my religion."

"Religion? You have no religion other than wine and boys, like me."

"It is never too late to reunite with God, to reaffirm one's faith."

"You think the Turks need to be killed?"

"For my faith—"

"And even if you believe that, which you don't, you think you're the one to do it?"

"To create the kingdom of God on earth."

"Listen to yourself, Antonio: one aphorism after another. How can I trust this? Observe clearly your embracing of the cross, this march east and east—backward into the past, because the time for knights and infidels was four hundred years ago. Call it what it is—suicide."

Pigafetta took a chair a safe distance from Carlotta and slumped into it. The servant appeared at the door with goblets and a carafe of wine, and Carlotta watched him pour out the wine, biting her lip. Then the servant was gone, and she drained half her glass, wiping her mouth with the back of her hand.

"I know you are brokenhearted for your captain, who, as I understand it, never loved you. Only as his friend. You will get past this—"

"You only say that because he was a man."

"No," said Carlotta. "I say this because you are a man. Grief is a young man's privilege. At your age, it is only loss and acceptance. This crusade—who are you killing? Turks? Arabs? You care enough about these people to kill them? And you are not a soldier. You told me you shot one Indian and then were pierced in the leg by a poison arrow. Turks and Arabs are not so strangely armed, and worse, they know you, their enemy, whereas those naked heathens know nothing at all."

Pigafetta looked out the window at the hazy blue sky. How could he argue for the importance of his decision when nothing had value, nothing was worth fighting for, so why not fight? How could this convince anyone? How had he convinced himself?

"You cannot stay in the wake of this Magellan, who, even in death, moves you by simply having passed."

"Many die having never been so moved."

"So you wish to die because of it? They will kill you. Infidels are superior to barbarians. It is an irrefutable fact."

"How simple the world is for you, Carlotta."

"You mean to insult me and scare me off." Carlotta laughed. "Simple? You, like young men, desire complication a virtue." She folded her hands in her lap; she was now serious. "Venice is your home. The doge is your friend and admirer, and they are publishing your book everywhere," she said. "Even the pope takes it to bed with him each night, to read about the giants and the native girls girdled about with nothing but their hair. You are not a man who needs a profession, but there it is: writer." She smiled. "There is only one problem with the account, and that is everything is somehow Magellan. Even after he dies, you're singing his praises, as if he is the wind pushing the sails and his cunning helps you outrun the Portuguese boats. Write another work, and this time—" Carlotta leaned forward and raised her eyebrows significantly. "You are the star! Antonio Pigafetta, native of Vicenza, nobleman, adventurer. Honestly, your Magellan never even made it around the world . . ."

And so she continued for some time, and as the moon waxed and waned, rose and sank, and the tides marched up and up, then back and back, Carlotta could still have been prattling on, sitting in her chair, demanding the servant bring more wine. It made little difference to Pigafetta. It made none at all.

10. Paradise

I will leave Pigafetta, nobleman of Vicenza, first writer of the modern world, standing on the battlefield. It might be Turkey; it might be the moon. He has just been thrown from his horse and is inordinately pleased to have survived this with no broken bones. The horse, smart thing, is returning to camp and is nothing but a distant drumming of hooves curtained by a poof of dust. Pigafetta's armor is heavy, and he dislikes how it chafes at the knees and shoulders. His sword is also heavy and he can barely lift it. It seems unlikely that he could use the sword to inflict harm on anyone other than himself; in swinging it about, he might dislocate his shoulder.

Pigafetta starts walking to the heart of the conflict, aware that where he now stands is somewhat peripheral. There is dust all around, and heat. He can hear the shrieking of the injured horses rise above the grumble of men at war and the tromp of their boots. Pigafetta feels irrelevant to this battle—to himself—and would gladly fritter away what could very well be his final moments in this state of carelessness, but he does not have that option, because Pigafetta needs to relieve himself. He knows the knightly thing to do would be to just let loose, let the urine trickle down his leg, pool into his shoe, and march on. That would save him from having to set down his sword and unburden himself, plate by plate, of this ridiculous carapace, and what if he is ambushed? He pictures himself turning—all gleaming metal above, all hairy pinkness below—and the surprise on the Mussulman's face. It would certainly be funny. Pigafetta finds himself laughing, laughing, and laughing louder. He walks in circles, deeply amused, dragging his sword behind him as if it is a toy, as if he is a drunk: the sword records his passage in the dust in erratic zigzags. How sad to be laughing alone!

And then, playing in his ear like a song lodged there against his will, he hears his friend laugh with him. Magellan is laughing too, *ha, ha, ha,* in his bawdy, flat way:

"'Tonio, what have you done to yourself, and all for me?"

He's laughing with Pigafetta, and although, so close that you can smell them, men are fighting—not just fighting, but dying too, and for God! For their faith! For the cross!—it is somehow still funny. These men have left their families behind, and little boys, their mouths turned down in sad little bows, will never know their fathers. Silken, perfume-choked hankies will be blooming with leaked blood and limbs will be left here and there, tossed around as the young discard their clothes.

People are dying and in pain—blood is spilled upon the plain.

But in this world, what could be so terribly serious?

Pigafetta, fumbling with his pants, looks up and surprises the infidel, who—his nose covered with some sort of veil—has crept up behind him. Oh, the hilarity of it all. Now the tears pour out the sides of Pigafetta's eyes, and Magellan laughs *ha, ha, ha,* and the infidel—who knows to fear madness in dogs but is not sure if the same holds in men—stands with his scimitar, gripped loosely as skilled soldiers hold their weaponry. Pigafetta sees him, and fans inward with his hands, in a gesture of welcome, an invitation: *Avvicinarsi!* And laughing all the while. The infidel does not laugh, but sees the easy kill. And Magellan and Pigafetta see no harm in a little more blood spilled. They see no reason to become morbid in this morbid situation. Soon it will all be over and there will still be love. Why shouldn't they laugh?

Paradise

I. Tragedy

Tragedy is waste. Tragedy is the reminder of human helpless-
ness. Tragedy invents God everywhere it chooses to appear.
Tragedy destroys God everywhere it chooses to appear. Tragedy
has its superstars. Tragedy has its victims. Tragedy forces people
to take stock of their lives [as if lives were pantries or mutual
funds] and find meaning in it. Tragedy is what forces people to
take stock of their lives [as if lives were pantries or mutual funds]
and find all essentially meaningless. Others' tragedy makes one
feel lucky—safe. Others' tragedy is what makes one feel lucky—
but for how long? Tragedy affects children because they are
not yet jaded and know how to fear. Tragedy does not affect
children because they have yet to learn fear. Tragedy takes no
hostages. Tragedy takes hostages. Jonestown is a tragedy that
took no hostages and holds me hostage. I was a child at the time
of the Jonestown Massacre and I feared Jim Jones. I am held
hostage by the Jonestown Massacre and I fear Jim Jones. Parents
comfort children by saying, Hitler is dead, Pol Pot is dead. I
comfort my children by saying, Idi Amin is dead, Jim Jones is

dead. Children find little comfort in these deaths, adults even less. There is always another monster waiting in the wings. This is what children teach adults, although no one needs to teach this to me. I have never forgotten.

II. In the Beginning

Who is Jimmy Jones? He is the child wandering the streets of Crete, Indiana, lunch sack in hand. He is the long face on the other side of the screen door, asking politely to come in. He is the son of [the long-suffering] Lynetta Jones. His father is a drunk. His father came back from the war damaged by the mustard gas. His father was in the nuthouse for five years. His father has no job, or beats him, or has hallucinations. His father's face shows pain. His father's face shows no pain. Something is not quite right with the father. Something is not quite right with the son. The mother is so busy with her housework and suffering that people are not sure if she is right or not. Jimmy kills a cat. The neighborhood children are scared. Jimmy has a funeral for the cat. The neighborhood children are scared. The cat goes to heaven. The cat tells Jimmy what it's like. The cat says, Jimmy, you're special. The cat says no such thing. Cats don't speak, especially when dead.

III. Monkey Time

He is the long face on the other side of the screen door, asking politely to come in. You say you don't need a monkey. Your whole life, you have lived without a monkey, and that's been all right. You agree that the monkey is cute and ask, although you're not at all interested, what kind of monkey it is. You let him, and the monkey, in.

"Ma'am," he says, "this is a white-faced capuchin monkey, as healthy and sweet as they come. He'd like to go sit on your arm."

"Would he, now?"

The monkey comes and sits on your arm and disarms you. This is a house without children, but not for lack of trying, and this monkey has a sweetness in its eyes. You wonder why you've always been scared of monkeys, have images of monkeys lighting on people's heads, scratching eyes, ripping pages from books, sitting on the brass rail at the foot of your bed, watching as you sleep—watching and thinking. But not this monkey. If this were your monkey, you'd call it Baby. You'd crochet a soft blue cap for it, and a jacket, and teach it to ring a little bell. When you said, "Naughty Baby!" this monkey would cover its face with its tiny hands. Now it's holding on to your finger and your fingertip is in its mouth, and it's chewing on your fingernail, holding your gaze [hostage] in its nut-brown eyes.

"Isn't that sweet?" says the young man who's selling the monkey.

"Do monkeys make good pets?" you ask.

"If you love them enough," he says, this seller of monkeys. "Do you think you could love this little guy enough to give him a good home?"

And now you're the one answering questions. What is this monkey on your arm, gnawing at your finger? And why can't you bear to part with it?

"What's your name?" you ask the man.

And we know the answer.

"Well, Mr. Jones, I swear you could sell paradise back to God himself."

There's some good-natured chuckling and the monkey chuckles too, which is a little unsettling. You remember you're the one who told your husband that you were just too busy to look after a dog. But now you have that Mr. Jones's monkey (he says Reverend Jones, but you're not yet ready to buy that) on your arm, and he has your money in his pocket—money that he says [crazy notion] he will use to start his own church.

And for weeks after, you'll have that dream that the monkey is sitting on the foot of your bed, ripping pages from the family Bible. You'll dream it and dream it and dream it and then wake up one day to find out it's really happening.

IV. Sanctuary

There is a safe place in the world. There is a safe place in the Midwest. There is a safe place in Indiana, in Indianapolis, on the corner of 15th and North New Jersey. At Peoples Temple, there is a safe place for you. There is a safe place for you old people, and you young people, and you black people, and you white people who don't mind being with black people. All can be safe here. Bring your elderly, and your people from the wrong side of the tracks, and your people from the right side of the tracks, then take a big hammer, just take it, and bust up the tracks and bring those too. Bring your aunts, your uncles, that uncle who works in insurance, that one who worked but is now too old, and bring his pajamas, and bring his life insurance policy. There will be a bed for him, and food, and a nurse, with medicine, who will always be there, doling out the medicine, making sure you don't just die in that chair in the kitchen by the screen door [that needs repairing] to get found by your neighbor when she wonders about that smell and all the flies buzzing round.

Give your watches, and your jewelry. Sign your checks. Go live in the Peoples Temple old folks' home, and when your relatives [did they ever ask you to live with them?] wonder what happened to your car, you tell them it's none of their business. When they ask you why you sold your house, what you sold it for, and where's all that money, you tell them it's none of their business. When they ask where you've gone, you won't even be there to tell them. They can all ask each other, sitting around the table at Thanksgiving [the only time you saw them anyway], why you went to Ukiah, California, and they won't know the answer. You're not there to tell them, and they won't know the answer, and even if you were there, you wouldn't be able to answer, because you're on a bus going to California, and, to be perfectly honest, you're wondering why too. And why the Reverend Jones would need that watch that once belonged to your father [the only thing of value he ever had] and where it is because you haven't seen it in a long time. But thank the Lord Almighty for faith, because if you didn't have that, right around now you might start feeling kind of foolish.

V. Hindsight

Was something done to him? Was he damaged? What was hidden behind those mirrored sunglasses? That smug and smirking confidence? That spitting, impassioned, fascistic, hell-splitting, heaven-dropping delivery? What inward look? What glance to past? What wrong pulled back the band of the slingshot to let loose with tenfold power? What crime against this man grew into this crime against humanity? What [who] else is responsible? Can it be his [drunkard] father? Can it be his [long-suffering] mother? Can it be his free will? His inability to exercise control? God whispering in his ear? The God delusion? Can he be important? Can he be unimportant? Excised from memory? Excised from history? History itself?

What is wrong with these people that there is something wrong with? What is wrong with Pol Pot and his Year Zero, his hobbled people marching backward through time, those dead babies in bags hanging from the trees? What is wrong with Idi Amin? Why does he sew his wife's legs on backward? Why backward? Two girls [my sister and I] listening to the radio all day during the Christmas holidays [summertime, 1976] will hear about Amin's pools and houses, wives and children, this wife, her legs. We will wonder what adultery is, but [this is instinct] know, and know not to ask our parents. Hitler's barking and hysterics, his butchery, his ovens, are dead in black and white. Be nice to Jews. But Pol Pot is killing children now. Idi Amin is killing people now, hunting them with lions, in the jungle. Jim Jones is building paradise now, building it in the jungle. You hold your plastic doll, sit in your underwear [Perth, 42 Celsius], and look at the TV, and think it is a window—a Narnia wardrobe—into Cambodia or Uganda or Guyana. That's bad, says Father. That's bad, says Mother, but they're holding back since they know [she knows war, he knows her] that things can always get worse.

VI. The Jungle

Jim Jones is in the jungle. Jim Jones has bought the jungle, bought the jungle for you, with all the money from your pay-checks and social security checks, with all the money from the watches and jewelry he sold, with all the money from selling your cars, because you don't need cars anymore, not now that you're moving to the jungle. You remember that when people are looking for hard-to-find things, they sometimes look in jungles. You remember Cortés searching around for El Dorado. He looked in the jungle. You remember Ponce de León looking for the Fountain of Youth. That was [why there?] in Florida, all jungle then, even though one look at Florida is enough to let you know he didn't find it. In fact, neither of them did, which is a concern, because Jim Jones is carting you and the rest of the "rainbow family" off to the jungle to find paradise. You're no theologian, but you know paradise isn't in the jungle. It's not in Guyana [is that really a country?] at any rate. He says he's taking you back into Eden, but wasn't Eden somewhere else, where all the biblical stuff happens, in Israel and Arabia? And isn't that all desert? When you try to remember, all you see is Charlton Heston dressed up like Ben-Hur, riding around in a chariot, and even you know, and you're no scholar, that the chariot races were in Rome and that Rome is in Italy.

You know this is not the right state of mind to be in while applying for a passport.

But everything is gone, except for Jim Jones. The car is gone. The house is gone. The bank account was emptied long ago. Your brother says he'll never speak to you again if you don't leave Peoples Temple—the same brother who called ten times a day for nearly six months—and who you know loves you. He says he's going to the papers, like some others. This is why you have to leave, before they do that thing that they will do, whoever "they" are and whatever "that thing" is. But that's okay. Remember, your money is still on Jim Jones. Why the hell not? This is the Jim Jones that built a church by selling monkeys, and if there's anyone who can build paradise in Guyana, you know it's him.

VII. Holocaust

Maybe Hitler did not invent the term, but one might say he owns it. Ten million died in Manchuria in the 1930s, more than in all of Hitler's camps [despite his best efforts], but there is no single name that ties up this particular campaign of murder. And that was before we cared if Japanese [yellow people] killed Chinese [yellow people]. Hitler wants to teach us that Jews aren't people, but he teaches us the opposite. He teaches us to avert our eyes from neatly stacked corpses, to feel unhinged [responsible?] for all the waste, to wonder if God is present everywhere in this dark spectacle, or present nowhere.

Hitler's score: 6,000,000 dead.

It is 1976 and in Cambodia, [brown] people are killing [brown] people. People are trying to unlearn, remembering the process of learning as a distant, lovely thing, and not really understanding how to reverse it. People are digging their own graves, and handing over their children to people they don't like, and it is Year Zero, even though they know [as they desperately try to unlearn it] that somewhere the twentieth century is speeding to its ferocious end—each year like a leg-flicking girl in a cancan line that gets smaller and smaller. Is this what the French have given you? Is it such bourgeois imagery that subverts the peasant revolution? People disappear, and to remember them, we have the pyramids of brilliant white skulls. Forget people. Unlearn people. Remember their clean and blameless bones.

Pol Pot's score: 1,700,000 dead.

We could blame the English and the vacuum left by colonial powers when they call it a day. That said, we could blame the

French for Pol Pot. But this is not about pointing fingers, pointing here, pointing there, pointing at ourselves, looking in the
mirror. This is about tallying scores, and right now we're taking
a good, hard look at Uganda.

The English did not create Idi Amin, the monster. The
English created Idi Amin, a monster. Idi Amin terrifies, but he
is like a child. Idi Amin terrifies because he is like a child. He is
Big Daddy. He is Conqueror of the British Empire. He throws
the bodies of traitors into the Nile, where crocodiles eat them.
He throws the bodies of innocent victims into the Nile, where
they clog the intake ducts of the hydroelectric plant. He is a great
athlete, but a sore loser. He is a great athlete who never loses. Do
not be his enemy. Do not be his friend. Be in Kenya, better yet,
England. Stay out of his reach, beyond the claws of lions, beyond
the snap of the crocodiles' jaws, beyond the range of firearms,
or orchestrated car crashes, or whatever he imagines—his sleep
of reason, his birth of monsters, his voracious reign.

Idi Amin's score: 500,000 dead.

Jim Jones has made a paradise in Guyana. He is an explorer, a
settler, a visionary. Jonestown is Jamestown. Jonestown is Ply-
mouth. He has big ideas, like Hitler. He has blind followers,
like Pol Pot. His rule is absolute, like Idi Amin. He is a monster
and he kills people.

Jim Jones's score: 913 dead.
What?
Jim Jones's score: 913 dead.
Is that all? Why should we care?
All right. How about this:
Jim Jones's score: 1.

Which was the number of people still alive at Jonestown
when he was finished.

VIII. Passion

Jim Jones does good things. He is a good man. He is also Lenin, and Father Divine, and sometimes Jesus Christ. The sun rises over Jonestown. The sun rises over Dad, who is also Jim Jones. He wants people to call him Dad, to write him letters: "Dear Dad, It would be so beautiful to die a very peaceful death with my family." They write letters back home, "Dear [other] Dad, we are teaching the children animal husbandry and farming. They are learning in the open air." They are learning to live in an agricultural society. They are tilling the fields, sowing seeds, and the sun is high in [Year Zero] Jonestown.

Jim Jones [Dad] speaks all day through the loudspeakers. He speaks of the bloodbath, of the massacre of all black people back home, of the rise of the Klan, of the evil of the Americans spreading like a stain across what you used to call home. But here in Jonestown, you are safe. Here you are learning to repair shoes and make soap and work in a sawmill. Here you are safe from television and racism and all those people who want to hurt you and Jim Jones, because they want to hurt you and Jim Jones. You are safe from your parents, your family, their interference. You are safe from leaving, because you have no passport. You are safe from wanting to leave, because you know Jim Jones [Dad] will kill you. You are safe from feeling bad about this because you are so tired from working in the fields that you don't think anymore. You are safe from feeling bad about this because you haven't felt anything in months, not since you moved to Guyana and learned to write letters: "Dear Dad, I think it would be so beautiful to die . . ." Although there's a twinge somewhere in the mind—like a shooting fever pain—that reminds you of something, or someone [yourself?], like when you smell corn bread and it reminds you of your grandmother.

The sun is high in Jonestown, and you have one hour to eat your watery rice soup for lunch. There was rice for breakfast, and there will be rice, with beans, for dinner. You remember liking rice, but that was the other you that had that ability. You can't like unless you can dislike, and here [Jonestown] you can't afford to dislike anything.

The sun is setting on Jonestown, and Jim Jones is going to Russia. You're all going to Russia, because the Russians love Jim Jones and the Russians love you and America is an evil place. You are all leaving Jonestown because Congressman Leo Ryan [who?] is spreading lies and rumors. You are all leaving Jonestown so that you will not be gunned down by Congressman Leo Ryan. You are staying in Jonestown so that you will not be gunned down, like Congressman Leo Ryan, who is lying facedown on the tarmac beside his plane. No one is sure of anything. Listen to the announcements coming over the loudspeakers. Just listen.

You are not going to Russia because there is no time, but you are still leaving Jonestown. You and your grandmother and your children are leaving Jonestown. Your husband and brother, they are leaving Jonestown. You are no longer building paradise on earth. You are no longer doing anything, and you wonder if all that will be left of your time in the fields, your faith and hard work, will be the sound of babies screaming, and parents wailing, and Jim Jones [Dad] talking crazy, his mind rotted with his God-like, barbiturate-hazy, heaven-and-hell thinking. And you think it's time to run. Run for the jungle, now before it's too late. Before you're poisoned or injected, before his men gun you down. You think that maybe you'll find something there [yourself?], like Ponce de León wanted to, and Cortés wanted to, and Jim Jones wanted to. Then you remember that none of them found any of it—not the Fountain of Youth, not

El Dorado, not Paradise. The whole mess might make you laugh, if all those people [now you too!] hadn't died.

IX. We Pray

Let us all say a prayer for the people killed at Jonestown. Let us all say a prayer for the 913 people who died at Jonestown. Let us all say a prayer for the 276 children who died, and their parents, who are also dead. Let us all say a prayer for the women and men, for that woman lying on the ground, facedown, with her arm draped over her child, her hand touching someone [grandmother?] who is also facedown, whose face we cannot see, who died at Jonestown. Let us all not drink Kool-Aid because it kills people, even though [at Jonestown] the people drank Flavor-Aid and it was the cyanide in it that killed them.

On the playground, let the Australian children ask in urgent whispers, "Your dad's American. Do you think he wants to kill you?"

Let us all say a prayer for the people killed by Pol Pot. Let us all say a prayer for the babies killed by Pol Pot, for the babies in plastic bags hanging from the trees like fruit or Christmas ornaments or bats. Let us all say a prayer for the people who are being killed, even though we've been told that in Cambodia it's Year Zero, and if it really is Year Zero, wouldn't most [all?] people not even be born yet? Just say a prayer, send it out, hope that God notices what's happening and fixes it quickly.

Let us all say a prayer for the Ugandans who are being killed by their leader, Idi Amin. Let us all say a prayer for Idi Amin's wife, because he killed her and cut off her legs and sewed them on backward. Let us pray for him, that he might become a better ruler, and not let anyone know that when we see Amin on TV, his shiny black face and enormous smile, that there's something to like about him and that [don't tell anyone, don't think it too hard or God will know] we might even follow him, even though we know about his wife. And that he's feeding people to crocodiles and hunting them with lions. Pray for the lions, who we like to think would not want to eat people unless they were really, really hungry.

Let us all say a prayer for Pope Paul the Sixth, with Jesus in heaven, and then—a month later—say a prayer for Pope John Paul the First, with Jesus in heaven. Then let us all say a prayer for Pope John Paul the Second, so that he lives longer.

Let us all say a prayer for Elvis, and then get into a fight on the playground when Phillip Murphy says he died with his head in the toilet.

Let us say a prayer, secretly, for Skylab, which crashed out in the desert. We're not supposed to pray for things [no souls], but we do anyway because there's something sad about the twisted bits of metal, the melted wires, the smashed glass. And we know that Skylab must have felt lonely out there in space, taking pictures for us, and we ought to have found a way to bring it home.

Pray for all of this because God is listening, and if he hears you praying, he'll know to protect you from being crushed when Skylab smacks into the desert, to protect you from Idi Amin's crocodiles and lions, and Pol Pot's Year Zero. From Jim Jones and his monkeys and religion, guns and Guyana, from his paradise, where everyone sleeps facedown and never wakes up.

Jim Jones is dead, shot with a gun [suicide?], but let's not pray for him. At night you'll imagine he escaped into the jungle, wonder if he's lurking in that dark corner beside the wardrobe, waiting quietly with his drink bottle filled with Kool-Aid. You'll dream of a monkey wandering into Jonestown, seeing it all so still. The monkey will trot across the bodies, pulling at belt buckles and other shiny things. The monkey will pull off buttons, put them in his mouth, and spit them out. The monkey will go through the pockets of the people who lie so still, looking for something [what?], but find them all—every one—empty.

The Solace of Monsters

Captain Zimri Coffin retired to his cabin with a book, as was his habit. His wife chose his reading material. He did not have the time to buy books when in port. As soon as he set foot on solid ground, he was already preparing to leave, his head occupied with whaleboats, harpoons, hardtack, barrels, whatever was needed for the yearlong or maybe longer voyage. His wife had started him on the novels. She was afraid he'd get lonely at sea, or worse, become overly familiar with the men, some of whom were Wampanoag, barely civilized, and capable of such intimidating silence that she (not justified, but passionate) thought they lived in some animated state between death and life. How this fit in with her views on God and heaven was unclear, but as Coffin burrowed into this new book, *Frankenstein,* he was beginning to see where she came up with such ideas.

"Silly woman," he thought. But he was fond of her. And the reading kept her alive in more than memory. He was not so much reading as reliving that eight-hour period when his wife had only risen from her rocker to give orders to the maid for his dinner. He could almost smell her in the pages.

Coffin was about twenty pages into the first of the three volumes—the point at which Captain Walton picks up Dr. Frankenstein, who is in dreadful shape, emaciated, half-frozen, gripped by a fever—when he thought he should turn in. The clock showed it to be nearing eleven and his lantern was low on oil, a good time to quit, but maybe he could go another ten pages without wasting himself for the next day's tasks. The water was slapping on the side of the *Dauphin* and she was at such a gentle roll—almost snoring herself—that it was not difficult to believe the *Dauphin* an exploring vessel, that he was not Zimri Coffin, but rather Captain Walton. That he was not involved in the dirty, unromantic task of boiling whales down to machine oil, but rather deep in the North Sea in pursuit of that somehow stationary yet elusive North Pole.

But out there lurked the monster.

Ten pages later, Coffin heard a beastly moan, and for a moment forgot altogether that he was floating in the warm Pacific, rather than bound in by ice in the frigid waters of the north. He moved the book from his face and stilled his breath. Yes. There was the moaning again, a ghastly, beastly moaning. After what seemed a long time, he put the book down and, picking up his pistol, got up from the bed. His door swung open silently.

On deck the ropes were creaking in the mainstays and the whaleboats, hoisted high, were swinging slightly as the boat rocked. A large, almost full moon lit the boards of the deck and a million stars peppered the sky. Captain Coffin stopped. No men were about, which was good, because no doubt he presented a ridiculous figure. He was wearing his slippers. Even the best-kept deck produced an occasional splinter, he reassured himself, and he did not have the toughened soles of the men, who went without shoes, springing up and down the rigging like monkeys, gripping with their toes. But there again was that beastly moaning.

"Uhhagh. Uhhagh," the creature moaned.

Captain Coffin slowly made his way around the main mast. There was the monster, huge and hulking, crouching over the side of the deck.

"Uhhagh. Uhhagh," it moaned again.

The captain squeezed his pistol. Then he let it hang by his side again. This was no Frankenstein. This was Asnonkeets, one of the Wampanoag, who was very large but hardly a monster.

"Asnonkeets, what are you doing about at this time of night?" said the captain, stepping out from the shadows.

"Sir?" said the man, and he spun around. "I'm feeling under the weather."

Coffin smelled the strong odor of rum.

"This behavior cannot be tolerated."

Asnonkeets lowered his eyes, and despite his extreme illness and usual expressionless gaze, there was the start of a smile. The Indian had noticed the slippers.

"All right. Belowdecks, now," said Coffin.

"But sir, I am very ill."

"I suppose no one wants you belowdecks."

The Indian pulled himself to full height, not to be threatening but rather as a gesture of politeness. "Am I to be sanctioned, sir?"

Coffin considered this. "No, but keep it down. I know you're unwell, but isn't there a way to . . . relieve yourself without such moaning? It's keeping me awake."

Asnonkeets nodded.

"I need you at your best. Let's just say that this is a warning."

"Thank you, sir."

As Coffin returned to his cabin, he pondered the fact that he could have cut Asnonkeets's rations or even had him whipped, but he'd been so grateful that he was the monster that he actually felt more disposed to toss him some beef, in with the usual salt horse. In this generous mood—half grateful that Asnonkeets was still on the deck upchucking over the port bow, keeping watch—Captain Coffin finally fell asleep.

The following morning dawned bright and clear. Captain Coffin stepped out of his cabin cheered by the warm sun, although his dreams had been dark—Asnonkeets stitched over, yelloweyed, moaning from the ice that trapped the *Dauphin*. Ice in the Pacific. He chuckled to himself. And there was Asnonkeets, clearly solid Wampanoag, no composite of dead criminals here, joking with the other men. He looked sheepishly at the captain, smiling almost warmly, and the men also seemed to look at him with a certain amount of approval, no doubt because of his generosity with the Indian. Coffin was feeling fatherly today, his heart full of goodwill, his emotions all jumbled due to the tortures of the previous evening. He walked confidently to the railing and swung his telescope to the horizon, optimistic that today (no worrying ice floes in the Pacific) whales would break that fine line, that their oily shadows would spoil the surface of the water. The first mate, Owen MacDonald, was busily investigating the integrity of the prow of one of the whaleboats, which looked a little soft. He had his pocket knife dug into the timber and twisted it.

"Captain, it will do until we reach Valparaiso."

Again, good news.

At the head of the mainmast, John Squibb, another Wampanoag, was roosted like an eagle. He had fine eyes and if there were whales he would sight them long before any of the other men.

Coffin turned to MacDonald. "What's our location?"

And the first mate rattled back the latitudes and longitudes, minutes and degrees, and it was all acceptable and as it should be.

Coffin looked back up the mainmast. John Squibb had unfolded himself and was stretched with his hand shielding his eyes from the sun. Coffin's heart beat in his chest and he waited—breath held—for the call "there she blows." But none came. Maybe it was another ship. "What have you got there, John Squibb?"

"Whaleboat, sir."

A tiny vessel, good only for chasing fish, in the middle of the ocean. Coffin went to the railing and raised his telescope. It was a whaleboat, and he thought he could make out the brushy tops of two heads just over its sides.

"All right," said Coffin, "let's go pick them up."

Shipwreck victims were not uncommon. Some boats were destined to sink. Some ships were just doomed. Large waves, like improvident hands of God, slammed them into splinters in the most inconvenient locations, like this, the Pacific, where one could only hope for flying fish to offer themselves, leaping into the boat, or for a shipmate to expire, the blood still running in his veins. And there was always the drawing of lots. Better to be trapped in the ice where seals and bears sometimes made an appearance. Coffin stuffed his pipe full and puffed heartily as he waited for his ship to draw alongside the small vessel.

But Coffin was not prepared for what he saw there. The two men were dead, and their boat was no stab at life, but more of a floating coffin. Scattered bones covered its planking. Captain Coffin looked carefully at the desiccated corpses—ulcered, leathery skin wrapped around their skeletons, the clothing rotted off their bodies, bleached by the sun and salt. His heart was chilled. How could one be frightened of monsters when men offered up such images of horror?

The boat rocked on the waves, at a knock and knock against the ship's keel.

The men of the *Dauphin* waited for their captain to give them some direction; they waited on his words, but he was dumbstruck.

"Ah," he said. His eyes were moist and he was deeply moved with pity. "We shall give them a Christian burial."

Asnonkeets, who was at Coffin's side, raised an eyebrow, then looked back at the boat. "Sir, not meaning to be disrespectful, but those men are alive."

"They are?" Coffin looked back into the boat and sure enough, awakened by the sounds of human speech, the men were slowly blinking, shivering to life. "It is a miracle! Praise merciful God!"

At first, Coffin didn't notice that the men did not share his enthusiasm. Seeing two shriveled specters afloat in an ossuary did not deepen their faith in this so-called "merciful God." Was this not a whaleboat? Was this fate not a frightening possibility? Were these starved men not the crew of the *Dauphin* in a dark mirror? But soon Asnonkeets and Garby—another harpooner—were descending on ropes like benevolent spiders, bringing up the survivors with startling tenderness, whispering gently, "You are alive. You are saved."

Coffin called the cook and demanded that he start a pudding of tapioca, because this was gentle food and all the rescued men could handle.

"What of the boat?" asked MacDonald.

"We'll tow it," said the captain. "We can sell it when we reach Valparaiso. Once the bones are out, someone might want it and we can start a charitable fund for these good men."

Coffin supervised the bathing of the castaways, who turned out to be none other than Captain George Pollard and Charles Ramsdell of the *Essex* out of Nantucket. Somewhere, out there in the blue wash of sea, was another boat with the first mate, Owen Chase, and a few other men. A third boat was also making its way to Chile, but they had lost sight of that one long ago. On an island deep to the west, three other sailors had elected to cast their lot (or decided to avoid casting their lot) trying to eke out a life on the occasional albatross egg. Pollard was eager to tell his tale, but Coffin had been firm. Rest first, then maybe later, if Pollard was up to it, he would join Coffin in his cabin, where he could tell of his ordeal.

At about five o'clock that afternoon, another ship was sighted, the *Diana*. Coffin knew the captain, Aaron Paddack, and it was soon arranged for Paddack to come aboard for dinner.

Coffin met Paddack's boat as it pulled up to the side of the *Dauphin*. "Coffin, you look good!" Paddack called as the ladder rattled down the *Dauphin*'s side. "And I'm done, on my way home with the hold filled to the brim. So I have a gift for you." Paddack swung his long legs over the railing and handed Coffin a cloth bag. "Tobacco, and smell it."

"How kind," said Coffin. He inhaled the contents of the bag. "Damp and sweet. And you look well. How I wish I was heading home." But really, he wished nothing of the sort. "Come and have a drink with me," he said. And after a hearty handshake, they made their way to the captain's cabin.

Coffin wasted no time telling Paddack about the men of *Essex*. "If Captain Pollard's up to it, he'll join us shortly. But I must say, he presents a frightful appearance. Quite wasted, and I'm not sure, but verging on the mad."

"What happened to the *Essex*?"

"He says a whale sank it. Smashed into the boat and crumpled the timbers. I've never heard anything like it, but he swears it happened, as does the other man. They've been afloat for three months, have navigated over three thousand miles."

"And how have they survived?"

"Their boat was filled with bones. We had to pry them out of their hands. When we gave them clean clothes, we found their pockets filled with fingers cleaned of all the meat. And the ribs, they were sucking, to get the marrow out. When we took these bones away, the men started sobbing, begged us to give them back their companions. They said we'd no right to take their friends away."

The steward set some pork on the table and the captains grew still.

"How are our guests faring?" asked Captain Coffin.

"Captain Pollard is eager to join you, sir."

"Well," said Coffin, and he stood up. He went to his chest and pulled out a clean shirt and a pair of trousers. "Give him these. I'm sure he'll feel more of a man when he's dressed for dinner."

"Yes, sir," said the steward. "Anything else?"

"Have the cook send up another bowl of the tapioca."

"Yes, sir."

"And give the men this," said the captain, "to be shared." It was a bag of his old, inferior tobacco that he no longer needed.

"Thank you, thank you very much, sir. From all of us."

After the steward was gone, Captain Paddack cast a bemused look at Coffin. "You are soft on your men."

"Yes, I am. And it's probably stupid, but I know no other way."

Captain Paddack picked up the volume of *Frankenstein,* which was on the shelf at his elbow. "What is this?"

"A frightening book. Terrible to read, especially at sea."
Coffin smiled. "You don't read novels, I assume."

"Novels? My wife does."

"How do you pass your evenings?"

"I have my ship's log and the navigation." Captain Paddack shrugged. "I must sleep better than you because I feel I have no time to spare."

There was a knock at the door.

"Come in," called Coffin, in a merry voice.

"Sir," said the steward, "I have Captain Pollard."

Captain Pollard held on to the steward's elbow, shuffling across the floor painfully, as if his bones were rubbing on each other, and collapsed into the chair to Coffin's right. Coffin's clothes were large on him, and Pollard folded up so much when he sat that his head was no higher than that of a boy. He had settled into that chair like a gull into its nest and his eyes held that same disquieting glitter. But as he looked first to Coffin's face and then to Paddack's, his expression softened into one of complete contentment.

"Good of you to join us," said Captain Paddack. He smiled at Pollard, but the shock was clear on his face.

"Yes, and I fear too good," added Coffin. "If you are not up to this, I assure you I will not be insulted."

"To sit in a chair at this good table," whispered Pollard, "is of great comfort to me, who have suffered much."

Coffin brought his chair up alongside Pollard's and helped him sip some water. "There's a good man," he said. There was another knock on the door. "What now?" called Coffin.

"Captain Pollard's tapioca, sir," said the steward.

"Bring it in," said Coffin. "Give it to me."

Coffin took the bowl and spooned a small amount into Pollard's mouth, which Pollard worked over like an infant.

"So," said Paddack, a forkful of pork by his mouth, "I hear your ship was stove in by a whale."

"That is true," said Pollard.

"Remarkable," said Paddack. "Must have been a big whale."

"A monster," whispered Pollard. "Rammed our ship. He came back and made sure that we sank, and most of us still in the herd, hunting among the cows. The sea was red and bubbling with blood. Owen Chase, my first mate, was still aboard repairing one of the whaleboats. He saw the monster—a bull ten leagues in length—but was scared to harpoon it, scared it would shatter the rudder in its anger." Captain Pollard raised his two wiry arms, which cast a long shadow on the wall behind Paddack's head. He inhaled a raspy breath and let his arms sink, folding them back into his lap. "Then it dove. The *Essex* sank quickly."

"Right," said Paddack. "That's quite a story."

"My poor man," added Coffin. "And what a miracle of good navigation and a merciful God have delivered you."

"Hang on," said Paddack, "why didn't you head for the Tahitian islands? They're a good deal closer than Chile."

"We'd heard," whispered Pollard, "that there are cannibals there. We feared . . ."

And then Pollard, mid-sentence, fell asleep.

"He'll come to in a minute," said Coffin. "He's been doing this all day, just a part of recovery."

Pollard stayed asleep for about twenty minutes, enough time for Coffin and Paddack to finish their meal, enough time for Paddack to speculate on the amount of baleen a whale's head large enough to sink a ship would contain.

"Be worth something, a whale that big."

"A ship-sinking monster," said Coffin, "does not interest me. I've enough to fear without that leviathan stalking the seas." Coffin stuffed his pipe, as did Paddack, and the cabin filled with smoke. Soon, Pollard, overcome by coughing, woke up.

"Captain Pollard," said Coffin, his pipe in his teeth, "can I offer you my extra pipe?"

"I've all I need," said Pollard.

Captain Paddack raised his eyebrows over Pollard's head, but Coffin politely ignored him. Pollard was digging around in the pocket of his pants. He came up with a short, wide portion of bone that he raised to his mouth, as if it were a cheroot, and began to suck on it.

"What, my good man," asked Captain Paddack, "is that?"

"This," said Captain Pollard, "is Barzillai Ray."

Later, when the moon was large in the sky, Captain Coffin escorted his friend back to the railing. He was sad to see Paddack go, because, even though he was insensitive and on occasion boorish, he was a friend to Coffin and always in good cheer.

"I must ask you," Captain Paddack said, laying a warm hand on Coffin's shoulder, "what is 'barsilarey'?"

"Barzillai, first name. Ray, last name. He was shipmate to the good captain. They were forced to eat him. I thought we took all the bones from Pollard, but he managed to hide that one."

"That chills me."

Coffin nodded. "Why keep the bones when their friends are gone? What comfort can that bring?"

As Coffin watched Paddack slipping over the water, the oars dipping in a soothing rhythm, the ocean dappled with moonlight, the sky calm and aglitter, he thought of the monster beneath him, spoiling the clear waters with its dark shadow, slowly mapping its vengeful way through the bottomless deep.

"Stay down there, beast," he said out loud. But his was a poor night's sleep. A light breeze combined with some loose rigging had set something to tapping—something that Coffin translated into Pollard crawling along decks, below his windows, tapping (but why?) with his bone. Finally, thrown into a panic of such heart-thudding, chest-restricted terror, Coffin had lit the candle, crept to his window, and peered into the hopeless, somber night. The face was there: eyes sparking in a dark face!

"Oh," said the captain, barely rescuing the candle, which would have fallen to his bed and lit it on fire. "Oh," he said again, recognizing the face, the eyes as his eyes—not wide with hunger, but with fear. He blew the candle out and returned to his covers. Little comfort, he thought, little comfort. But his mind wandered to the whale circling below him, while far to the north, the scientist's monster loosed his howl into the sparkling frozen wastes and this was, finally, enough to send him off.

His Actual Mark

I. 1840 and North of Adelaide

Edward John Eyre forays into the interior, northward, to where Sturt before him, and others since, suspect an inland sea. There is naught to confirm this, although a large body of water presents itself. *To stymie me,* he thinks. The lake—Lake Torrens—has a wet sparkle that tantalizes broken men and broken horses, for how long can they continue without finding water? But Torrens is a salt lake. A lake of salt! The novelty of this, after months of pushing through scrub and mountain and watching the horses stumble on the uneven brickwork of rocks, does not intrigue. A salt lake does not terrify—which might wake him up. A new danger, previously unimaginable, is both stunning and enervating. He thinks of his father, vicar of Hornsea, who talks often of God—the omnipresent God: Eyre, who has never before felt God's presence, knows it here, at the perimeter of this salted lake, when hope is ebbing. On the lake's edge, with the only sound the wind rattling the few leaves offered by the stunted trees, God is all about and patient, breathing silently, witness to everything.

At twenty-four years of age, Eyre will lead the expedition—but no further, merely back to Adelaide, to stave off more death. He wonders if he has accomplished a great deal, but it is possible that nothing has been achieved but for the wasting of horses and time.

Eyre decides to head west. No one has made it to the western colonies overland. As far as Eyre knows, no one has tried. Cattle and sheep are taken by ship to the southern port city of Albany, and then driven the remaining few hundred miles to Perth. Sea voyages plague livestock with disease, and once in Albany there is the problem of hiring drovers from the few unoccupied members of the population: drunkards, convicts, drunken convicts, desperate men, bored blacks who've never before ridden a horse, inland blacks who've never before seen a horse, and others, so many others, with nothing to commend them. Eyre knows this, as he has managed such journeys, managed to find the drovers, standing in the heat of almost comic intensity, with the eucalypts waving their fragile fingers in it as if to pantomime breeze, with the magpies coughing in the dust.

II. Eyre Managing Such a Journey

Albany! The men stare hungrily as if Eyre's pockets bulge with banknotes, as if he too isn't desperate after investing in these sickened sheep and piteously lowing cattle—as if he too doesn't wonder if he were the fool, just like these men who try to gauge just what sort of idiot would show up with cattle, would consider hiring them?

"Who can ride a horse?" asks Eyre.

And all raise their hands, except one young black on the end, an unsmiling sort of aborigine, which Eyre has been warned is just the sort that steals your grog and evaporates into the bush the moment you're asleep.

"What are you doing here," asks Eyre, "if you don't know how to ride a horse?"

A thought. "I know where I'm going."

Eyre considers this. "You know the route to Perth?"

The youth nods.

"Many people know the route to Perth."

"But I know different."

The boy's voice (he looks no more than fourteen) is thick, and he delivers his words in a long garbled stream, as if it were one word. This is a skill of Eyre's: understanding the black man's delivery of the English language, and if he weren't feeling judged by those large black eyes, Eyre might have a self-congratulatory moment.

"That's Wylie," the harbor master says, appearing at Eyre's side. "You'd do well to have him with you. He can find water and has a good sense of direction."

"Any caveats?"

"Not really. The vicar's been trying to convert him for over a year with no luck, so don't bother. And his leanness is misleading. He consumes a lot of food."

Eyre hires Wylie and a couple of others. With losses counted, overlanding cattle from Albany to Perth is still a success. The trip back to Albany, unencumbered by the herd, is uneventful. Wylie, who has said all of five words to Eyre over their months of shared labor, has asked to accompany Eyre back to Adelaide.

"But all your people are here," says Eyre.

"My problem," says Wylie.

Eyre considers overnight, the map of Australia unrolled across his knees. A suggestion of placement and location, hypothesis and desperate guesswork, a place for Eyre to make his mark—his actual mark—driving the lines of ink, drawing the earth itself. Wylie isn't the most industrious worker, nor is he particularly cooperative. For an aborigine, and one so young, he doesn't need much company, spends his time at rest looking inquiringly at the leaves waving above him or at the line of horizon dancing in the heat. He is a mystery, says Eyre romantically, he's an idiot, he says sympathetically, he's just a boy away from his people, Eyre says, barely more than a boy himself and also away from his people. But Wylie does seem to know where he is going: when a flooded river diverted them on their way to Perth, he knew just where to go, just as, later, when absence of water was the problem, he had no trouble finding it.

"Wylie," says Eyre the next morning, "I would like you to assist me in exploration."

"Expiration?" Wylie asks.

"*Explor*ation. Going into the far reaches of the desert, and other places," says Eyre, but he falters, because, all of a sudden, he can't remember what exploring is.

"You go with sheep?"

"No sheep," says Eyre.

"Cows?"

"No cows."

"Why you going?"

"To take a look and then make a map for others."

Wylie nods. "How's the food?"

"Good," says Eyre, "until it runs out."

Some of Wylie's people show up to send him off. None of them seems to know what to do, as if there is no precedent for one of their own leaving, and on a boat, of all things. Then someone remembers to laugh, and they all laugh and pat him, lovingly push him and slap his arms. Which results in more laughter, but after that, and with little ceremony—Wylie has all his possessions on his person—he boards the boat and they sail away at good speed from that far-flung spot that is Albany to that other far-flung spot that is Adelaide.

III. Sentimental Geometry

Something about his sense of balance makes Eyre want to think that Adelaide is in the center of the southern Australian coast. But it's not. All the colonies are crammed together in the east, hugging the shores, clinging to the rivers, while the broad continent happens mostly to the west—a bald expanse, wide open, as if it has nothing to hide. Across this great divide, a Western toehold, although this might as well be its own island: the land that separates Albany and Perth from the east is as uninterrupted as an ocean.

E. Alfred Delisser, when surveying the plain twenty-five years hence, will note the absence of trees. He will pronounce, *"Nulla Arbor!"*—the spartan landscape inspiring a Roman moment. And after that, a millennia of schoolchildren in scratchy shorts and restricting frocks will be enlightened that "Nullarbor" is not an aboriginal word at all, but yet again the work of the English invoking the language of their conquerors upon conquered terrain.

The natives call it "Oondiri" or "no water," finding trees—there or not there—irrelevant.

In the 1950s, the British will test nuclear bombs there and request that all inhabitants (who could inhabit this place?) move away, but the Spinifex Wangai tribespeople are hard to find. This place of desolation (bomb it!) looks like home to them. After years of watching the sun sink into the earth, they'll see its little sister burst from within it. Having been in this one place since the dawn of time, they'll wonder if they have been waiting for this, like the white man who came—fish-like—from the sea, or the camels who appeared shortly after, lunging peacefully across the desert.

And Eyre, in 1840, when he looks at his map, sees it as *nulla*-complete, and if he were forced to call it into existence by thrusting a name upon it, he might call it "No Ink," since that's what *he* finds remarkable, and because his Latin is restricted to a few, seldom-uttered prayers.

Since his failure to the north, followed by another failure to the north (why does he entertain these northward thrusts?), Eyre faces west. He has first gone northward to Spencer Gulf, pushed onward, returned the same way, essentially erasing all progress, turned west, then headed back south: a triangle. He is walking around in triangles, which is no better than walking in circles—although the degrees are distributed differently. He knows the sum of the angles of his peregrinations equals 180 degrees. He knows the sum of his peregrinations equals naught. As he waits at Streaky Bay for supplies to make the big stab westward (a ray pushing from its point of origin), he's grateful that the funding is still coming, although he's supplying half the horses and a significant amount of provisions. Cape Catastrophe and Anxious Bay lie to the east, Denial Bay to the west.

Wylie, who has missed the earlier exploring, down with some undiagnosable aboriginal malady, arrives with other supplies, and Eyre—along with fresh horses, bread, medicines, flour, tea—now has direction. The horses stamp idly in the dirt, soft noses dilating, eyes kindly. Eyre holds one's harness, saying, "easy, easy," to which the horse responds with the backward nod and nod that is the equine's gentle agreement. Eyre knows that many of the horses will perish on this trip. He might too. But it's hard to feel sad about his perishing—cold fear accompanied by arrhythmia and trickling sweat, maybe—but sadness? No. Although he does feel sadness for the horses. In the dust, Wylie squats flat-footed, elbows hooked over his knees. The sun that rises coldly in the past boils downward in the future.

"That's where we're headed, Wylie," says Eyre. He attempts a paternal tone, which he thinks appropriate to both his age and race, but the delivery is off and he sounds unsure and almost amused at the prospect.

"I know that place," says Wylie.

"You do?"

"Going home, right?" asks Wylie.

"I suppose, if we're successful."

Eyre can tell by the look on Wylie's face that he doesn't know what "successful" means and hopes this is not just a shortcoming of language, but rather an innocence that knows no failure. He hopes that Wylie understands honest progression, uncolored by valor or tragedy: just the before, when one isn't there, and the now, when one is.

But he is not there yet.

And why would Wylie's understanding of a situation determine anything?

"You thinking?" asks Wylie.

"Certain things concern me," says Eyre.

Wylie wrinkles his nose, unimpressed with concern, and worry, and all preludes to the English overcoming of inertia. If they didn't have all these men and all these horses, and therefore all this provisioning for all these men and all these horses, there might be no cause for "concern."

"Too many of them, men and horses," says Wylie.

"That is your opinion," says Eyre, he hopes with enough disdain to communicate that Wylie's opinion was not wanted.

"Too many," says Wylie.

Later, after a profound loss of both horses and morale, Eyre will send nearly all of the party back to the east. He will stand at the head of the Great Australian Bight and squint at the brilliant white continent extending in an unobstructed plain, bewildered by the drop of limestone cliffs to pounding waves, waves clawing at the rock face—at the continent itself—clawing it into destruction. Here, with one's throat thick and parched, you must raise your voice to be heard above the surf. Here, even Wylie looks alien, not something that could deftly be inserted into the landscape with a few expert strokes of watercolor—black natives holding black spears with black legs at right angles, chasing prey: kangaroos to be jotted in with a few strokes of red or gray. Here, they are all extraneous. Here, at the blank spot where God ran out of ideas and couldn't be bothered with trees and billabongs and more wildlife than the distant screech of birds digging in the sand, Eyre feels as if he's wandered onto an empty stage, poorly costumed and with no lines rehearsed.

Eyre enters stage right with eleven equines (nine horses, a Timor pony, and a foal), Baxter (his trusty-when-not-drunk foreman), Wylie (a native from the west), and Yarry and Joey (two natives from New South Wales as bound and indistinct in all reports as Chang and Eng). He would like to exit stage left, but that lies several hundred miles to the west across Significant

Hardship. He wonders if this is suicide, and still wonders as he lifts his left foot and then his right—the mode of executing this stage of exploration, or expiration, as Wylie still terms it—left then right, all the way out of Significant Hardship and into History.

IV. Significant Hardship

To write the story of Eyre and Wylie is to stand on the firm plane of History and look back across the desert, much as Eyre, in later years, looks back across his life, trying to sight through more recent regret to this simpler, heroic time. Eyre's journey is assembled into an epic of great deprivation, friendship, sentimentality (Eyre writes of his weakened horses, "Whenever we halted, they followed us about like dogs"), fortitude, trust, luck, fear—all those elements of rich stories that we tread and tread like song lines are tread and tread, that we rehearse in our minds in the hope that life will provide for us a similar stage upon which to tread and tread (here come Eyre and Wylie across the Nullarbor!) with equal distinction. And if not that, perhaps populate our dreams with adventure, or our moments of rest with a perspicacious wonder more befitting a valuable consciousness than merely what needs next be done.

Eyre, Wylie, right, left, right, left.

But what happened to the others?

When last observed, our intrepid explorer, Eyre, accompanied by his faithful overseer, Baxter, and three native boys—Joey and Yarry, of New South Wales (although they call it something else), and Wylie, of the Swan River Settlement (who also calls it something else)—are struggling across an expanse of desert, having nearly expired due to lack of water, after having nearly expired due to lack of water, after having nearly expired due to lack of water. This is a dry and barren place. One horse has been killed and eaten, although Eyre could not bring himself to touch it. The English do not eat their horses. They adore their horses, withholding much affection from their fellow man in order to maintain this pure, unadulterated love for God's speechless beasts. What distinguishes Eyre from other English is the fact that he extends this sentimental attachment to his natives, wishing that they not be in pain, feeling responsible for their hunger and thirst. Baxter heaves a sigh skyward.

Baxter is an alcoholic who distinguished the first stretch of the journey by falling off his horse. He had been dragged out of a grog shop (the things spring up along the new trails like forest mushrooms after rain), feeling the beast of liquor roaring in his veins, the sky whirling above his head (or was he whirling?), and suddenly the ground—old friend—racing up to meet him. Oh well. There's nothing to drink in the desert—regardless of your inclinations—and what is he doing here, following Eyre across it? It's easy enough to get from Adelaide to Perth. You go by water, like all civilized creatures. It's only the blacks who go crawling across the scabbed back of the continent, like fleas on a sick dog. He's been wanting to turn back for weeks. And each time Eyre has persuaded him to continue, saying that he does not know how much longer they need travel. One can only hope that the halfway point has been passed, and that to return would increase the journey. But Eyre has said that several times to Baxter, and each time they've struggled on through weeks that might have brought them home again.

It was five days previous that Joey and Wylie ran off. They took their spears and some bread. Baxter said that thieving savages were welcome to the desert, and Eyre had gently reminded him that Wylie and Joey had that small amount of bread coming to them anyway. Eyre! All this misplaced goodwill! Didn't he know that blacks can't ration? Of course they'd eat the bread whenever they felt the slightest want of it, or tired of carrying it, or had nothing else to do. And when they appeared on the horizon, Wylie leading, Joey's face like a collapsed bellows, Baxter was not surprised. He could have put the time in his log even before the trip had started: when the thieving darkies take off, when they come back begging for more food.

Eyre—how could he be so artless *and* so accomplished?— was moved by this display of mercenary fawning, as profoundly heartened as he'd been disappointed at their thievery and abandonment. But what's Baxter to say? It's not as if Eyre listens to him, and even though he's not a drunk right now, he's used to being treated like one: humored and ignored. Life would be simple if Eyre were not so respectable and kind. Baxter is momentarily annoyed with himself for finding kindness and respectability of value. Could valuing these traits kill him? There's a good chance.

"Eyre," says Baxter.

"Baxter," says Eyre.

"Can we go home now?"

"England's that way," says Eyre, pointing farther west.

"Very funny," says Baxter.

"You look tired," says Eyre.

"I am tired," says Baxter. "I'm tired of walking the length of this stinking continent."

"I'll take the first watch," says Eyre. Although it was Baxter who was slated for this shift, the rest will do him good, might cheer him. What value, though, is cheer? Conversely, how is one supposed to continue without it? Eyre rises from his place by the fire and goes to find the horses that—though hobbled to prevent wide roaming—still manage to get around. They need to, since there's not much to eat if they don't find it themselves. And Baxter, despite the night chill, finds himself drifting off, his last thought a wonder of what tomorrow might bring if these savages don't kill him in his sleep.

Eyre was searching among the low shrubs in the utter blackness, responding to the occasional crush of twigs that he hoped was caused by horses and not by snakes, when he heard the gunshot. His first thought was that Baxter had awoken and, worried that Eyre was lost, fired a shot to reorient him and bring him home. Eyre listened. No other shot was fired, but finding the horses satisfied in their present location, he decided to return to Baxter to let him know that all was right. But all was not right.

There's Wylie zigzagging through the darkness, coughing and weeping, bringing his hands to his head, flinging them out. He searches for Eyre in the murky moonlight, each shrub appearing to him a crouching assailant, each branch shaken by a cold wind moved as if by hostile hands.

"Mr. Eyre," he yells, and his call bounces in the void.

"Here, Wylie," says Eyre. "Here." As if *here* is anywhere.

And then they stand but ten feet apart.

"Baxter is dead," Wylie says. "They killed him."

"No," says Eyre. How could one think this of Joey and Yarry? "No one has killed Baxter." But in saying the falsehood, he has accepted the truth.

What's to be done? Eyre takes stock of his diminished supplies, notes the disappearance of firearms, the only one left defective: there's a cartridge lodged in there somewhere. He needs this rifle if he is going to survive. By the fire, he cleans the piece, looking at Wylie, thinking, *Can I trust you?* And Wylie thinking back at him, *You don't really have a choice.* And there's Baxter, poor soul, wrapped in a blanket, since you can't bury people in solid rock.

Wonder. Wonder.

What if. What if.

Boom!

That's the gun going off, since there was a little gun-powder nestled around the stuck cartridge, just enough to get it going. That *boom* nearly took off a part of Eyre's skull, nearly killed him, nearly left Wylie in the middle of the desert. You can picture it: Eyre, his legs still folded up from sitting, his arms flung out, his skull leaking blood onto the thirsty rock. There should be a bird cawing into the wilderness, this call standing in for a departing soul, although there are no crows here, and therefore no caws. Perhaps we should consider the cry of a cockatoo? "In the wake of that fatefully expelled bul-let, naught was heard but the cry of a cockatoo." Cockatoos probably squawk—although some speak. "In the wake of that fatefully expelled bullet, a cockatoo was heard to utter, 'There goes Eyre's soul. There goes Eyre's soul.'"

As you ponder all this, Wylie and the horses wait pa-tiently, wonder, what now? And what if it ended there?

Because it has to end with Eyre: what could be less note-worthy than an aborigine in the desert? Would this end satisfy the needs of history?

Maybe.

Haven't you heard of Burke and Wills? The two, despite Burke's leadership, made it from Melbourne to the Gulf of Car-pentaria, but didn't make it back. The rescue party hung around in the middle of nowhere (Burke and Wills having traveled on to the edge of nowhere), and then left a few hours before Burke and

Wills showed up to deliver a few expletives (undocumented), to blunder hopelessly (documented) up and down Cooper's Creek, wasting supplies, time, and energy, to expire despite the gifts of food from the aborigines who were all about them and thriving. And a few years later we have Scott freezing to death on his way back from the South Pole—shouldn't it be enough to reach a place?—who held on proudly to the bitter end and never lost his spirit, although, given the circumstances, he really should have. Scott and Burke and Wills are all part of history, and history finds them of more interest—seats them up close to the host at Perpetuity's table, with Eyre placed further down, almost invisible.

Boom!

Well, that bullet really wakes Eyre up. "Gun's working," he says to Wylie.

And Wylie nods.

Get to your feet, Eyre. You've a long way to go yet, and Baxter doesn't need you fawning over his remains. As far as Wylie's concerned, it's a waste of a blanket, although he does stand in respectful silence as you tug the blanket to cover Baxter's feet, revealing his face, and then tug the blanket to cover the face, revealing his feet. And then repeat this. Twice.

Guilt. Responsibility. Eyre makes a mental note to never fail those who put their trust in him, to not fall victim to his innocence—which is of no value—at the expense of those loyal to him. "That was bad of Joey," says Eyre, "to shoot Baxter."

From the patience on Wylie's face, Eyre knows the boy is concerned about him. There are some things Wylie doesn't understand, like valor, but there are other things that Wylie knows better. Despite native simplicity, an aborigine can get just as crazy as an Englishman, crazier if you lock him up. Wylie thinks Eyre's mind is slipping. That's what Eyre sees on Wylie's face.

"Baxter's all right now," says Wylie.

"Back with his people," says Eyre, and rises to his feet. He hopes this notion of being back with one's people is something that Wylie believes in, because it might be: the sentiment seems to incline toward the native. And Eyre sincerely hopes in this possibility of belief since he does not hold faith in any such thing. He knows that Baxter is gone, his juices destined to evaporate, the blanket destined to crumble, the bones there to be cleaned by predators, and then sand, and then carried off by the unknown or just left with no witness.

Struggle on, Wylie. Struggle on, Eyre. Get a move on.

Eyre pauses and puts his cracked hands on the knees of his torn pants. He turns a weary head and looks out of his spot on the desert. Does he suspect his future in Jamaica? His fall from grace? Does he imagine that he will be singled out as a killer of blacks? An entitled squire and racist monster? Could he ever guess that famous men will attack him, and famous men will champion his cause, that even after all the charges have been dropped he will be unemployable? That after years of courting History, Eyre will be desperate to escape her attention? Maybe he does guess at this, because he's sitting down again, exhausted. Eyre thinks he's dying, but just as that bullet missed its mark, so will this moment pass.

Wylie, finding himself ahead, circles back. He extends his hand and Eyre grasps it. There's a moment here. Wylie is pulling Eyre up and Eyre is feeling him do it, and there's warmth in Wylie's hand and generosity in his face and patience. Eyre knows that Wylie will never desert him. Eyre knows that Wylie is good. For one moment Eyre feels his heart swell and a false strength take hold of his bones and muscles, because he loves Wylie, this savage, this kind boy.

"Wylie," says Eyre, "you have saved me."

And Wylie yet again finds this unremarkable.

V. The *Mississippi*

Not far to go is not close enough. Eyre has been wandering as though in a dream—a very bad one—for several weeks, so when he first sights the boats in the harbor, he thinks them to be an illusion. Why not? Just a short half hour ago he had a thought that the landscape had dreamed him up, and when it thought better (the landscape, thinking), he would vanish from it. He tried to explain this phenomenon to Wylie, who gave him that frank look—a white man would have shaken his head nervously—to let Eyre know that the thought was, well, unhinged. So Eyre looks out at the boats, unsure of how to approach the subject, or figment, with Wylie. But there is no need for such concern.

"Food!" says Wylie. "Food!"

And Wylie leaps around, briefly forgetting that such expressions of joy—joy itself, perhaps—is a wasting of valuable resources.

The boats are small, rowing boats, and Eyre wonders what would bring such boaters to the curbstone of the known to entertain themselves in such a frivolous way. But there they are, rowing to and fro, maybe six of them, in the broiling sun, and not an umbrella to be seen.

"Such small boats," says Eyre.

"For the big fish," says Wylie. "You know, the big fish!" And he flings his arms open to indicate that the size of such a fish is beyond his illustration.

"You mean a whale?"

"Yeah, I think so," says Wylie.

So they're whalers, and that would make sense, as it would make sense for Eyre to leave his ponderings and make some sense as well. Eyre does his best to shake off his unbecoming hallucinatory demeanor, which has actually been very useful—a cradle to rock permanent dementia to sleep—in exchange for an English fortitude.

Soon Eyre, his English fortitude, and Wylie are down on the beach shaking hands with a Captain Rossiter, who shakes back, accompanied by his gift of salvation. The *Mississippi,* which slides into view at the promontory, is indeed a whaler, and the rowboats deployed earlier were not involved in sporty leisure, but rather industry. Twelve days Eyre and Wylie spend among these men, mostly French, although Rossiter is English, eating and sleeping with a roof above, which, Eyre at least, will choose over earth beneath. The *Mississippi,* that small embassy of Europe, rolls beneath him, for all is progress in the Western world, all is movement, and isn't that what Eyre too is about: moving across this great, still continent, creating a necessary disturbance?

Finish up that soup quickly, Eyre. Put down the spoon! You're not done yet.

Eyre and Wylie recover quickly and, newly outfitted, determine to finish off their journey. The horses too, rested and watered, are eager to put an end to things, aided by the magical gift of horseshoes fashioned from harpoons.

Eyre should have known from the rain that he and Wylie were reentering the English side of things. After struggling through some of the driest terrain in existence, he and Wylie now travel ankle-deep in water, with so much precipitation that one wonders if it is worth remarking where the water has collected (about one's ankles), and where it is in the process of collecting (everywhere else). All the sound is muted and the thousands of droplets striking all around create a uniform cacophony. Surely,

Eyre thinks, each sound of each droplet must be as individual as the structures of snowflakes. But this wall of sound can also be one sound—or at least one composition. This is how Eyre occupies himself as he follows Wylie, who is now always two steps ahead.

"Wylie," shouts Eyre, "where are we?"

Wylie shrugs. "I know where I'm going," he says, which is surely more relevant.

Later, as they descend the Stirling Range and see Albany before them—a perverse and suspect diorama—Eyre will fall to his knees, as close to complete collapse as he's ever been on this journey. Wylie, resting his hand on Eyre's shoulder, will say, "Things are good now."

And, to some extent, he'll be correct.

Eyre and Wylie stand in the sheeting rain at the edge of water that has already burst its banks. They watch as things speed past on the river's back: branches, whole trees, a steer with its legs in the air that is at least a harbinger of civilization.

Normally there would be a few people about—farmers, settlers, idiots—but the weather has driven everyone indoors. It's still that reliable trio: Eyre, Wylie, the elements. And then, from across the river, a human voice, calling out. Listen! No. Yes. It's gone. But there it is again: definitely a human voice, someone hailing them. Wylie's face goes from its usual passivity to joyful wonder. Through the scrim of rain, Eyre can make out the man on the opposite bank—a native—waving his arms enthusiastically. He can hear the choking happiness in the man's voice, sent out in wave after wave of welcome. Wylie turns to Eyre, extending his arm to assist—are they really going to ford this river?—and Wylie says, "My brother."

Cross the river, Eyre, please. It's been so long—over a year since you left Adelaide with the crowd cheering you on. And after all that hardship, what's a river? Just one last thing: a job worth starting is worth finishing. Is that your adage? Well, if it wasn't before, it should be now.

VI. His Twilight

To him, this is a fine day for fishing because the house is filling up with people—his daughter, his sons, in-laws, grandchildren— whom he prefers from a distance. He moves across the shorn grass, lately arena for the spectacle of tennis. The house sits broad where it has sat for many years. The wind tugs at his greenheart rod (newly outfitted with a click-check brass reel) making progress, as he juggles tackle box, lunch kit, bucket, less swift than he'd wish it. Wylie would have indulged himself only his two hands. Wylie. Where is he now? What is he now? A variety of ether?

Eyre's eighty-four years, an extra burden, slow him. As does the ridiculous fence and the ladder-like steps straddling it that he must also straddle. His trousers grip him as he maneuvers, but he drops only the bucket. Still, the field rolls out in front of him, embroidered over with cow pats and prickle plants, and after (and if) he manages that, only then the peace of the riverbank, its gin-clear waters, and fish swimming it. Eyre recovers his bucket. He recovers his breath. He looks across and sees, through shoulder-to-shoulder trees, the flash of light that is reflecting water. A moment here, he thinks, a moment here to ponder his final steps, to gather strength. To convince himself this final distance is worth its winning.

He is in Tavistock, Devonshire.

The year is 1901.

He has been retired for twenty-seven years, too long unemployed. Unemployable. His thoughts swarm briefly and settle, like flies on a cow pat.

"I'd like to be of assistance, if I may."

Who has said that? Eyre turns to see a young man standing backlit by low sun. Who is it? By the stance, casual, Eyre assumes it's someone he knows or someone who belongs there, although no servant would be so jaunty in his posture.

"Grandfather?"

John, Eyre's grandson, has ferreted him out. The previous evening, the boy had brought up Carlyle at the dinner table. Carlyle! Dead and buried, along with all the troubles, buried at least at Eyre's dinner table where polite conversation and general delicacy have left such provocative subjects unexplored for many, many years. John wanted to know, what did Eyre think of Carlyle's notions of heroes and great men? Eyre had deflected the question with a tepid response about Carlyle being a forceful sort of gentleman. And influence on John Stuart Mill, although they later disagreed.

"What makes you think I need assistance?" says Eyre.

"You dropped your bucket."

"The wind and this gate have made it all—" says Eyre, handing over his bucket and lunch kit, but keeping his tackle box and rod.

"The gate exists because the cows kept eating all the flowers."

The cows, chewing, chewing, chewing, support this.

"Why," says Eyre, with an old man's scowl, "have you followed me?"

"I am your grandson," says John.

To which Eyre repeats his question. Which is disingenuous, because Eyre knows what the boy wants. "You, John, like the others, ask all the wrong questions. You ask about Carlyle and the Eyre Defense Committee. You ask about Mill and his Jamaica Committee—formed to convict me, and not for the wrongs done by me, but for all the victimized negroes in all the colonies. I put down a rebellion. The negro Gordon was no smiling victim. He was sharp as a tack. He could have wiped out all the settlers, if not handled swiftly. His training was as a preacher. People followed him, and his followers killed twenty-four civilians. I authorized his hanging, yes, I did, and for that was prosecuted as a murderer."

"You yourself were nearly hanged," says the grandson.

"Nearly hanged for being governor of Jamaica at a time when Mill and Carlyle wished to engage in debate. They wished to play tennis. I was merely the ball, battered and practically irrelevant."

"I don't understand," says the grandson, and he lands his leather oxford deep in manure, which is funny to Eyre: only a gentleman—because, recent development, that's what his descendants are—would wear such shoes in a cow pasture.

"Let me explain it clearly," says Eyre. "I was governor of Jamaica. A Baptist minister, a colored man named George William Gordon, started a rebellion, which I put down quickly and effectively. That should have been the end of it, but Mill thought to make of me an example. To him, I was an aristocrat who felt himself beyond the reach of the law, when I was neither aristocrat nor criminal. Carlyle came to my defense. The case was brought to court three times, and each time the charges favored no trial."

"Surely there is more to it than that?" asks the grandson.

"It was as I've stated," says Eyre. "What ought to have been a small legal matter tried in relevant courts in Jamaica became an English circus. In the Jamaica Committee, there were

Mill, Bright, Darwin, Huxley, Hughes, Spencer, and nine thousand more. John Stuart Mill, with his rights for women and all others weak and defenseless, chose to attack me, as if I were their scourge. On my side, I had Carlyle, whose knowledge of the French Revolution made him something of an expert on rebellion. I had Dickens, who wondered at the ability of men like Mill to champion the cause of distant negro rebels when the streets of London were choked with diseased prostitutes and their starving children. I had Ruskin, whose eloquence exposed the unchecked lawlessness of gentlemen in England, and therefore the hypocrisy of my persecutors. And Tennyson, who . . ." And here Eyre struggled, because he knew that Tennyson wrote poems, none of which he'd read, and thus seemed a weak note to end on. Who else had come to his defense?

"Charles Kingsley came to your defense, Grandfather."

"And made a hash of it."

"And Hamilton Hume wrote a book of your accomplishments."

"Which was filled with so much false detail and conjecture that I came to be questioned on matters that had once been accepted as truth."

They were now reaching the brace of trees that marked the final descent to the riverbank.

"The truth is the only thing that matters, which is why I pursue it, Grandfather, with you, who is the only one I trust to make it clear."

Was Eyre really as old as all that, to make his grandson press this case with all the doggedness of one who may never get the chance again?

"Mill vilified me, and I was exonerated, and then the courts, the people, whoever 'they' are who have such power, vilified him. If you wish to know the truth, know this: I am an explorer who started as a cattleman. I was never a gentleman, not one to receive the deference accorded, nor the criticism. I did best when alone."

"Which is why you've settled here," says John. He gestures about as if Devonshire is a wilderness, not a patchwork quilt of this farm and that pasture, as if Dartmoor, with its ponies and left-and-right-sloping vistas, edges the abyss of unknowing, as if they are blanketed in the silence of the Maker instead of hearing the blast and blast as hares expire at the hands of hunters.

Eyre sets down his tackle box and, stashed in the bushes, finds his three-legged wooden stool. He sits and opens the catches of the tackle box, sees the neat compartments and their temptations of glass-eyed chubs, kidney-shaped metal lures, even a fur-covered mouse lure, and the four treble Devonshire lure, which he ought to try, being in Devonshire, but thinks too fancy for him. "When I was sixteen," says Eyre, choosing the fluted spoon, "my father suggested that I go to Australia. My choice was between that and purchasing an army commission. Both were good options for a man in my position, the son of a vicar, but the army was filled with people! Australia, to my understanding, was not."

"Well that is true," says John.

"Not entirely," says Eyre. "There were people there, people like me, young enough to desire hardship and experience. And there were others, government officials and the like— gentlemen! Although often poor, or perhaps not sophisticated enough to be of value in India: gentlemen adequate to the task of governing in Adelaide and Albany and Wellington." Eyre hears the bitterness creeping into his voice and looks to see if his grandson has noticed it, which he has. "And there were natives!" he hastily adds, although there was nothing more important to Eyre. "But when I arrived in Sydney, at the age of sixteen, younger than you—"

"Not much," John protests, flattered his grandfather knows his age.

"Young enough," says Eyre. "But older, too." Eyre scowls again. "Do you know what it is to ride for six months through the world's roughest terrain, with no guarantee of grazing and water for your herd, of water for yourself and your horse? Do you know what it is to trust the morning to bring a day worth living, to trust the black man to share his knowledge, to share his friendship with you, to lay your gun upon the ground when faced with a dozen raised spears? Do you know what it is to lead when you don't know where you're going?" Is his grandson edging away? "I could tell you a story," says Eyre, "that would give you nightmares."

"I'll return after breakfast," says John. "To hear it."

Eyre, smiling, has regained his solitude. No one's interested in exploration. His memory of Wylie says *expiration,* and Eyre wonders if the food will be good.

"Tell your grandmother," Eyre shouts to John, who is quickly crossing the cow pasture, "not to concern herself with having me fetched for lunch."

Eyre is momentarily reflective. How could he know what waited across that other river, in those final meters that led— and at the same time—to both history and the future? How different is this river and its positive, reliable trickle, the silver fish within it, the splash of a frog returning to it, the reflected willow tree behind his bearded, gray, reflected face. He casts his line and the lure, sparkling, flips into the depths of the water. He draws it back slowly, but then loses the will to continue, his eyes trained on the horizon that presents itself on the opposite bank, a horizon of unnatural green meeting brilliant blue, flat, distant, and irrelevant, a horizon that he will never reach nor try to, just there to torment or comfort, just there to split sky from land, north from south, past from present. The white light across the bank begins to rob all color, and the elements—trees, grass, shotguns blasting—disappear, like stage props shifted by invisible hands.

Full Circle Thrice

Once!

This earth: a ball, a plaything. The surface, in this age—
Exploration teetering into Reason—a driving spit of black
ink dividing solid and liquid. This America, claimed by Spain,
raided by England, inhabited by natives. This beast of Panama,
neck stretched, holding to the southern continent by its teeth.
These trees, a fleshy mass heaving with monkeys, weighed down
with garish, jewel-soaked birds. A red flag tied with ribbons
raised high and in its wake, a host of thieves, men all marching
and marching still, marching to sack Portobelo: burglary on a
large scale. And in this host, our hero, William Dampier, who
steps to one side of the column of men and sits on a rock. He
squints up at the sun, and Lionel Wafer—his friend and fellow
scholar-buccaneer—thinks he might be winking. At whom? At
God maybe? And why not?

   "And why stop here, William?" says Wafer.
   "I have a stone in my shoe."
   "A stone?" Wafer laughed. "When you must stop, you
get such a look about you, as if stopping itself—the need to

stop—were a constant stone in your shoe, your whole life, worrying your foot."

"There is no need to stop, Lionel. Magellan taught us that."

"So you would go round and round—"

"And round again."

"And after that?"

"Sit down somewhat dizzied by the accomplishment."

Darién!

Dampier takes off his shoe and returns the offending stone to its land of issue: Darién. He puts the shoe back on, shoulders his weapon, his twenty pounds of powder, his salted beef, his rum. He and Wafer rejoin the march, Dampier having aged in the last five minutes, wisdom adequate to that task, however irrelevant to much of his life.

"What weighs so heavy on you?" asks Wafer.

"On me? This weapon and the person I will use it on when we reach our destination. Why cannot man just travel? Why must one be a priest or soldier, or buccaneer? Why cannot one just board a boat to see what lies after the great remove of ocean?"

"Would you have no profession?"

"Can this really be called a profession?" Dampier thinks. "I march to attack the Spaniards, and after all this"—he gestures at the jungle as if it has sprung up merely to stymie his progression—"I look forward to having enough gold pieces to sign up for a similar venture. Or maybe we could camp awhile and, when the good people of Portobelo have managed to replenish their coffers, sack them again."

"Maybe the life of a buccaneer is not for you."

"It's not for anyone," says Dampier, a little laugh, "but I can speak like this and no one disagrees. It is a life without hypocrisy. Is that not worth something? Sacking without conversion. The good people of Portobelo ought to thank us for dropping in and not insisting on that final humiliation."

"We leave them as we find them."

"Although a little less well off, or dead."

Who is this William Dampier? An orphan. A failed businessman. A seasoned traveler, and still only twenty-three. I would like to say there is a sense of destiny about him, that greatness, like some buzzing halo, stands about his head; that the finger of God extends downward and then, one, two, three, pokes a rubbery staccato upon his stinking hair: this one, this one, this one. And the history writers flock and scribble. But it is not greatness, more a displaced refinement of intellect: a cunning. But strangely packaged. He is popular with other men. He likes to drink, but stays a good bottle of rum behind the others, and after the drunken fisticuffs and rough encounters with rough women, he is still there and not so poorly used—that weary smile and extended arm: he picks you up, cracks a joke at your expense, and then, hands firmly upon your shoulders, pushes you into a more productive hour. He is all right, this William Dampier. I like him well enough.

I hover by his ear, a listener, conjurer, and spy.

Dampier holds forth on a variety of subjects and Wafer fills, like a cup, to overflowing. Dampier, of whom Coleridge will say, "Old Dampier, rough sailor, but a man of exquisite mind," then sit to pen his mariner's tale. And Swift—a man not easily impressed—will have his Gulliver claim him, "Cousin

Dampier," kin. Over the buzz and thrum of insects and the incessant, succulent drip of jungle sweat, I hear his laugh: one note, loud, confident, yet not so humored as world-weary.

"My dear Wafer," says Dampier, "the sea is the great equalizer."

"Surely war," says Wafer, "and not the sea?"

"And so it is," says Dampier, swatting something, this gnat, this thought, against his bare and sweating neck. "The sea, war, hunger, death, love, knowledge."

"Surely not knowledge. That's naïve. And even hunger. Hunger must find one to equalize, and there are many people beyond the reach of hunger, although not appetite. And knowledge, William . . ."

"True, true," says Dampier, a tight-cornered smile on his face. "What are the many keys that unlock knowledge: reading, for one, a challenging companion," and here Dampier nods at his friend, "and all of these tucked safe in Privilege's pocket."

"Right, sir, right you are. Perhaps instead of knowledge, we can place the unknown."

"The unknown," says Dampier, and he chuckles. "The unknown the great equalizer? The unknown will be mine."

"As you dispense with it."

"People want its perimeters—my favorite place to hang my hat."

Dampier lives to observe and his behavior defines this age.

Lionel Wafer fancies himself something of a writer, and so Dampier has given him this Darién, this neck: the tough part of the bird. Dampier has no need of it, and, as observed by Wafer, Dampier is a man on the move and will doubtless have some other place to write about: a newer place to bind in vellum and sign his name. Wafer, being wise enough to recognize Dampier's superior gifts, has accepted the Panamanian Isthmus with gratitude and acknowledges Dampier's right to the rest of the world.

Mindanao!

When savages start stuffing you with food and keep you by the table, it could be something other than hospitality. Perhaps providence, and not your providence, their providence, for the pigs are all about and small, and this Swan, Captain Swan to be precise, really ought to be more careful. He could feed this village for a month, and, if he keeps consuming their food at the current rate, he might have to, for there will be nothing else to eat. And if the men keep at the village girls with the same enthusiasm, the population will double, and with villagers significantly larger—whiter too—than those standing about the doorways and animal pens, with hoes, sticks, and other primitive tools: things looking less like farm implements, more like weapons.

"Sir!" says our Dampier. "Perhaps you are done with lunch and we might discuss our departure."

"Lunch? Isn't it still breakfast? I just sat down," says Captain Swan.

"You sat down several weeks ago, a fact that has been noticed by the men and, of more concern, our host."

"The sultan delights in my presence," says Swan. "And I delight in his."

"The men are restless and the monotony of the passing days is perhaps only interrupted by your visits to the ship, where you entertain by picking one from the pack to flog."

"You criticize me," says Swan. "That's insubordination."

"You are a captain who does not sail," says Dampier. "That's madness."

"You are a navigator who cannot bear stillness."

Swan offers Dampier a cushion on the floor beside him, a wooden plate, a stew of chilies, coconut, and chicken. "When we were still escaping the Pacific, all the men were patched with scurvy, blundering around the decks as if already dead yet still in motion. They were threatening to eat us—both of us, the officers! They are a mutinous lot. I know that look. You think you would have made a less attractive meal."

"True," says Dampier, "I am as lean as you are lusty and fleshy."

Swan, as if to prove this point, licks through his fingers. "All the while, you had your eyes fixed on the sky, then on the horizon—that shift of ninety degrees held all the interest for you, because we were in motion."

"A navigator is one who navigates."

And through what treacherous waters has Dampier navigated? He has already been labeled "pirate," and now must make his way through the straits of his life a criminal, but a necessary one, for who else dares to sail at the edge of knowing? And as he watches a sailor angled over the edge of the ship, line in hand, sounding for depth, our Dampier knows the true danger is not the coral clawing at the soft wood of the ship's keel, but the wigged minions back in London—authority! justice!—keeping the benches of court warm with their fleshy arses, the air redolent with the belch and stink of money, meals, and privilege.

Better to stay abroad, even if one's company is drunks, sodomites, and thieves. Better to keep company with the blank page and the ink scratching on it, the lines, the turn and turn of sheets, the manuscript growing thick as Dampier catches the unknown, slams it onto the page as if he has killed an insect. He writes, "In this Island are many sorts of Beasts, both wild and tame; as . . . Guano's, Lizards, Snakes, &c. I never saw or heard of any Beasts of Prey here, as in many other places." He writes, "The Winds are Easterly one part of the Year, and Westerly the other. The Easterly Winds begin to blow in October, and it is the middle of November before they are settled." He writes, "Here are also plenty of Sea Turtle, and small Manatee, which are not near so big as those in the West-Indies." He writes and writes and writes.

Later, with Mindanao receding, Swan stranded, and the Spice Islands wafting their magic just over the horizon, Dampier has a moment to contemplate his future. Although it was not his idea to leave Swan behind, he will no doubt be held accountable for it. The British authorities condemn and punish with great enthusiasm: payback for those who dare to spend so much time beyond their reach and imagination. And who is this mad crew anyway? The surgeon has already tried to make off into the wilderness—the jungle filled with Indians and daggers preferable to this lot—but they kidnapped him back. But he was the surgeon. Surely the loss of a navigator will not bother so much.

A Most Outrageous Storm!

The storm came out of nowhere, a blackened margin thickening in the northeast, and the wind, which had been "whiffling" about from one part of the compass to the other, appeared behind the cloud: zephyrs, cheeks puffed, a curling blue-gray plume of wind extending from their puckered lips.

"Sir," says Dampier to Captain Read, his current master, "we're in for it."

"In for what?" says Read, his little round nose twitching anxiously.

Moments later, as Dampier is thrust this way and that, his greasy locks flattened about his shoulders, a horizontal dumping of water first at his right, then left, he feels "it" to be adequately described. He holds firm to the railing to avoid being washed away. In his mind, he composes, committing to memory, ". . . the Rain poured down as through a Sieve. It thundered and lightened prodigiously, and the Sea seemed all of a Fire about us." The men are baling anxiously and Captain Read is scampering fore and aft. But something in this evil weather feels vindicating, and should one bother to look Dampier's way (yet no one does, navigating being something of a luxury in the current circumstances), they would see his calm expression, although one eyebrow is merrily raised, his mouth pulled to one side—jaunty! Because he senses with the instinct that overrides reason, a quality of all true navigators, that they are blowing off the edge of the map.

New Holland!

A flat expanse of fine white sand, a fiery sun, and two men—one long and lean, one pudding-short and compact—face off against each other.

"Where are we indeed," says Dampier.

"You're the navigator! You tell me!"

"Captain Read, sir, when we were in Manila, did I not say, 'Here we are in Manila.'"

"Yes, but—"

"And when we reached the coast of China, did I not re-mark, 'Why, there's China, right where we English left her!'"

"Yes, but—"

"And did you not say, 'Jog us down to Celebes,' and did I not point the way?"

"Yes but—" and here Captain Read had paused, so had he predicted interruption, but none had come, Dampier having become distracted by a sight over and beyond the captain's head. "Dampier, you are a most vexing man!"

"Well proven."

"Do you have no desire of learning where we are?"

"That interests me!" says Dampier. "Learning where we are is far more provocative than knowing. Indeed, I believe us to be the first Englishmen in this place, although perhaps the Dutch have been here before."

"So you have a suspicion?"

"I suspect this to be New Holland."

"What do you know of this New Holland? What is there with which to provision ourselves? Are there natives? Are they friendly?"

"They are not friendly and are most savage."

"Really?"

"Their Hair is black, short and curl'd, like that of the Negroes; and not long and lank like the common Indians. The colour of their Skins, both of their Faces and the rest of their Body, is coal black, like that of the Negroes of Guinea. They have no sort of Cloaths, but a piece of the Rind of a Tree ty'd like a Girdle about their Waists, and a handful of long Grass, or three or four small green Boughs full of Leaves, thrust under their Girdle, to cover their Nakedness."

"How come you to know so much of these savages?" says Read, and seeing Dampier's gaze, which is focused in the offing, somewhat of a distance sighted past his shoulder, Read turns. He is startled to see a group of savages has crept quite close.

The savages are shaking wooden spears, cudgels, some variety of a flattened wooden elbow—most primitive and incapable of harm—yet Read (it must be the spectacle of the unknown) shrinks back in fear.

"Not friendly," says Dampier. "Most savage."

Of the Australian aborigines, Dampier informs himself and, therefore, the world, and, therefore, whatever "the world" at that particular time happens to include: certainly not New Holland, which—in addition to being in a state of transition from fantasy to fact—knows all about its inhabitants and requires no informing. He writes:

> The Inhabitants of this Country are the miserablest People in the world. The Hodmadods of Monomatapa, though a nasty People, yet for Wealth are Gentlemen to these; who have no Houses and skin Garments, Sheep, Poultry, and Fruits of the Earth, Ostrich Eggs, &c. as the Hodmadods have: And setting aside their Humane Shape, they differ but little from Brutes. . . . They did at first endeavour with their Weapons to frighten us, who lying ashore deterr'd them from one of their Fishing-places.

What else?

> In the Midst of this Distress, I observed them all to run away on a sudden as fast they could, at which I ventured to leave . . . wondering what it was that could put them into this Fright. But, looking on my left Hand, I saw a Horse walking softly in the Field; which my Persecutors having sooner discovered, was the Cause of their Flight. The Horse

started a little when he came near me, but, soon recovering himself, looked full in my Face, with manifest Tokens of Wonder: He viewed my Hands and Feet, walking round me several Times—

My mistake! The second of these accounts is, of course, not Dampier, but Swift, for as Dampier discovers, striding about the previously—at least not by the English—unstrodden sand, there are no large animals, certainly nothing capable of bearing a burden such as a horse, intelligent or otherwise.

The natives have turned from hostility to curiosity. After a gift of rice boiled with turtle and manatee, they have seen the English to be, if not friendly, mercantile: requiring something of them that makes their murder unprofitable. What this something might be is difficult to determine. First the crewmen pushed upon the natives an assortment of dirty vestments of the kind that they wore. A few of the native men put these on, to the great amusement of their kinsmen and companions. So clad, these men turned to the English, who are all in a fussy pantomime involving some barrels of water, which—or so the New Hollanders suppose—need transporting to their ship. This mad display has been going on for the better part of half an hour and is certainly not so entertaining now as it was at its start.

"Ritual?" suggests one native to his friend.

"Really? The presentation seems a bit base for that." The two men watch as, with embracing, beckoning gestures, Captain Read endeavors to bring them closer to the barrels. "Maybe they are proselytizing."

"You know what?" suggests his friend.

"What?"

"I think they mean for us to carry the water for them."

"Really? How did you come up with that?"

"Look at them."

Together, the natives look as Read, all agitation, mimes the levitation of a cask. He points vigorously at them, asweat and muscles twitching, all this mimicry taking great effort—possibly more than carrying the water themselves.

"They can't possibly think that." The first native smiles in disbelief. "Why would we do it?"

"I think because they have made us the gift of these foul garments."

"Well they can have them back," says he, quickly shrugging his shirt from his shoulders.

"They certainly can!" concurs his friend, and shakes his foot free from a trouser leg. "These English," he adds, "they're worse than the Dutch!"

Later, with New Holland slipping over the horizon, Dampier pens:

> . . . we found some Wells of Water here, and . . . thought to have made these Men to have carry'd it for us, and therefore we gave them some old Cloaths; to one an old pair of Breeches, to another a ragged Shirt . . . But all the signs we could make were to no purpose, for they stood like Statues, without motion, but grinn'd like so many Monkeys, staring one upon another: For these poor Creatures seem not accustomed to carry Burthens.

Another Most Outrageous Storm!

What small craft is this that floats upon the waves—no, founders!—wait, is that it yet again? It is more of a log than a craft, and our men are soaked and disoriented, the stars coyly

veiled behind thick cloud, a cheeky wind scampering about
to play first at the west, and then at the east, and the waves—
such waves! The canoe first climbs upward, then plunges
down, and Dampier through it all cursing and cursing at first,
which is a comfort, but then quiet as he contemplates what
might be his final moments: he imagines himself descending
to the ocean floor, his hair extending upward like a damp
flame, his solemn expression as curious fish stop to watch his
progress.

He has done many things in his life that he now regrets. With affecting sorrow Dampier, as an entreaty to his
maker, now recalls the wife he deserted. Poor good woman!
He shakes his head in shame, but looks upward cautiously—is
there any indication that his maker is actually listening? Have
his penitence and humility gained him favor? Because these
good thoughts are already being replaced by thoughts truer to
his nature: Dampier does not regret leaving the woman at all.
Indeed, his only regret is marrying her in the first place. What
was he thinking? She was not an unattractive person. Did this
recommend? In fact, the novelty had been her willingness to
marry him. Who chooses a pirate, even one book-learned like
Dampier, to be her husband? What flaws does such a woman
conceal? The obvious: an evil temper, a love of drink, a passion for indolence. Is his maker still listening? If he knows all,
does he not know that she was an insult to her gender? Why
did the maker, in all his graciousness, make her in the first
place? A cautious look heavenward—could God be watching, a togaed giant asprawl on a nimbus couch?—but there
is no such thing, just the fearful waves, his friend Hall, who
marooned himself along with Dampier—Captain Read having become insufferable—and a few Malays, who—although
knowledgeable of this type of boat and region—suffer from a

nerve-wracking fatalism that makes it impossible to determine if, firstly, such canoes as this can survive tempests and, secondly, if land is within their grasp.

"Do you know where we are?" Dampier yells at one of the Malays.

"Still at sea!" the man shouts back.

And Hall, half dead and stinking like a dog, can't help but laugh. And once he's laughed, finds it so pleasant an activity that he keeps at it, laughing and laughing, madness being preferable to this drawn-out fear.

For one second, the clouds part, and Dampier sees the stars for the first time in days. He grabs his pocket compass and makes a quick calculation.

Surprise, surprise. He might survive after all.

And Dampier, a look of triumph clear upon his face, reassigns his maker once more to the far back, dimly lit row of his consciousness.

The Bloody Flux!

Surprise, surprise. The battle is not over, his bowels still being at sea regardless of his feet standing on solid land. But he is not standing, rather lying down, and as his clouded mind conjures his waking dreams, our hero Dampier is not sure which is more fantastic: his phantasms or that which, as his journal bears him out, he has actually encountered. As surely as Archimedes sat in his tub displacing the water, so does our Dampier displace all knowledge that goes before. He writes and writes and writes and whom does he write against? Pliny! Pliny, who has given us old "umbrella foot" of the antipodes! Pliny, who believes in the "pegasi" of Ethiopia and the three-foot locusts of India! Pliny, who believes that having a naked, menstruating woman walk around an orchard protects the apples from insects! Pliny, whose gift for plausible fictive exposition has stood these last fifteen hundred years, and now it is Dampier who must debunk the great Roman.

In his sweating fever he sees the man (Pliny himself!) sit upon his bed.

"Do you know me, Dampier?" he says.

"Yes, sir," says Dampier, "and I know you for a fool!"

"That assertion puts you in small company."

"You say that Europe is bigger than Asia and twice as big as Africa."

"My calculations are on the page."

"Your calculations consist of adding length to breadth!"

There is a moment during which the two men blink at each other and Pliny adjusts his toga, which he is sitting on in such a way that it's tugging at his shoulder.

"How do you know me to be so false?"

"By going. I see with my own two eyes. How come you to so many errors?"

Pliny rubs his eyes. "I have gone nowhere. I wrote what others saw, or what they thought they saw—"

"And by committing to print these falsehoods have perpetuated a millennium of ignorance!"

"Where is the wrongdoing committed? When they saw and saw incorrectly? When I took pen to paper? Or when they read? It does not start with me, Dampier." Pliny folds his hands in his lap, looking down the length of Dampier's dysentery-ravaged frame. "What makes you so special?"

"I observe and then I write it down!"

"Yes. You are the first to do this, the very first."

"William," comes a weak voice. It's Hall, who is suffering down the other end of the long hut. "If you must speak, speak quieter, for your madness is keeping me from rest."

Madness? For of course Pliny is not there and has been displaced, not by reason and observation but rather air—still air, with a mosquito circling lazily through it.

Bencouli!

This fort is rotting to pieces and the governor of this place, soft too, in the head, his mental constitution undermined by heat. Or is it drink? Or is it both? And Dampier, our naturalist friend, has found himself the unnatural job of "gunner." He is a good shot, as are most pirates who make it to their thirties, but he has now spent five months gunning and writing, with the only entertainment the occasional surprise attack from the Malays— whom he guns—and the petty tyranny of the governor—of whom Dampier writes, "I saw so much Ignorance in him, with respect to his charge, being much fitter to be a Book-keeper than Governor of a Fort . . . I soon grew weary of him, not thinking my self very safe, indeed, under a Man whose humours were so brutish and barbarous."

So pop goes the gun. And then reload. And then pop. Who is he shooting? Well, the Malays are not mounting a surprise attack, and the gun is angled toward the sea. Pop. Reload. Pop. This would be a much better moment if he were at sea, shooting into the land—better yet, onboard a ship: "In the empty immensity of earth, sky, and water," although safely harbored in modern literature, "incomprehensible, firing into a continent." At least this futility would symbolize something, for these islands in some way do comprise a dark continent, not *the* dark continent, but dark nonetheless. Dampier's shooting into the water is futility that symbolizes futility, which cancels out the symbolism, making it just what it is: meaningless shooting. And at whom is he shooting anyway?

Is it the Dutch? But the English are no longer at war with the Dutch. We're all friends now, except the Malays, who, from a cluster of village huts at safe remove from the fort, announce with a vehement politeness, "We're victims." And right they are!

Dampier looks up from his porthole and wipes his hands on the rough cloth of his shirt. "No longer at war with the Dutch? Then what am I doing here!"

You're wasting your time, friend. How long has it been since you were home? It must be twelve years. You left with the scrappy whiskers of youth upon your upper lip, and now look! All the stubble of manhood casts a dark shadow about your jaw, and some of this is gray. You left to find your fortune—

"I left to leave," says Dampier, and he packs his journal and his papers carefully. But he does miss England. "What was there in London?"

What is there now?

In the corner of the room there is a movement, and I see that Dampier is not alone.

"Come, Jeoly. We are leaving. That must please you a little, my prince."

From the darkened shadow a slight figure steps. He is young, maybe twelve years old, and tattooed from head to foot in brilliant swirls, coiled vines, marvelous birds. He blinks, and from the pattern of his skin the two dark eyes stare out, unmistakably natural, sad. His mother, despite Dampier's best efforts to nurse her, has died of a fever, and he has been Jeoly's only caretaker. Jeoly too has been sick. He nearly died along with his mother, first of fever, then of grief.

"Where are we going?" asks the prince.

"To London! London is a great city with buildings and people and things that you have never seen before."

"It is very cold in London," says the prince, "and I am sure I will not like the food."

From the deck of the ship, Prince Jeoly watches the islands of his youth disappearing into memory. And Dampier? He is hidden belowdecks, as his departure has become more of an escape. The governor withdrew permission allowing him to leave, and Dampier dropped from a porthole of the fort with only his journal and a few other papers on him. His books—valuable—and furniture—expensive—he left, along with the fort and governor and whatever has occasioned their presence on godforsaken Bencouli to be reclaimed by the jungle, to return to anonymity and irrelevance—irrelevance, that is, except to its original inhabitants, who didn't like the English there in the first place.

London!

Dampier cares for Jeoly—this is clear in his writing, and should not surprise, since the English have always done well by their pets. He brings his prince with him up the winding, stinking alleys, directs him around the steaming piles of horseshit and waste-filled gutters, stamps his boot angrily to shoo the rats so that the two can pass across the threshold of the alehouse, in through a wave of heated tobacco and stale-ale stink, along the dark hallway with its cobwebbed beams and grunting patrons. With sweating whores. Through to a quieter dining area, a place closer to the fire.

The boy's eyes are all agog with filth and spectacle, yet still he notes Dampier's reticent behavior.

Our pirate sits upon a bench opposite the prince, who, as predicted, finds his stew of beef gristle (has it gone off?) not much to his liking. The prince peers into his bowl, his face returned to him, distorted in the congealing gravy. In this, his mother would have found an omen.

"Eat," says Dampier with some gentleness. "Look how big we English grow from such food."

"And look how far you go to find better."

Dampier smiles, but there is little to cheer him of late. He finds his finances wanting, the clink of coin on coin too pronounced when not muffled by the substantial presence of others. He makes a tidy stack of currency upon the table. He swings a boot over the bench to straddle it so that he is not looking at his little prince.

"It is a neat stack, William," says Jeoly. "Too neat. You mean to sell me."

"No," says Dampier, "no, no." But his eyes roam the ceiling because he cannot decide which is kindness: truth or subterfuge.

"Sell me now," says the prince, "for I will not survive much longer."

"Are you not well, my prince?"

Jeoly shrugs. "Is this how you English treat your princes? I know I am a slave. And that makes me smarter than you, William."

"How so?"

"You think yourself free."

One afternoon, when the weather is fine and the dampness not so noticeable, Dampier is walking back from his printer (Yes, printer!) to his room when he thinks to have a celebratory beer. An alehouse presents itself and within it Dampier presents himself, and soon, within his long, tapering fingers, a beer presents itself. As he's licking the foam from his lip, he looks up from his drink and sees a poster displayed upon the alehouse wall: *The Painted Prince!* Dampier takes his cold drink in thoughtful gulps.

"Sir," says Dampier to the publican, "that painted prince is dead."

And, wiping the surface filth into filthy circles with a blackened rag, the publican nods, which he thinks generous enough for such a comment.

And Twice!

The second circumnavigation was to be his undoing, but only because its inception had been Dampier's glory, Captain Dampier now, in command of the *Roebuck*. The *Roebuck*'s charge was to menace French ships and collect information. Dampier was pleased to have finally escaped being a pirate, although even he—who knew through qualification (which helped with the Royal Navy) and suffering (which appealed to his sense of justice) that he had earned it—felt the whole thing to be somewhat ironic. When the charge of piracy was leveled against him upon his return—destroying whatever reputation he had managed to cobble together on that first long voyage—he could not have been surprised.

Captain Dampier is busy writing, yet he raises his head to answer this charge.

"What is the difference between a pirate captain and one of the English Royal Navy?" he says. "Two things: the pirate menaces everyone, not just those enemies of the Crown, and the pirate publishes as buccaneer, not scholar. Although perhaps the running of the ship is more democratic in the former."

Surely you mean the latter: the Royal Navy.

"I certainly don't," says Dampier, and he lays down his pen to spend some time with this and me and my lack of understanding. "The pirate defines justice through equality: what's good for him is good for me. The Crown defines justice through adherence: if this is not done, it will be punished. So you decide. Choose as you like. I don't care."

That's sour grapes, Dampier, because of your court-martial. I know all about Fisher.

"Fisher? Has history bothered with him?"

I'm afraid so, even though Dampier left from his works—mentioning only in passing "the Refractoriness of some under me"—any mention of Fisher. But Lieutenant Fisher, Dampier's second-in-command, was his undoing.

"Do you find me so undone?" says Dampier, and he looks offended.

But let's return to a time when Fisher was still on board the ship, before Dampier deposited him in a Portuguese prison in Bahia. Dampier had little control in choosing his crew, and he knew that many sailors were pirates and vice versa—in truth, piracy versus sailoring was factored in degrees; the factions beloved of simpleminded people like Fisher had no business on board a ship. Fisher disliked being second-in-command in general, and in particular to a known buccaneer. These things he let be known, and he is on record these long years since as having called Dampier everything from an "Old Dog" to a "dissembling, cheating rogue." And Dampier is on record for beating him about with his walking stick—as ridiculous then as it would be now—and, in response to Fisher's angry threats, responding that he did not care "a farthing for what your Lordships [can] do to [me]."

Dampier desired to be a captain not to rule over men, but in order not to be ruled, there being no way to avoid both these situations without returning to piracy. Being a pirate interfered with his career as a writer and explorer. What he really liked to do was make maps—maps of things never done before: obvious things, such as certain stretches of the west Australian coastline; and inventive things, such as the winds, which had certain noteworthy characteristics, and tides, which operated with some regularity. All of these were of value to the mariner. And who before had thought to map the wind?

The trade winds blow at an acute angle on any coast, and Dampier is wondering how best to communicate the specifics of this situation when there is an aggressive pounding on his door. Dampier is silent, hoping that the person might leave, but of course whoever it is knows him to be in his cabin: this is a ship, where else could he be? After a second series of thumps, Dampier responds with a weary, "Enter."

And Fisher enters. "I must report a breach in authority."

"Really?" says Dampier. But he doesn't look up from his papers. "Is that all?"

"The nature of the breach," says Fisher.

And Dampier is not sure how to respond because this is not a question. He finally says, "Yes?" as it is clear that Fisher has no intention of leaving until he has communicated the details of the transgression. Dampier watches Fisher speak, his mouth and jaws in rapid exercise, the hands over here, then over there, a righteous angry flush about the cheeks, the fists at the sides, then in conscious, punctuating gestures in the air in front. A fleck of spittle catches the light. And then another. Could that be sweat collecting at the man's temples? Why has Dampier never noticed just how short Fisher is— diminutive—a fact underscored by the tall boots? He looks like a uniformed mouse. And then Dampier realizes that Fisher has fallen silent.

"So what you're saying," says Dampier, "is that you wished to issue beer and the purser refused?"

"Of course that's what I've been saying."

"And this is important?"

There is a moment during which Dampier sincerely hopes Fisher has seen the light, but he suspects this to be unjustified optimism, and is right.

"You are a captain, and as such must maintain authority."

"Yes, but not an abstract authority, an authority to maintain order. And I fail to see the necessity of serving men beer."

"The breach is not in the men being deprived of beer, but in the purser refusing my order."

"This is a breach of authority that represents a breach of authority, but also maintains order. Perhaps the men are better off without the beer."

"Then you must order that, in order to have me order the purser not to issue beer, who must obey said order."

"Then I do just that."

"But sir, that cannot be done."

"Why?"

"Because my order has already been disobeyed!"

"I don't have time for this," says Dampier. "Go away, and that's an order."

It is hard to blame Dampier for having Fisher locked up in a Brazilian prison, but surely he saw his reputation would suffer. The judges found Dampier's treatment of Fisher to be extreme, his defense of fearing mutiny without justification. They fined Dampier all the proceeds from his journey and said he was unfit to command any of Her Majesty's ships.

"Is this Fisher business of interest to anyone?" says Dampier. "And who are you? Why bother to write my tale when others of far more prominence have done it justice— justice that has stood the test of time? What do you think you can bring to my equation when Swift has brought pen to it already? What bastard do you hope to birth from humping the margins of Defoe?"

I know of Swift, and Humboldt, and Coleridge, but what of Defoe?

"I dropped Alexander Selkirk off on my second journey and picked him up on my third. So perhaps one cannot credit me with the story of the maroon, but for putting a start and end to it, that is surely me. And since the book is what is important, then that is surely me, since the story needed a beginning and an end, Selkirk just supplying the middle: his demand to be left on the desert isle, his regret as the ship sailed off, his ability to survive until I rescued him. But let me tell you one thing: Selkirk did not survive because he was a noble soul, but rather because he was the most stubborn, ill-tempered, fiery, blighted soul, and nothing could kill him. But were it not for me, who bothered to pass by and bring him on board, who deposited him in London, where he soon returned to drink and fisticuffs and syphilitic women, his story would have died among the goats and turnips and sea lions of islands."

Fair enough.

And Thrice!

I feel compelled to tell you that Dampier did indeed make it a third time around the globe, as sailing master to privateer Woodes Rogers on the *Duke*. Had he survived his arrival, he would have achieved the prosperity that he pursued all his life. But he died a drunk, which is a shame, considering he had spent so much of his life amongst alcoholics without affliction; consider his drunkenness a choice. As he grabbed the bottle, he thought, "Why the hell not? What is there to be sober for?" And haven't we all felt that way?

So let's not bother with his final months, characterized by a chill misery. Let's leave out the Thames, her clippers and slavers and sloops bobbing tantalizingly, paused before they journey off into history, literature, art, and politics. Let's leave the gin drinkers, and poxed lovers, and dimwitted royals, and crooked merchants, the shit-slicked London streets, and tubercular whores, and set Dampier back at sea, where he was always more comfortable anyway.

I would love to ask him what he thinks, but I doubt he would respond kindly to me, so instead I send in a man of the cloth—a missionary of sorts—who perhaps has been working among savages somewhere (although it might be too early for this), and is headed home to rejoin his wife. We are already in deep night, and the only light in the captain's cabin is a flickering lamp that intermittently flares, illumining the corners of the ceiling, but most often burns from below, lighting up Dampier's drooping features as though he were the subject of a painting by Joseph Wright of Derby. And the missionary, sitting back in his chair in shadow, leans forward only to speak, his face revealed as he does, then lost again as he sits back, leaving Dampier to appear alone while he speaks, as he declaims *into,* no, *against* the dark—a beacon to vanquish abysmal ignorance.

Dampier, who feels the end of his life approaching and, as a man of no faith, senses the futility of the future.

Dampier, who has been taught that he is the only one to be trusted—he and his own eyes—and that brotherhood, companionship, and trust are but self-perpetuating myths or, worse, luxuries: things valuable only to those in power, whom others dare not cross, or to savages and those living in abject poverty, who have nothing to lose.

Speak, Dampier! Speak, while I can still hear you, before I lose you to history.

History!

Dampier clears his throat. Although it is plain that he is hobbled—tongue, thought, and senses—by drink, he still has a few useful words to share. What are you thinking, Dampier? What keeps you now in motion?

"It is my fate to trust only the stars, those bitter shards sunk deep in night's abysmal, gawping bog. The stars keep me in motion. A navigator is one who navigates. But my life is lived in knots and naughts—a speedy tangle of days amounting to nothing. Am I taking this voyage, or is it taking me? Am I drinking this bottle, or is it drinking me?"

I tap my man of the cloth on the shoulder, for it is his turn to speak, and I would feel bad if Dampier were declaiming to nothing but the stinking, still air of his cabin.

"But life is not so void of meaning," says he, who may or may not be a missionary, startled to attention.

"Don't talk to me of God, for I will smash this bottle against your head and give you visions."

"But what of—" and here the chaplain stops, for he means to speak of love, but seeing Dampier's dissipated state, the very air around his head corrupted by proximity, the bitterly curled lip hoping for a vindicating violence, he substitutes the less contentious—"family?"

"Family?"

The chaplain proposes, "Perhaps a wife." Although seeing Dampier's countenance, the thought of someone cleaved to that, cleaving to that, even clinging, even a louse, seems impossible, absurd. But what relation to one so stiff in solitude would not offend? What would comprise solace to one so locked within disdain? A thought: perhaps molestation would offer a relief, a distraction, from the stilled thoughts that press upon the pirate's soul. But what guise would this molestation take? The chaplain's thought circles back, for the answer is, of course, a wife. Dampier—his eyes bloodshot and drooping, the pouches beneath them weighted with a low-burning, unrelieved, and general grief—exudes an assertive, skeletal awareness.

"Perhaps a wife," repeats Dampier, not bitterly, but lightly and without anger.

He had been listening. "So were you never married?" asks our man of the cloth.

"Certainly not. Never. And I know Never, for I did stand there once, and so situated, understood her borders. Never! I know her hectares marked off by my fences. For I am wed to her. She is my wife!"

The chaplain sips nervously at his brandy, and watches Dampier's head droop, and droop, and then, with a hollow thunk against the table's rough wood, he falls to sleep. Carefully the chaplain places his half-full glass against the table and, rising from his chair, contemplates the distance to the door. For surely this is madness. Madness, yes, for drink has never been so complicated.

His End!

Our brilliant buccaneer and naturalist has, in the grip of drink, wandered off the page. If you wish to see him, there is a painting hanging in the National Portrait Gallery in London. Beneath the painting is the inscription, "Pirate and Hydrographer," and maybe it's the smell wafting up from this that has set the dour expression upon his face. Dampier is unhappy, of course, to have been so stuck—to him no less an ordeal than the "painted ship upon a painted ocean," words that he also inspired.

Since our friend Dampier spent his final days in London, we can presume him to be buried in a damp square of ground, his bare bones laid out in proximity to the bones of others, an uncaring population passing by above, as equally uncaring moles and worms pass through: an end befitting a buccaneer whose brilliant writing and adventurous soul fed the brilliance of others, with this result: he is outshone by his fictionalized self, without even the benefit of being the author of that which threw him into shadow. Ultimately, the fact that Dampier was so intriguing during his life has left him buried in time, tossed out with the historical detritus: Gulliver and Crusoe and the Ancient Mariner sit in the center of the page, and Dampier—the foundation of it all—peers, lips pursed, from the margins.

"You fool," says Dampier from his grave, his jaws working admirably without the aid of muscles, his bad teeth bare for all to see, the skull like any other, since—whatever Dampier might have thought before—death is the real equalizer. He says, "I am not a character, but a writer. A writer happy to be such, not desperate like you, who for a reason unknown to me has felt the need to put herself in her own story. My book is still on the shelf of every library. I do not need to be hero, only author. Gulliver is welcome to command whatever tale he wishes and does not impugn my work, nor steal my thunder. Shut up, just shut up. You don't know what you're talking about."

All right, Dampier, I can take such criticism. But nothing shuts me up. And I am not happy with this end: London, graveyard, presumed Christian burial. We can do better.

We're on a lonely stretch of coastline, and I think it must be the western coast of Australia because it's very hot and very dry and alien to most, but familiar to me, who has seen it. A stiff wind is blowing on the shore. We're floating along bird-like in the air, but we throw no shadow. There's a point of interest on the beach, but the sand seems uninterrupted, so initially we're not sure why we focus on this place. Then, yielding to the force of wind, we see the sand sift away to reveal a skeleton, bleached by sun, buffed clean of any meat or tendon, elegant, and alone. And this is you, Dampier. We draw close and pause at our fallen buccaneer, our mood reverent, our steps careful. We fall to our knees: how much of our understanding do we owe to this man? (Are you happy now? Is this better?) Oh, Dampier, great explorer, naturalist, to have you still with us, "man of exquisite mind"! But what is that sound? I hear a strange singing. We bring ourselves closer, almost touching the vaulted hall of your ribs. It's the wind singing through you, the very wind of which you wrote, that shifting, impossible power upon which your life depended, that unpredictable force to which you presumed to bring understanding—the wind has loosed itself about you, making of your skeleton a mouth. But what is it saying? What could it say? Ah. Now it speaks clearly, and I make out at first one word, then more, then a flood as it plays upon your bones:

". . . we left Captain Sharp and those who were willing to go with him in the Ship, and imbarqued into our Lanch and Canoas, designing for the River of Santa Maria . . ."

And it's your story, Dampier, the whole thing, put down exactly as you wanted it.

Periplus

I. Embarkation

In the final days of 1959, a Jesuit Scholastic sits at a desk in the seminary library. He is twenty-four years old. Outside, a death knell sounds on the frenetic fifties, while the sixties wait twitching in the wings. In the library, all is peaceful. Or is it merely quiet? Does he care? He must. Regardless of whatever philosophical bent is endemic in the role of seminarian, he is only twenty-four years old—young—and the world, that unwritten void beyond the tall walls of the seminary, still belongs to him. Here, in the print, all is quiet. Silence holds fast. Silence is what precedes the slam of a book, the accidental grind of a chair across well-waxed floorboards. Silence follows everything, is the destiny of everything. The pencil is sharp. His notes already fill an entire legal pad. He writes with the confidence that never fails him in independent endeavors, in moments of solitude:

> With perhaps the exception of the mysterious Euthymenes, of whom little is known, the first recorded navigator of the

west coast of Africa is Hanno the Carthasinian, whose voyage is reported to us in *The Periplus of Hanno*.

He makes a note in the margin—*this will need citation*—and wonders about the *Periplus*—the "wandering around"—and what he knows from where he sits: mapped worlds blocked horizontally, realms stacked one upon the other, the specter of evolution. Time—a length of rope wound round and round and round it all. Print: words uncoiling as if they too were twisted out of hemp, pausing and then restarting while read: a hushed unspooling as his eyes sweep right and right, the length of the page. Words: carried like oil lamps, illuminating a little in the darkness.

The seminarian silences his breathing.

He uses his own stillness to better understand the rapidly expanding boundaries of time and narrative and domain. No breath, no movement, but he hears his heart—his clock—and remembers the marking of blood through his own tributaries: his personal *periplus* over which he has no control, that circulating, that wandering around, which will stay with him until his heart no longer marks the second.

There was another young man once—a merchant sailor. Was it really he? He remembers being on a ship—his watch, he was quite alone—peering into the darkness in case something should appear. The world was rolling on beneath him as he bobbed atop it and he felt the rocking of the waves, but not the earth bowling under the ship's prow, although that was his understanding of what was happening. The blackness was even, and the much-pierced veil of sky, the stars burning hotly through, presented a false stillness. He was the point of reference, the entry, the relevant word, the moment, the now: the circumvolving earth and greater clockwork of the heavens used him as fulcrum and center point.

There was a thought: I am what makes it all happen.

There was another: I am without meaning.

Which was Sturm und Drang? Which rationalism?

This is all very funny, and he laughs. He knows that while the fifties and sixties—with their attendant dances and tunes and sexual mores—play on outside, he is happy in his library. This is reprieve.

On the wall is a painting—a respectfully muddied oil of Saint Ignatius relinquishing his sword, giving it up to God. He is no longer soldier, not yet saint, not yet founder of the Jesuits, not yet inspiration to the seminarian (yet to be born, yet to be inspired); he is merely a disillusioned soldier—receiver of injuries, survivor of prolonged recoveries—who is determined to follow in the path of Saint Francis, although Ignatius (or Íñigo) is not a big lover of animals and likes his shoes, as future Jesuits will like the occasional Mercedes-Benz. In the picture, Saint Ignatius has fallen on one knee; on the other, a sword is miraculously balanced. Something hidden behind a woolly cloud has caught his attention. The saint's face is a confusion of awe and decision and duty.

Did Ignatius, falling upon his knee, politely wait for God to appear and accept the gift of peace, inaction, and identity shedding: a gift of willful innocence (as if the battle and bloodshed had never happened) and a new man? Was this his destiny? Did destiny contradict free will? Free will, that gorgeous flawed and slippery cliff's edge upon which all men travel, defines both him and his relationship to God. There is a response to this that he should know cold, that should save him from having to parse out what is faith—not to be questioned—and what sits in the brain like sand in an oyster: the stuff of meditation and philosophy.

Destiny. Is that something to fear or something to dream on?

Our seminarian stares hopefully at the picture of Ignatius, as though the answer might exist within it.

"This painting will not help you," says Ignatius. "It is but a metaphor. A lot of good art and," he looks around at the dun-colored sky, the static rendering about him, "even much average art is composed in such a way as to tell the story rather than present a specific moment in time. It would be unfair to restrict a painter in a way that a writer would never submit to—to submit to the reality. I never fell upon my knee like this. Our brotherhood of Jesuits was not formed with my arms flung wide, my mouth open. We were an intense lot and met in Saint Denis in Paris. It was a meeting of the minds . . ."

All right. All right. No more daydreaming. Take the pencil.

It is your destiny. Take the pencil.

II. Influence

Our seminarian writes "destiny" in the margin, and for one moment it stays upon the page until deemed irrelevant and erased. He writes:

> This account, which is extant only in its Greek translation, was originally engraved in Punic on a bronze tablet set up at Carthage, from where Hanno and his party set forth, probably about 500 BC, on a voyage of colonization and, most likely, exploration.

He considers "most likely" and wonders if "unavoidably" would be more appropriate. He writes "hegemony" in the margin, and the word briefly asserts its influence upon the paper before he erases it.

Hanno's bronze tablet was installed in a temple dedicated to the god Chronos—Old Man Time himself—whom the Carthaginians rather liked. A bronze tablet ensured the words of Hanno a significant march into the future. Where is Hanno's tablet now? No one really knows. Instead, we have various other people on Hanno. Pliny on Hanno. This book that informs so much of the seminarian's paper: *Ancient Greek Mariners,* by Walter Woodburn Hyde. So: Hyde on Pliny on Hanno. And now him: Murray on Hyde on Pliny on Hanno. And somewhere down the road, someone else will jump on board—most likely, perhaps unavoidably, on a journey of colonization and discovery.

III. Scholarship

How has this young man found his way into this library? Man's job is to find his way back to God, and perhaps a seminary is an obvious place—a place for an unsophisticated mind, let's not forget his youth—to start the journey. Perhaps it was his grounding in the classics—all those *A*'s in Latin and Greek. This paper, if he could only make himself write it, will no doubt also be a success—a success unlike Carthage, which flowered in 500 BC, which is why he picks this vague, rosy-fingered chunk of millennium for Hanno's departure, and then, in 146 BC, following the Third Punic War, was wiped from all but history.

When was Carthage established? Well, Queen Dido, princess of Tyre, founded Carthage, and Aeneas found *her* sometime after the Trojan War. So if we look at the dates of the

Trojan War we can approximate. Eratosthenes says Troy fell in 1184 BC, Herodotus 1250 BC, and Douris 1334 BC Let's go with Herodotus, he thinks. Everyone else does.

It was Book Four of the *Aeneid* that got him interested in Carthage in the first place. Aeneas must leave his lover, Queen Dido, because the gods have decided that he is to found Rome. "Leave now, Aeneas. Found Rome!" And in response, no doubt: "Can't somebody else found Rome? And what's the big deal if no one founds it? There are plenty of cities already in existence. What's wrong with Carthage?"

What if the gods had agreed? What would have happened then? Well, Book Four would have been the final book of the *Aeneid,* and Rome would have never been founded, which would no doubt have affected the history of the papacy, and Ignatius, and therefore our seminarian. What if the gods had said, "Quite right, Aeneas. Back to bed with you! Sorry for the bother." Was all possibility and direction contained in Book Four?

That was the book he almost knew by heart, but of course, come the final exam, the passage to translate had been something all together different: the passage on Laocoön. Was that from Book One? Well, it had to be one of the early ones because Laocoön's tale is really that of the Trojan Horse, and his suspicion of it, and the gods yet again favoring Greece over Troy.

Laocoön, high priest of the Trojans, does not trust the Greeks. After ten years of siege, why would he? He says:

> . . . equo ne credite, Teucri. Quidquid id est, timeo Danaos et dona ferentes.

Which translates as, "Do not trust the horse, Trojans. I fear the Greeks even bearing gifts." And we say something similar, although we trust horses and not Greeks. To underscore his justified concern, Laocoön throws a spear at the horse and Minerva (the Greek's Athena, but this is Virgil), in a rather unsubtle cover-up, sends two serpents up the beach to strangle him; the result is that his "fillets soaked with saliva and black venom," something our seminarian was understandably nervous about as he penciled his translation on the final, but this was quite correct. A few lines down, Laocoön's cries of suffering are "like the bellowing when a wounded bull has fled from the altar/and shed the ill-aimed axe from its neck." "Fillet" and "bull" and "horse" suggesting a metaphorical unity that trumps mere narrative, and indeed our translator was as on his mark as Laocoön himself.

In another account of Laocoön's strangulation by snakes, this of the Hellenistic poet Euphorion of Chalcis, the presence of the horse was coincidence: Poseidon had been waiting for Laocoön to present himself on the beach since he'd offended the god by having "marital relations" in the temple in front of an important cult statue. The snakes are payback for Laocoön's wild ways, and Ulysses, who has just dodged the spear tip and now, peering past it through a narrow slit between tempered steel and frayed wood, sees the snakes in hasty slither and the ensuing struggle. He turns to his companions and says, "You won't believe what just happened!" Since there's nothing much to do inside the horse, the other Greeks listen, and they do believe, because they've been through quite a lot. Although, as we well know, they're in for even more.

IV. Departure

Our seminarian taps the tip of his pencil upon the paper. "Leave, Hanno!" he wills his subject. If Hanno never leaves, he will have nothing to write about. And Hanno, lazy in his imagination, finally stirs. Our seminarian writes:

> The voyage took about thirty-seven days before Hanno decided to turn back at a point which has been greatly disputed, but which is now generally believed to be around Sherbro Island off Sierra Leone or Cape Palmas . . . There is no description of the return trip.

In fact the details of the journey are vague to the extent that it has been suggested that Hanno intentionally confused them. This has to do with Carthaginian hegemony—and a desire to befuddle Greek competitors. Hanno, like Laocoon, knew not to trust the Greeks.

The Greeks are powerful adversaries.

The seminarian looks at the picture of the sculpture of Laocoön in his book on Pliny. He reads what Pliny has to say about it, "it was to be preferred to all that the arts of painting and sculpture have produced."

He remembers Father Tedeschi, an art historian now returned to Rome, speaking about Michelangelo's first view of *Laocoön and His Sons*. The year was 1506, and some Roman citizen, while digging around his vineyard on the Esquiline Hill, had discovered the entrance to a long-forgotten niche. One can only imagine his amazement as he peered into the darkness, blinking against it, until the group of figures—monumental Laocoön and his struggling sons bound together by writhing serpents—thrust their unspent anguish upon the Renaissance. And Michelangelo, who no doubt standing there and processing Laocoön's torqued torso and blistering muscles, the expression evident not only in the pained faces of the figures but in every finger digit and calf tendon, thought to himself, *The Greeks are*

powerful adversaries. In this particular case, the Greeks being Agesandros, Polydoros, and Athanadoros of Rhodes, to whom Pliny attributes the sculpture.

I would go further to guess that Michelangelo, sweeping back to Trastevere and the ongoing torments of the pope—who had enlisted the Florentine to paint his chapel ceiling—swung between elation and annoyance at this feat of marble. Gone was the eternal complacency of the *Apollo Belvedere,* which he had skillfully bested with his *David*'s prolonged internal struggle, balanced against the splinter of time before action. This *Laocoön* was a composition that spun under the force of gaze, that pitted man against monster, his best self against his worst, his spiritual against his physical, and all the while under the eyes of gods who, worse than indifferent, were determined to do him in. As is often the response of artists who admire the work of others, this sculpture—this *Laocoön,* by three dead Greeks—seemed to have been expelled from the earth to spite him. As surely as Minerva sent her snakes to snare the priest, so had his God chosen to reveal the statue, miraculously torn from this cleft of the earth, and—a miracle, considering the march of time—all in one piece, as torment.

"Not to torment me," thought Michelangelo, "to do me in!"

What will he pit against this statue?

What will the Renaissance have to stand against this work of ancients?

How can the present engage its ticking, slipping second against all that has gone before it?

"No wonder I have headaches and constipation," says Michelangelo. "God damn those Greeks!"

"And Carthaginians!" adds the seminarian. Why engage the classical world? It's not as if the hegemony of the Greeks is still an issue, nor do we stare past the Pillars of Hercules with awe and ignorance. There is Morocco and Mauritania and just more. What was it like for Hanno, who with his bronze tablet addressed a section of world where land bled to water and water to sky?

The seminarian's eyes wander across the picture of Saint Ignatius again. He feels that he should fall upon his knee and offer his pencil. Would God take it if he stated, "Being scholar or saint is not my thing. I'd like to try soldiering"?

But someone has entered the library and is shuffling on leather soles among the stacks. Our seminarian closes the picture of the *Laocoön,* snaps the covers upon its distracting influence, not wanting to be discovered so entranced by something other than his paper. He looks at his notes. The first section is the introduction—clearly a good place to start—but he's not altogether sure what he's introducing. Maybe he should move to the next section, Pliny on Hanno, which is—if nothing else—where the intriguing matter will be placed. Pliny, writing five centuries after the time of Hanno, writes of the Carthaginian explorer three times. Our seminarian glances over his notes, flips back to the history, and writes:

> In the final passage, Hanno, *Poenorum imperator,* is said to have reached the Gorgades Islands, where he came upon the people with hair all over their bodies, whom the *Periplus* calls γορίλλασ—gorillas, but whom Pliny refers to as Gorgons.

V. Monsters

The seminarian is under the impression that these hairy people were neither gorillas, nor gorgons, but rather pygmies. Much of Hanno's information came from the Lixitae, and their word, "gorel" was a broad term for describing diminutive man-like creatures. The term could refer to a baboon, or a pygmy, or maybe even a dwarf. It is a term based on size, probably refined by familiarity—or in the case of this term, the absence of familiarity. Of course, now he's merely positing.

But what if . . . of course, Hanno wrote in Punic. And he is translating out of the Greek into English in much the same way that, at some point, some like-minded Greek translated out of the Punic. But a Greek would not have used the word "gorilla" for what we now refer to as gorillas. Aristotle provided neat, fixed terms. For ape, he had πίθηκοσ, pithikos; for baboon, κυνοκέφαλοσ, kinokephalos; for monkey, κῆβοσ, kivos. So why use "gorilla," should Hanno not be encountering something new?

But what if Hanno was making it all up? Hanno writes of rivers and tracts of land in constant blaze, islands within islands, a fire-spewing mountain that seemed to touch the sky.

Pliny has his fanciful unicorn moments, and Hanno might too. The seminarian looks at the *Periplus* and reads:

> . . . and in this lake another island, full of savage people, the greater part of whom were women, whose bodies were hairy, and whom our interpreters called *Gorillæ*. Though we pursued the men, we could not seize any of them; but all fled from us, escaping over the precipices, and defending themselves with stones.

This did not sound like a gorilla to him. Didn't gorillas stand their ground, beat their chests, roar? Or was this a vestigial belief left over from his Saturday viewings of Johnny Weissmuller's Tarzan as he subjugated leopards, lions, gorillas too, and the truth, in the admirable pursuit of firing up the imaginations of young boys and bored housewives? He returns to the text.

> Three women were however taken; but they attacked their conductors with their teeth and hands, and could not be prevailed upon to accompany us. Having killed them, we flayed them, and brought their skins with us to Carthage.

Were they human or animal? Attacking with teeth and hands sounds human. Having hairy, flay-worthy skins does not. Can these characteristics stand side by side?

The seminarian sifts through his stack of scholarship: the Frenchman who says that volcanoes appear and disappear in the course of history; the American woman who says that there might well have been gorillas in that region at that time: scholars searching for a possible reality to be—or to have been—reflected in the *Periplus* of Hanno. Hanno is undeniably vague. An infinite number of stories can be read into what he provides—extant only in its Greek translation—which has had its own *wandering around*: first brought west in the fifteenth century by a cardinal, most likely from Constantinople, in the decade after the city's fall to the Turks, then passed from a Basel convent to a Protestant scholar during the Reformation, then—as a result of the Thirty Years' War—carted off as Catholic booty to the Vatican, and now—in replica—before him on his desk in Shrub Oak, New York.

How many people have approached this document of 630 words and found volumes within it? How many words wash up against that original telling—conceived to neatly fit upon a bronze tablet—approaching and approaching in hopeful, scholarly erosion? Could this ever lay bare the truth?

Or are all these people, these scholars, attempting to find a reality to fit this tale? From this fiction, will they find a fact? Will they invent one? From this hairy gorilla, will they create a pygmy prototype or a migration of apes? A missing link? Is this scholarship? What is his paper trying to do?

Is he also composing reality from art?

"Mister Murray," comes a voice. It is Father O'Donnell, himself an ancient, with one foot already in the afterlife. The old priest smiles benignly and possibly senilely, but if this is one of his earthbound days, he'll be razor sharp. "How is your paper coming?"

"It started out well," begins the seminarian, "and now I no longer know the purpose of scholarship."

"Excellent," says the old priest. He pats the seminarian's head, then shuffles back to lurk behind reference.

"Excellent," repeats the seminarian quietly. Is this one of Father O'Donnell's days of senility or lucidity? He weighs the options and admits to himself that it could be either. Our seminarian has no idea whether he is sinking into a maudlin ignorance or achieving enlightenment. He looks at his translation—a solid, acceptable endeavor, that, turning words into other words. Or maybe it's not, but the last thing he needs is another great abstracting truth to wrestle with.

His eye dawdles over the page, resting at the final passage: ". . . an island like the former, having a lake, and in this lake another island . . ."

"Islands within islands," he repeats to himself. And then an insight. He will not argue with Pliny, he will embrace him. He will write about Pliny, and who's the other guy who has so much to say on Hanno? Arrian. There's his paper.

THE PERIPLUS OF HANNO
ACCORDING TO PLINY AND ARRIAN

Not according to me, he thinks. He's carting boulders, not making mountains. He's creating another lake in which to put all the other islands and lakes and islands.

VI. Extant

Pliny seems to have a handle on Hanno, although he hasn't checked his facts. He seems to think that Hanno sailed from Cades to Arabia—Pliny's convinced that Hanno circumnavigated Africa—a fact that is contradicted in the *Periplus* itself, which states that the party was forced to return. Hanno concludes: "We did not sail farther on, our provisions failing us." The seminarian makes a note to address this discrepancy, which suggests either that Pliny did not have an account of the *Periplus* as he wrote, that it had been a while since Pliny had read the account, or that Pliny found it a much better story should Hanno have actually have traveled from Cerne (somewhere just past the Pillars of Hercules) all the way back to Arabia.

Was Pliny making his life impossible or giving him something to write about?

Our seminarian knows that Pliny's great contribution is his *Historia Naturalis,* and that although he cannot always count on Pliny to be right, neither can he count on him to be wrong. Pliny is right maybe half the time factually, and all the time culturally. He's more interesting when he's wrong, when he writes of owl-eyed Albanians with flaming-red night vision, or King Pyrrhus who, with his swollen big toe, has the ability to heal all manner of ills. And accuracy had a different meaning then. Preserving knowledge in print was what excited Pliny—putting everything down—and had he not, we would have lost our gold-mining griffins of the far north. All that would remain is our goats and horses and sheep that present themselves now much as they did then: in a field rather than in the imagination. It's still a tremendous accomplishment, even if he relied on others to supply the information, and had a judgment-impairing affection for the weird animal and odd cultural practice.

Ironically, the one event that Pliny is famous for actually having witnessed, he never had a chance to write about. This was the cataclysmic eruption of Vesuvius in AD 79, which cautioned the outlying communities first with a cloud that appeared like "a pine tree, for it shot up to a great height in the form of a very tall trunk, which spread itself out into a sort [*sic*] of branches." Pliny, hearing of the cloud, decided it merited a closer view. He launched his galleys from where he was staying in Misenum and headed across the Bay of Naples. This short journey, initially envisioned as one of scholarship and perhaps journalism, developed poignancy as the danger of the erupting volcano became impossible to ignore. Pliny was attempting to rescue people from Stabiae when he was overwhelmed with poisonous gases. Pliny suffocated. Two days after the eruption, his body was found, still, yet seemingly unharmed: the effect of toxic fumes.

What account we have of that fateful event in Pliny (the Elder)'s life is provided by his nephew, Pliny the Younger, who witnessed his uncle's fatal embarkation but had the good luck to stay ashore. And this is what remains of Pliny's journalistic urge—his death, and a rather good account of what went down, furnished in a letter from his nephew to Tacitus.

There, in the book, by the account of Pliny's death, our seminarian sees a drawing of a plaster cast of three citizens of Pompeii, captured in their last moment, upon a set of stairs. He finds something artful about the composition rendered in quick frenetic lines, something aesthetic in how the geometric shadow of the steps offsets the rough human forms upon it. The three bodies form an *L*-shape, with the top-most figure seated, almost

lying on his back. The second figure forms the angle of the *L,* knees pulled up, his head sheltering beneath the thigh of his friend. And the third figure—the base of the *L*—is passed out facedown, a hand resting on the step above, as if he has never given up hope of reaching his destination: *Sleeping Beauty* forms, frozen in AD 79. They carry that moment with them, tacking it directly to our own—a pleat dissolving the years that separate the instant of their death from this of his viewing.

What would Michelangelo have had to say about it? Would he have been moved by this confrontation with the ancients? Would this interaction with capricious and uncaring gods—a grouping of three figures—without the skill of Polydoros, Athanadoros, and Agesandros to intervene—have moved him? Would Michelangelo have been as moved by people as by art? Is *The People on the Stairs* any less art than the *Laocoön*? What is the role of intention in art?

He thinks of one story: eruption, stairs, asphyxiation. And the other: Laocoön of the venom-filled fillets. Laocoön and his sons: extant in Virgil. The people on the stairs: extant in plaster. But in the end it's only impression: the gorgeous grouping of the people on the stairs achieves what it does, like the Laocoön, through artificial appeal.

The seminarian looks up at the clock. He has only another hour to work today and after that it's dinner and litanies and meditation. He looks at his paper—*Pliny and Arrian on Hanno*—and wonders if it's possible to get some sort of digression on the nature of art in there, which he decides is impossible. But it does amuse him, and he needs to amuse himself: all this time alone intended to make one dialogue with God often has the added effect of making one dialogue with oneself, as if there were another of him seated beside, cracking jokes and laughing in turn.

"Enough," says the seminarian, and he forces himself back to the *Periplus*. "Start at the beginning," he wills himself, and reads Hanno's opening line yet again.

"It was decreed by the Carthaginians, that Hanno should undertake a voyage beyond the Pillars of Hercules . . ."

VII. The Pillars of Hercules

Always the Pillars of Hercules! How tidy to have lived in the ancient world, where these pillars stood as literal markers between known and unknown, where so little was understood and recorded that one, standing upon the Rock of Gibraltar, could say, "Here is known!"—then point off into the North Atlantic and say, "There is unknown!" The Pillars of Hercules were the edge of the world, the ancients being a little more complicated than men in the Age of Exploration. One sailed through the edge of the world and into the unknown, rather than off the edge of the world and into oblivion. He remembers studying something about the Pillars of Hercules somewhere, a picture exists in his mind: two pillars and a galleon sailing through it. Of course, this looks nothing like the actual pillars—Hercules would never have created anything so baldly architectural and smooth. Instead, there is the Rock of Gibraltar and its corresponding Moroccan mountain—either the Monte Hacho in Ceuta or Morocco's Jebel Musa.

Our seminarian wonders, despondently, whether such pillars still exist. Or has everything worthwhile been observed and catalogued, illustrated and recorded? Is scholarship a desperate attempt to fling up more pillars—more barriers between known and unknown—only to sail immediately through? Is it necessary to create the unknown? Our seminarian closes his eyes and imagines himself sailing through these pillars, from a world of cool green and blue into one of heated red and orange.

And then he imagines *looking back* and seeing his youthful self, the moment suspended as if viewed within a crystal ball: his cheek lying on an open page, his fingers loosely holding the pencil, his life unspooling ahead of him as he blinks against the dust of books and wonders what could possibly be important or unimportant. He is that young. The thought that he himself is a history, that the passage of time will be recorded in his face, his limbs, his slower heart pushing blood through the tributaries of his body, it all seems impossibly distant. Impossible.

VIII. The Golden Triangle

And here, in northern Thailand, the heat is formidable, but as a man who has worked and studied much of his life in Asia—near forty years—he is accustomed to it. He is taking a vanload of philosophy students from the University of Southern Maine wandering around Thailand on a voyage of discovery, mostly concerned with Buddhism. The students find the heat intense, the Thais (who are not intense) intense, even the food. He amuses himself by thinking of what it must be for them to live minute to minute in such a state of stimulation. He sees one young man snapping pictures of children, some girls looking at woven goods—bags and blankets—for which they will pay too much.

"Doctor Murray," says one girl. "Why is it called the Golden Triangle?"

"Well, famously, because of the opium trade. But we will say that we are here because it is the place where Thailand, Burma, and Laos all meet. And for that it is worth looking at."

The girl, smart enough but too practical for scholarship, looks first to the left with frank suspicion, then back over her shoulder. What can he teach this person, who has never had a question that she did not want answered?

"So the borders are right around here?"

He nods patiently.

"What's the river?"

"That's the Mekong. The confluence of the Ruak and Mekong is not far from here."

"Oh," she says, not impressed. "And what's over there?"

She points toward Burma, and that is probably the answer that would satisfy her. She points to the west. She points to the West from the East. He knows the response cold, but then he doesn't. He remembers being a sailor on a ship and the earth bowling up beneath him. He remembers living west, the sound of books slammed shut, the approach and loss of car radio music, popular music, coming over the seminary wall as he walked between buildings. He remembers being young. And then suddenly he remembers all, as if his entire memory has become suspended before him—this moment the portal to everything that has gone before. The world spins back and back, unleashing a pool of wrinkled event.

"Doctor Murray," she says, "Doctor Murray." And she looks concerned.

The sky is more white than blue and he wonders if it is always like that, and, if it is, why he has never noticed it before.

"Doctor Murray," she says again.

"Over there?" he says.

She nods, but she's forgotten her question.

He gestures with conviction. "Over there? Over there is everything."

Balboa

Vasco Núñez de Balboa ascends the mountain alone. His one thousand Indians and two hundred Spaniards wait at the foot of the mountain, as if they are the Israelites and Balboa alone is off to speak with God. Balboa knows that from this peak he will be able to see the western water, what he has already decided to name the South Sea. He takes a musket with him. The Spaniards have been warned that if they follow, he will use it, because discovery is a tricky matter and he wants no competition. The day is September 25, 1513.

Balboa ascends slowly. His musket is heavy and he would have gladly left it down below, but he doesn't trust his countrymen any more than he trusts the sullen Indians. So he bears the weight. But the musket is nothing. He is dragging the mantle of civilization up the pristine slopes, over the mud, over the leaves that cast as much shade as a parasol but with none of the charm.

Balboa is that divining line between the modern and the primitive. As he moves, the shadow of Spain moves with him.

Balboa steps cautiously into a muddy stream and watches with fascination as his boot sinks and sinks. He will have to find another way. Upstream he sees an outcropping of rock. Maybe he

can cross there. He tells himself that there is no hurry, but years
of staying just ahead of trouble have left him anxiety-ridden. He
would like to think of himself as a lion. Balboa the Lion! But
no, he is more of a rat, and all of his accomplishments have been
made with speed and stealth. Balboa places his hand on a branch
and pulls himself up. He sees the tail of a snake disappearing
just past his reach. The subtle crush of greenery confirms his
discovery and he shrinks back, crouching. In this moment of
stillness, he looks around. He sees no other serpents, but that
does not mean they are not there. Only in this momentary quiet
does he hear his breath, rasping with effort. He hears his heart
beating in the arced fingers of his ribs as if it is an Indian's drum.
He does not remember what it is to be civilized, or if he ever
was. If ever a man was alone, it is he. But even in this painful
solitude, he cannot help but laugh. Along with Cristóbal Colón,
backed by Isabel I herself, along with Vespucci the scholar, along
with the noble Pizarro brothers on their way to claim Inca gold,
his name will live—Balboa. Balboa! Balboa the Valiant. Balboa
the Fearsome. Balboa the Brave.

Balboa the gambling pig farmer, who, in an effort to escape his debt, has found himself at the very edge of the world.

Balboa stops to drink from the stream. The water is cold,
fresh, and tastes like dirt, which is a relief after what he has been
drinking—water so green that the very act of ingesting it seems
unnatural, as though it is as alive as he, and sure enough, given
a few hours, it will get you back, eager to find its way out. He
has been climbing since early morning and it is now noon. The
sun shines in the sky unblinking, white-hot. Balboa wonders if
it's the same sun that shines in Spain. The sun seemed so much
smaller there. Even in Hispaniola, the sun was Spanish. Even
as he prodded his pigs in the heat, there was Spain all around,
men with dice, men training roosters, pitting their dogs against

each other. But here . . . then he hears a twig snap and the sound of something brushing up against the bushes. Balboa stands.

"I give you this one chance to turn back," he says, raising his musket as he turns. And then he freezes. It is not one of the Spaniards hoping to share the glory. Instead, he finds himself face-to-face with a great spotted cat. On this mountain, he'd thought he might find his god, the god of Moses, sitting in the cloud cover near the peaks, running his fingers through his beard. But no. Instead he finds himself face-to-face with a jaguar, the god of the Indians. He knows why these primitives have chosen it for their deity. It is hard to fear one's maker when he looks like one's grandfather, but this great cat can make a people fear god. He hears the growling of the cat and the grating, high-pitched thunder sounds like nothing he has ever heard. The cat twitches its nose and two great incisors show at the corners of its mouth. Balboa raises his musket, ignites the flint, and nothing happens. He tries again and the weapon explodes, shattering the silence, sending up a big puff of stinking smoke. The cat is gone for now, but Balboa knows he hasn't even injured it.

And now it will be tailing him silently.

There is nothing he can do about it. He should have brought an Indian with him. The Indians have all seen the South Sea before, so why did he leave them at the foot of the mountain? They have no more interest in claiming the South Sea than they do rowing off to Europe in their dug-out canoes and claiming Spain. But Balboa's hindsight is always good, and no amount of swearing—which he does freely, spilling Spanish profanity into the virgin mountain air—is going to set things straight.

He is already in trouble. His kingdom in Darién on the east coast of the New World is under threat, and not from the Indians, whom he manages well, but from Spain. Balboa had

organized the rebellion, supplanted the governor—all of this
done with great efficiency and intelligence. What stupidity made
him send the governor, Martín Fernández de Enciso, back to
Spain? Enciso swore that he would have Balboa's head on a
platter. He was yelling from the deck of the ship as it set sail.
Why didn't he kill Enciso? Better yet, why didn't he turn Enciso over to some Indian tribe that would be glad to have the
Spaniard, glad to have his blood on their hands? How could
Balboa be so stupid? Soon the caravels would arrive and his
days as governor (king, he tells the Indians) of Darién will be
over. Unless, Balboa thinks, unless he brings glory by being the
first to claim this great ocean for Spain. Then the king will see
him as the greatest of his subjects, not a troublemaking peasant,
a keeper of pigs.

Unless that jaguar gets him first.

Balboa looks nervously around. The only sound is the
trickle and splash of the stream that he is following, which the
Indians tell him leads to a large outcropping of rock from which
he will see the new ocean. Insects swoop malevolently around
his head. A yellow and red parrot watches him cautiously from
a branch, first looking from one side of its jeweled head, then
the other. Where is the jaguar? Balboa imagines his body being
dragged into a tree, his boots swinging from the limbs as the
great cat tears his heart from his ribs. He hears a crushing of
vegetation and ducks low. He readies his musket again. "Please
God, let the damned thing fire." He breathes harshly, genuflect-
ing, musket steady.

The leaves quiver, then part. There is no jaguar.

"Leoncico!" he cries out. Leoncico is his dog, who has
tracked him up the slope. Leoncico patters over, wagging his
tail, his great wrinkled head bearded with drool. Leoncico is a
monster of a dog. His head is the size of a man's, and his body

has the look of a lion—shoulders and hipbones protruding and muscle pulling and shifting beneath the glossy skin—which is where he gets his name. "Leoncico" means little lion.

"Good dog," says Balboa. "Good dog. Good dog."

He has never been so grateful for the company, not even when he was hidden on board Enciso's ship bound for San Sebastian, escaping his creditors, wrapped in a sail. No one wondered why the dog had come on board. Maybe the dog had been attracted by the smell of provisions, the great barrels of salted meat. The soldiers fed him, gave him water. Balboa worried that Leoncico would give him away, but the dog had somehow known to be quiet. He had slept beside Balboa, and even in Balboa's thirst and hunger, the great beast's panting and panting, warm through the sailcloth, had given him comfort. When Enciso's crew finally discovered Balboa—one of the sails was torn and needed to be replaced—they did not punish him. They laughed.

"The Indians massacre everyone. You are better off in a debtors' prison," they said.

Balboa became a member of the crew. When the boat shipwrecked off the coast of San Sebastian (they were rescued by Francisco Pizarro), Enciso had been at a loss as to where to go, and Balboa convinced him to try Darién to the north. Once established there, Enciso had shown himself to be a weak man. How could Balboa not act? Enciso did not understand the Indians as Balboa did. He could see that the Indians were battle-hardened warriors. The Spaniards had not been there long enough to call these armies into existence. Balboa's strength had been to recognize this discord. He divided the great tribes, supported one against the other. His reputation spread. His muskets blasted away the faces of the greatest warriors. Balboa's soldiers spread smallpox and syphilis. His Spanish war dogs, great mastiffs and wolfhounds, tore children limb from limb. The blood from his great war machine made the rivers flow red and his name, Balboa, moved quickly, apace with these rivers of blood.

Balboa is loved by no one and feared by all. He has invented an unequaled terror. The Indians think of him as a god. They make no distinction between good and evil. They have seen his soldiers tear babies from their mothers, toss them still screaming to feed the dogs. They have seen the great dogs pursue the escaping Indians, who must hear nothing but a great panting, the jangle of the dogs' armor, and then, who knows? Do they feel the hot breath on their cheek? Are they still awake when the beasts unravel their stomachs and spill them onto the hot earth? Balboa's dogs have been his most effective weapon because for them, one does not need to carry ammunition, as for the muskets; one does not need to carry food, as for the soldiers. For the dogs, there is fresh meat everywhere. He knows his cruelty will be recorded along with whatever he discovers. This does not bother him, even though one monk, Dominican—strange fish—cursed him back in Darién. He was a young monk, tormented by epileptic fits. He approached Balboa in the town square in his bare feet, unarmed, waving his shrunken fist.

"Your dogs," screamed the monk, "are demons."

As if understanding, Leoncico had lunged at the monk. Leoncico is not a demon. He is the half of Balboa with teeth, the half that eats. Balboa has the mind and appetite. Together, they make one. It is as if the great beast can hear his thoughts, as if their hearts and lungs circulate the same blood and air. What did the monk understand of that? What did he understand of anything? He said that he was in the New World to bring the Indians to God. So the monk converts the Indians, and Balboa sends them on to God. They work together, which is what Balboa told the monk. But the monk did not find it funny.

How dare he find fault with Balboa? Is not Spain as full of torments as the New World? The Spaniards are brought down by smallpox at alarming rates in Seville, in Madrid. Every summer the rich take to the mountains to escape the plague, and in the fall, when they return, aren't their own countrymen lying in the streets feeding the packs of mongrels? Half of all the Spanish babies die. It is not uncommon to see a peasant woman leave her screaming infant on the side of the road, so why come here and beg relief for these savages? Why not go to France, where, one soldier tells Balboa, they butcher the Huguenots and sell their limbs for food in the street? Why rant over the impaling of the Indians when Spaniards—noblemen among them—have suffered the same fate in the name of God? In fact, the Inquisition has been the great educator when it comes to subduing the Indian population.

Why take him to task when the world is a violent place?

"May your most evil act be visited on you," said the monk. "I curse you."

The monk died shortly after that. His threats and bravery were more the result of a deadly fever than the words of a divine message. Did the curse worry Balboa? Perhaps a little. He occasionally revisits a particularly spectacular feat of bloodshed—the time Leoncico tore a chieftain's head from his shoulders—with a pang of concern. But Balboa is a busy man with little time for reflection. When the monk delivered his curse, Balboa was already preparing his troops for the great march to the west. His name had reached Spain, and the king felt his authority threatened.

He is the great Balboa.

But here, on the slope of the mountain, his name does not seem worth that much. He has to relieve himself and is terrified that some creature—jaguar, snake, spider—will take advantage of his great heaving bareness.

"Leoncico," he calls. "At attention."

Not that this command means anything to the dog. Leoncico knows "attack," and that is all he needs to know. Leoncico looks up, wags his tail, and lies down, his face smiling into the heat. Balboa climbs onto a boulder. Here, he is exposed to everything, but if that jaguar is still tracking him, he can at least see it coming. He sets his musket down and listens. Nothing. He loosens his belt and is about to lower his pants when he sees it—the flattened glimmer, a shield, the horizon. He fixes his belt and straightens himself. He stares out at the startling bare intrusion, this beautiful nothing beyond the green tangle of trees, the *Mar del Sur*, the glory of Balboa, his gift to Spain.

Balboa, having accomplished his goal, luxuriates in this moment of peaceful ignorance. He does not know that his days are numbered, that even after he returns to Darién with his knowledge of the South Sea, even after he has ceded the governorship to Pedro Arias Dávila, even after he is promised Dávila's daughter, he has not bought his safety. Dávila will see that as long as Balboa lives he must sleep with one eye open. With the blessing of Spain, Dávila will bring Balboa to trial for treason, and on January 21, 1519, Balboa's head will be severed from his shoulders. His eyes will stay open, his mouth will be slack, and his great head will roll in the dust for everyone—Indians, Spaniards, and dogs—to see.

Last Days

It seems most credible that our Lord God has purposefully allowed these lands [Mexico] to be discovered . . .
so that Your Majesties may be fruitful and deserving in
His sight by causing these barbaric tribes to be enlightened and brought to faith by Your hand.

— Hernán Cortés, 1519

During the last days of the Aztec Empire, Nezahualpilli, ruler
of Texcoco, went to meet with the king of the Aztecs.

Nezahualpilli had a bad feeling about his meeting with
Motecuhzoma the second. He had reason for concern despite
and, perhaps, because of his ability to see the future. Motecuhzoma had called on him because of Nezahualpilli's skill as a seer,
but Nezahualpilli saw nothing good in the future, and it took no
trance, no rare herbs, for him to see that things were not getting
better. For years he had managed a modicum of autonomy for
his small island state, his kingdom within a kingdom. Tenochtitlan dominated without challenge as it had done since the days

of his father, but this great kingdom of the Aztecs was in danger of crumbling, disappearing as the revered Toltecs had before them, and in Motecuhzoma's desperation he had begun casting about his own kingdom for an explanation. Motecuhzoma worshipped the hummingbird god, Huitzilopochtli, and Motecuhzoma's palliative efforts were mostly comprised of human tribute. Casting about for explanation was a violent process.

Nezahualpilli, his head bowed in thought, realized that he was not alone. He raised his head and saw his favorite attendant standing calmly, still, as though stillness was a pleasure afforded him much as stillness must have pleased trees and rocks. "How long have you been there?"

"A time," said the attendant. "I thought you were sleeping."

"Have you news for me?"

"You will be pleased that I have none," the attendant smiled, "but your bath is ready."

"Is it hot enough?"

"For you, my lord, yes. The servants have an inferno raging on the outer wall and when I threw my dipper upon that of your bath, a great sizzle issued forth producing a billowing cloud of steam upon which floated aromas of great and pleasing variety—"

"All that, really?" said Nezahualpilli.

"Yes, all that, today as yesterday, as the day before, as all the days reaching back as long as I know, since I, a mere orphaned boy, came to this house and found myself the gatherer of firewood for this same bath of which now I am the steward."

"A nice history," said Nezahualpilli. "And now you will do me the favor of scrubbing my back."

As promised, the bath was hot and Nezahualpilli spent longer than usual seated in its embracing mist, inhaling its soothing vapors. The water trickled down the stone walls of the enclosure. He felt his water god near and everywhere. In Texcoco, the cult of Quetzalcoatl was flourishing, although in secret. The feathered serpent had been favored by the ancient and wise Toltecs. More of consequence, Quetzalcoatl did not demand human sacrifice, as did Huitzilopochtli. And years of rivers running with blood, corpses rolling down the canted steps of the Great Temple, and feasting on elaborate stews made with the flesh of one's own countrymen had resulted in widespread and justified despair. The Texcocons and other vassal states were not hardened by years of tribute to the humming bird, they were worn down. Quetzalcoatl was a god concerned with regeneration, more appealing, especially when Huitzilopochtli demanded beating human hearts to perform such basic functions as sending the sun across the sky.

"More steam," Nezahualpilli instructed, and his servant flung the dipper of water again and again against the heated wall.

There was something suspicious about Huitzilopochtli—an insecurity (like Motecuhzoma's own) that made him want victims and then more victims. After all, was there anything as ridiculous as an aggressive, bloodthirsty, carnivorous hummingbird? Nezahualpilli watched hummingbirds daily in his garden—tiny suspended jewels hovering about the plumeria, sipping nectar. How could one reconcile this with the god of Tlacaelel and the Aztecs, who demanded life after life and threatened total darkness?

Nezahualpilli had been there at the consecration of the Great Temple in 1487. He had witnessed the columns of slaves and citizens, children and warriors, snaking through the streets. One after another they were sacrificed at the hands of the nobles. Ahuizotl himself (who had ruled before the unfortunate collapse of the northern dam) had sacrificed for close to an hour until his arms grew tired. It was not easy work to plunge an obsidian blade into a struggling man's chest, to pull his heart out from the tangle of vessels and dense muscles.

During the entire ordeal, Nezahualpilli had sat on his chair behind a curtain of flowers wishing himself to a peaceful place, where water trickled endlessly down the stone walls of his temple and men sat in quiet dialogue with the ruler of the One World, his god, Quetzalcoatl, god of Venus, who disappeared with the morning light and then, each evening, was triumphantly brought back to life. His god was the god of resurrection, not hopeless blood-letting and infinite death.

Nezahualpilli drank more than his share of coca juice that day and in the days that followed, but he could not numb his senses. Even bitter mushrooms could not disguise the reek of decomposing bodies and jellied mounds of clotted blood filling the streets of the capital. Even back in Texcoco, the stench was vivid and inescapable. When Nezahualpilli asked Tlacaelel how many had been sacrificed, the great general and true ruler of Tenochtitlan had no exact figure. He estimated somewhere near eighty thousand.

"Enough," he said, and then louder, over the hushing steam, "Enough!"

This was to be the second time Nezahualpilli had met with Motecuhzoma, and he feared he would be held responsible for this dire second installment of prophecy.

Nezahualpilli felt the weight of his cloak descend on his shoulders. He nodded at his two attendants and they continued with his wardrobe, setting a heavy, feathered headdress in place. The weight of his cloak, the weight of this headdress, the weight of his years, and the knowledge that the kingdom was doomed . . . that he could sink back into the great lake from which all this had been born! The boat was ready for him to make the trip to Tenochtitlan. Maybe he would sink like a stone. Maybe that would be better for all of them.

Was it his fault that he could divine the future? He saw what he saw, he did not make it up, and when his prophecies were fulfilled, he felt no joy in his accuracy. He would have loved to be wrong, wrong about the Aztecs' defeat at the hands of the Tlaxcalans, wrong about ominous fireballs falling from the skies. Most worrisome, his final prophecy—that the great city of Tenochtitlan would fall, and all its inhabitants and their children and vassals would be annihilated—had yet to pass. Maybe he was wrong about that. All this was to occur in Motecuhzoma's lifetime, not his. In fact, the only comfort Nezahualpilli had was his age. He would be dead when it all happened. Maybe Motecuhzoma would kill him, although he doubted this because he was already close to death. The other seers and necromancers had been stripped naked and set in cages to starve when their prophesies failed to please, but Nezahualpilli, in addition to being old, was a blood relative of Motecuhzoma's, so he did not fear that.

Nezahualpilli paused by the side of the water. All around him, the islands of the city constructed by the Aztecs stood as monuments to their power to overcome nature. Crops were harvested on the *chinampas,* fields dragged up from the lake that were barely above water level. Fresh water flowed in from Chapultepec in two stone aqueducts. Great dams held the salty flows from the mountains at bay, but soon it would all be just part of the great chronicles of Aztec history. "Take my elbow," Nezahualpilli said to a young attendant. He stepped onto the flat platform of the boat and sank into the chair that was set upon it. "Go, go quickly," he instructed the rowers. He found it difficult to leave his palace anymore, to see the columns of children being led to the temple, to hear their mothers weeping. He closed his eyes, not wanting to witness the nobility leading their slaves, Aztec citizens, back from the market, eager to butcher and eat them. Was it no wonder that this kingdom was doomed? In his mind he called on his god, Quetzalcoatl, who was his only comfort.

Quetzalcoatl, return before we are all dead. Return and save us.

Nezahualpilli was not demanding the impossible in his prayers. Quetzalcoatl, revered by the Toltecs, had lain in the shadow of Huitzilopochtli long enough, and there was a prophecy that he would come again. The ancient Toltecs, with whom the Aztecs tenuously linked their lineage, had disappeared without explanation. One day these great beings would return with their god, coming from the east to the One World, and when that happened, there would be little that the Aztecs could do. Quetzalcoatl and his retinue of Toltecs would be recognized because they would accept the gifts of their land to which they had a righteous claim. They would eat the food offered to them and accept the rich gifts, and this would let the Aztecs know that their days of supremacy had ended.

Nezahualpilli covered his face with a feathered fan and fell to sleeping. He was old, and this practice for death, sleep, was comfort.

Finally, Nezahualpilli reached Motecuhzoma's palace. As he walked through the stone archways that led to the throne room, the torches flaring and sputtering, the metallic stench of blood rising off the stone in the heat of day, he was struck by the silence in the palace. The hiss of flame and soft step of the barefooted steward were the only things that intruded on the ominous quiet, on his dark thoughts.

The monarch was sitting on his throne surrounded by his dwarves. Usually, his dwarves and acrobats amused Motecuhzoma, but lately their purpose had been to listen to his increasingly insane ranting. Nezahualpilli had heard that the dwarves were Motecuhzoma's closest confidants. They crouched around him like evil, wisened children. It was said the king wanted to escape to the hills, that he wanted to die. What kind of ruler was this? Motecuhzoma was unaware of Nezahualpilli's approach. His eyes were closed and he appeared to be napping.

"Lord," said Nezahualpilli, his eyes respectfully lowered, "you summoned me."

Motecuhzoma's eyes snapped open. "Oh, yes," he said. "I need to ask you some things."

"You have your own seers . . . "

"Fools, all of them."

"But you surround yourself with jesters," said Nezahualpilli.

"Because they are not hypocrites," said Motecuhzoma. "There are fools. And there are fools who are fools."

The dwarves—Nezahualpilli counted eleven—looked up at him, offended. "I did not know we had so many stunted men in our realm," he said.

"A sign," said Motecuhzoma. "Things are not right. The women bring forth dwarves, and just yesterday a two-headed pup was born in Tlatelolco. They brought it to me. I saw it."

"Two-headed dogs have always been born, my lord."

"And has it ever come to any good? Did the birth of a two-headed dog ever mean victory in the provinces, or an end to this drought, or," and here the monarch sobbed, "a long reign?"

"You are upsetting yourself needlessly. I have heard you sent your seers to all corners of Tenochtitlan to find these perversions of nature—"

"I did. And here they are." Motecuhzoma spread his hand over the heads of his dwarves. "And you said to look in the sky, and I did, and a great ball of fire fell. And you said to not wage another Flower War, and I went against the Tlaxcalans and saw my warriors flayed and strung from trees for target practice."

"That is true," said Nezahualpilli. "But today I have nothing for you. No dog. No dwarf. No whirlpool sucking at the lake."

"Because all that has happened. But what does it mean? Last week, lightning struck the temple of Tlaloc, but there was no rain, and he is the rain god. What does that mean?"

"It means it did not rain."

"And the earth shakes and quivers. Our temples wobble as if they are made of reeds."

"The earth shakes because we live on a lake."

"And what of the fire in the Temple of Huitzilopochtli?"

"Where there are torches, there is often fire, my lord."

"Not good enough, old man. You know things that you do not tell me."

"And you defy my reasoning," said Nezahualpilli wearily. "You place your trust in me, but just this year you ordered me to march my army against the Tlaxcalans in retribution for your loss, then ordered the Aztec warriors to pull back. My armies were destroyed and two of my favorite sons are dead, which is what you desired for me. In the months since my first visit to warn you of the dangers faced by our great city, you have reduced me from a leader of the Triple Alliance to the lowest of vassals. You have snuffed whatever autonomy I had. Even my desire to worship the god Quetzalcoatl is denied—"

"But this is why I've called you here. Repeat that prophecy," said Motecuhzoma. He half-covered his face with the feathered fan and watched.

"This is not my prophecy," said Nezahualpilli. "I heard this from the priests in Cholula."

"Tell me," said Motecuhzoma. "Tell me what they foretell."

Nezahualpilli sighed. "Quetzalcoatl will return. The Toltecs will be with him. They come to reclaim this land. As the reign of the Toltecs once ended, now it is time for the reign of the Aztecs to end. We will recognize Quetzalcoatl from his lordly attire, the marvelous beasts that will be at his command. He will accept our gifts of food and treasure, for are they not truly his? Is not everything the land brings forth the property of Quetzalcoatl?"

"Go on," said Motecuhzoma, "why stop there?"

"Because that is all there is."

"What about your other prophecy?"

"We've been over that before, and recently."

"Are you refusing to repeat it?"

"No, my lord," said Nezahualpilli. He took a deep breath. "Be forewarned that in a very few years, our cities will be laid to waste, that we and our children and our vassals will be annihilated. Do not lose faith or become anxious about what will happen because it is impossible to evade. I am comforted only by the knowledge that I will not see these calamities and afflictions, as my own days are counted. And because of this, before I die, I wish only to warn you as if you were my own dear son."

"Is that it?" asked Motecuhzoma.

"Yes, my lord."

"It's shorter this time." Motecuhzoma lowered his fan. "Yes. I'm positive that it's shorter."

"Yes, my lord."

"Why?"

"Because, my lord, the rest of the prophecy has already come to pass."

"But why not say it?"

"Because, my lord, a prophecy only deals with the future. You can't have a prophecy that deals with things that have already happened. This goes against the very definition of 'prophecy.'"

"I see," said Motecuhzoma. "I see very clearly. What is left of the prophecy is inescapable doom, but you are wrong. Yes. I have no doubt about it. You are wrong, and do you know why?"

"No, my lord."

"Because I am no longer merely the leader of the Aztecs. I am a god, supreme ruler of the universe and heavens."

Nezahualpilli was momentarily stunned. He had witnessed this claim before, and had seen the commoners prostrated along the street—forbidden to gaze at Motecuhzoma—when the monarch chose to leave his palace, but Nezahualpilli had always thought this to be some variety of political maneuvering, just as he'd always thought the bloodthirsty cult of Huitzilopochtli was a good way of frightening the whole valley into submission and keeping the warrior population down in the vassal states. But looking at Motecuhzoma now, Nezahualpilli saw that the king had succumbed to a powerful dementia. Truly, there was no hope for the empire now. He heard the death knell, the drums of defeat, but realized it was only his own heart pounding in his ears with the unhealthy force typical of men his age.

"Well, my lord," he said, "I'm sure Quetzalcoatl will see you as a great adversary."

Unfortunately, the prophecy would prove to be true. The only trope the great emperor, or god, was capable of tossing in Quetzalcoatl's way would be the bloody clinging to a lost empire, a network of fissures and plumbing choked with bodies, a brilliant, fecund breeding ground for the conqueror's seeds of progress, seeds that burst in suppurating ulcers, seeds that filled one's lungs with the oil of their own organs and left them struggling for breath. The citizens of the great city burst apart with gunfire, burst like the dry puffer mushrooms that appeared after the rain, fell to the ground riddled and pitted with bitter blacking and dirty blood.

But that version is already known.

What if Nezahualpilli is actually a capable soothsayer, what if he sees the dwarves sitting anxiously (or drowsing unaware) about the throne of Motecuhzoma and he says, "Slaughter them all and make a stew." And by eating this stew, Motecuhzoma is, in fact, transformed into a god. And when Quetzalcoatl does appear, what if Motecuhzoma, ruler of Tenochtitlan, now newly incarnated as a god, rather than showing up with tasty food and a treasury's worth of gold, instead makes no such mistake of hospitality.

Let us arm him with the sun in a small pill, something he can throw down at the foot of the conqueror, and then let it bloom in all its power at the feet of these two men, annihilating them, spilling its brilliance into the city, burning up the slopes of Popocatepetl and Iztaccihuatl and to limits the ocean, then into the ocean, where all the fish begin to fall, as if enchanted, to the bottom of the water, to lie upon the sand until the sand itself is consumed by this brilliant power, until the very histories stretching forward and backward, all that mankind was and hoped to be, are eradicated, snuffed, burned quickly, until the only scent is that of the scorched numbers, 2006 and 1968, AD 33 and all those BCs, and everything is burned until. Until.

And now all is white, and we can start again.

On Sakhalin

You ask yourself for whom do these waves roar, who
hears them during the night, what are they calling for,
and for whom they will roar when you have gone away.
— *The Island of Sakhalin,* Anton Chekhov

Outside, the wind is running up and down the street, setting
every shutter to a questioning rattle. There is grit and dust
suspended in the air. In the distance, the watchman calls out
mournfully and, with a sudden drop in wind, a not-too-distant
drunkard—deeply sincere and off-key—sings the response.
There is oakum stuffed between the rough-hewn walls of the
governor's house to prevent drafts, and the walls look as though
they are sprouting hair.

He and the governor are talking of the indigenous peoples. He realizes that he is not—not indigenous—and considers
briefly this unnatural state of being.

"They're very primitive," says the governor. "Not much
to them."

"Perhaps," he agrees. "But all my life I've been surrounded by Russians, although there were Greeks in Taganrog."

"Taganrog?" says the governor. "On the Sea of Azov?"

He nods. "That's where I'm from"—a past so distant as to be implausible. "They say these aborigines don't look like the Japanese, or the Mongolians. They say these natives are altogether different."

"Well," says the governor, "the Gilyak have faces round like the moon, and their fingers are long—tapering, not quite human." The governor toys with a loose button on his vest. "And this interests you?"

"I am a doctor."

"But you are here to take a census?"

"Yes."

"Is that the job of a doctor?"

"I will record medical statistics," he says. A census of the penal colony might be useful—he'll count the lot of them: convicts, settled exiles, peasants-in-exile, freemen. Then turn his attention to each individual and their catalogue of ills: malignant protrusions mean a chemical influence; that jerking walk, the presence of syphilis. And then he'll count the dogs. And the fleas on the dogs.

"But you have not yet seen our natives?" asks the governor.

"Not up close, just from the side of the boat," he says, "shouting up. Three men holding geese that they had shot."

"Not shot. Killed somehow, crawled up to the goose and strangled it. They don't have guns—unless we've hired them as guards. Did you buy the geese?"

"I think the captain did, for a matter of kopecks."

"Well, good for him, supporting the local economy. No doubt the savages have spent it, and in the magical way of Sakhalin, geese have been transformed into vodka."

Conversation drifts back to the census, and the governor agrees that such a thing might be useful. He says a man has been found to take him around, to give him his bearings. Ivan Petrovich Sobolev.

"He's pleasant enough," says the governor. "He'll keep you from losing your way, although how lost could you get? We are on an island."

The governor has been letting him stay at his house, which is good, for there is no hotel. He stands on the street, his eyes lighting from one space to another, his gaze shifting and shifting, since there is little to hold one's attention for more than a second here in Sakhalin. Before his departure from mainland Russia, he made the requisite appearances in drawing rooms, drawing out the requisite letters of introduction, but it seems that none preceded him, his arrival a surprise—how curious that the popular story writer should show up in this unpopular corner—followed by an effort to conceal that reaction. Perhaps the mail was lost, which would not surprise him. He has forded rivers to get here and seen the sacks of hopeful letters born upon the backs of those lost on the Kozulka, those no longer welcome in the real Russia. And what is in those letters? Of the prisoners, news of ill-timed births and predictable deaths, maybe portraits of home life. He thinks of his sister Masha sitting on the overstuffed couch, her legs splayed out, since there's no one to see, boot heels on the carpet, a half-finished letter to him resting on a book, her unfinished thoughts hovering about, as she picks dog hairs off her skirt while composing in her head. Will this letter bring him hope? Of course not. There will be news of some new financial catastrophe or some woman who wants some thing that he will not want to give. Suddenly the howling wind, singing at the cable, seems like good company. He takes a cigarette from his case and wonders how one lights something in this wind. As if on cue, a criminal bumbles up to him (criminals wander here, tolerated and aimless, as, he's heard, do the sacred cows of India) and says,

"Sir, this takes my skill."

Which makes him think his neck might soon be efficiently snapped or his wallet stolen, but soon a light flares forth from a match rendered invisible by the flame, as if this convict's skill is the ability to conjure little balls of fire from his cupped hands.

The sun is rising in Sakhalin. The sun is rising here, in the east, unremarkably, and setting elsewhere, unremarkably. The sun is rising over the broad road where nothing is happening, and for one moment he imagines that he is rolling under the sun, as if, here in Sakhalin, one can feel the spherical nature of the earth, this diurnal winching connected to the distant subterranean creak, which he knows is actually mine-related, but on this morning—somehow disconnected from unspooling time—could be ascribed to the ratcheting of ropes and pulleys angling Sakhalin to better feel the effects of that distant source of heat. He cannot remember waking to the company of his thoughts. Usually, there is some pacing outside the bedroom door—his mother with a fresh catastrophe, his father brandishing an icon, his brother Kolia begging for work that he will not complete although the commission will be his, and the advance on the commission will be his, and the money—soon spent on morphine and vodka and perfume to combat the reek of his aging mistress—will disappear without the required illustrations or paintings completed. And then he will wake to the pacing of the footsteps of Kolia's creditors, although they will not be outside his door, rather down the street. But he will still hear them.

Stop. To think of Kolia this way has become a fantasy, something he can still conjure in the early morning with his thoughts rising isolated and of their own accord. Kolia is dead. He feels it now. He follows a bird making horizontal progress across the sky and holds a deep, deep stillness.

The man sees him struggling to remember the name, and offers, "Ivan Petrovich Sobolev," with an outstretched hand. "I am to take you to see some of our remarkable prisoners," he says. His collar is frayed, his jacket shiny with wear, elsewhere shiny with dirt. The man has a direct demeanor and is prickly and resigned in equal parts, and simultaneously: as if one is seeing two sides of a coin at the same time.

"Thank you for escorting me."

"Nice to be thanked," the man says, "but I don't really have a choice. I'm one of them."

"You are a prisoner?" he asks.

The man shrugs. He might have asked if the man were a count and received the same response. There's a moment of silence between them. The man says, "Don't you want to know what has landed me here?"

"Not everyone here seems to know. Besides, you might be wrongly convicted."

The man raises his eyebrows and his eyes grow merry. "If that is the case, then I am wrongly convicted of forging banknotes. I thought you might like to know. If I were wrongly convicted of murder, you might be concerned that, at a future date, I might be convicted, wrongfully, of killing you."

The humor is welcome and he smiles. This is a large man with a large shadow. One of his hands could easily span the good doctor's neck, such bear paws incongruous with the nimble, inking work of forging banknotes. He takes his cigarettes from his pocket and thrusts one into Sobolev's right hand. Sobolev turns to him, smiles, looks around at the mist burning up in the sunshine.

"Looks like it might not be such a bad day after all," says the forger. "Although it's hard to tell one day from another." He draws thoughtfully on his cigarette and, puffing his cheeks, expels the smoke with force.

"What do people smoke here?" he asks.

"Here?" Sobolev shrugs. "Whatever can be smoked. I think it is most often Japanese, but there is little choice." The forger considers. "The choices I've made have left me with few choices."

He thinks of a few maudlin responses. He could address the pleasant weather, the man's good health. These would be things to say.

Sobolev watches as though reading his thoughts. "Should I just take you around?"

He nods.

"You will ask these people questions?" asks Sobolev.

In response, the doctor produces the form that he has had printed here on the island. The information is basic but has provided him a sort of passport into the houses and fetter blocks and souls of Sakhalin.

Sobolev holds the paper. The form asks for age, place of birth, when the individual arrived in Sakhalin, religion, if one can read, who taught them to read, and other simple facts.

"I'm interested in literacy," he says.

"Here?" says Sobolev.

"Yes." Perhaps it is remarkable.

"And they fill this out?"

"Yes."

"Who will read this?" asks Sobolev.

He shrugs.

For one second, understanding flickers in the eyes of his companion. Sobolev nods at the form and hands it back to him.

"The house of Pishchikov is over there. Perhaps he is home. He does not talk that much, but he will fill out your form." Sobolev considers him thoughtfully. "You are not as I expected."

And what was that?

"Rumor is that you're not so much a doctor as a scribbler of stories in the papers. Is that true?"

"Friend, it depends on what is called for. If a man is ill, I'm more of a doctor. If a man is bored, I'm more of a writer."

"Good enough," says Sobolev. "This is a love story, our Pishchikov. Come!"

Sobolev takes long strides. He follows. On the verandah of a government building, a small group of Gilyak men have gathered. Moon faces, long fingers, and direct gazes. A sleeping dog that lounges by them begins to wag its tail, thumping a drumbeat on the wood, although what has caused this response—some thought of pleasure—is hidden in the dog's dream. He thinks of the forms in his satchel. Could he approach these men, with their long, tapering fingers and broad, flat cheeks, with this need for answers? Would they respond?

Sobolev stands some fifty yards down the road.

"Pishchikov! Pishchikov!" shouts Sobolev, as though he is asserting Pishchikov's importance over this gathering of Gilyaks. But now he sees that Sobolev is merely shouting into Pishchikov's house. He walks quickly to join him.

Sobolev pushes open Pishchikov's door into a poor cabin with a dirt floor, rough table, timid bed. "He's not here," says Sobolev. "Too bad. He has a clerical job with the police. Can you believe that? Pishchikov working for the police, and he's a murderer. It's a wonder anyone knows who to arrest around here. And I'm a tour guide!" Here, Sobolev smiles.

Sobolev has an appealing smile with big teeth. He thinks this Sobolev must be much liked by women, and wonders how this Ivan Petrovich Sobolev manages here in Sakhalin, where all the women are selling themselves, where even the freemen's wives are prostitutes for lack of other industry, and any girl over the age of thirteen can be guaranteed to have a price ready for you. This poor room has nothing sinister about it. There is a cloud of the pathetic here—now he is inventing—and perhaps regret. A woman's photograph, worried by mold, is nailed to a wall above the table. "What is this Pishchikov's crime?"

"It involves," says Sobolev, "a Turk, a wife, and a whip. And it ends badly."

"How so?"

"Well, this woman falls in love with a captured Turk, and Pishchikov—who has access to the Turk—helps her to see this Turk, brings this Turk her love letters, is so kind and generous and solicitous—" and Sobolev pauses. "I can't remember what happens to the Turk, but he leaves the story, and the woman falls in love with Pishchikov because he was so kind and generous when the Turk was around. This is an educated woman, with a college degree. I say that because around here all the women are prostitutes, even the ones who aren't. This *educated* woman bears for Pishchikov four children. And is close to nine months with the fifth when Pishchikov, and God only knows why, thinks of that Turk who all those years ago so inflamed her with passion." Here Sobolev thinks of his last statement. "Maybe she just—" and

Sobolev makes an obscene gesture, because "inflamed with passion" seems ludicrous here, or maybe anywhere. "He whips her for six hours. They say the woman was flayed, skinless, when he was done. Is there something beyond dead? If so, she was that." There's a moment of silence. "And now he's a clerk for the police."

This Sobolev has told the story well. He looks at the picture of the woman, stern and not quite pretty, nailed there. "And who is she?" he asks.

"Who else?" says Sobolev. "The wife, of course."

There's a silence, during which both men look about the room.

"Well," says Sobolev, "more sights?"

"What is there to see?"

Later, fortified with some Japanese vodka purchased from a freeman, Sobolev and the doctor and the forms—none yet filled out today—zigzag across the main street in the town of Dooay on the island of Sakhalin. They have had a little bread and cheese, a little conversation, a little humor, which is salve in this plain place.

"Sofia Blyushtein, better known as Golden Hand," says Sobolev, "you be the judge of her beauty. She somehow convinced the guard in Smolensk to run away with her, and they ran here and there, and where they ran, money disappeared and people had their throats slit. But I don't know how she ended up in a prison in Smolensk, only of her escape and subsequent crimes. Here, on Sakhalin, she is connected with parting Yurkovsky the Jew from 56,000 rubles. How? The money was gone and there she was, either guilty party or accomplice. It was never figured out. And it was also never figured out how Yurkovsky managed to acquire so much money. A look at his wife says that she didn't help to earn it: for something of that nature to occur, she'd have to pay the entry fee herself! And trading timber to the Japanese, well, maybe some money, but not 56,000."

"It is a large sum of money," he says.

"Even to me, who has been accused of making it."

They stop before the tall door of the prison. The smell of urine and excrement stand here, blown—but not away—by the wind. He looks up at the door and feels that stiffness in the neck from holding his head at that angle. Anxiety. That is this feeling. Being a doctor has mostly worn that away. He has seen the death of children. He has been choked by his own blood. Still, here, looking to the top of the door—and that smell—has made his heart begin to pound. Sensing this, Sobolev thrusts the cheap bottle of vodka into his hand. He takes a mouthful. A beating on the door produces the guard, who—through a barred portal—looks down at the doctor and across at Sobolev. The door is unbolted.

The guard steps aside. "This way," says Sobolev. He follows.

In the gloom of the long room, one can make out chains on what appears to be an enormous and low-slung table, but which he knows is a sleeping platform. In fact, at the far end, coughing and coughing, chained in place, a man is curled upon it. At first he wants to ask what this man is doing in the prisoners' block all alone when the other men are out in the coal mines, but he—this is the doctor speaking—knows the man is dying.

"Cells are this way," says Sobolev.

He follows through the narrow passage. There are cells on either side, and from one he hears a dry cough followed by the clink of fetters. Wind whistles through a gap between roof and wall. Sobolev pauses and peers into the grilled window of one of the cells. Sobolev shrugs and gestures with his head, in suggestion that he take a look. And so he peers inside and startles a man, heavily fettered, sitting on the side of his bed sipping tea;

the man holds the cup delicately, and a saucer is balanced on his knee. The man nods politely and he nods back.

"Come." Sobolev marches down the hall with knowing strides, looks into one cell, turns, and leans against the door. "She's in there. No great beauty now, but you can sort of see what the big deal was."

He is struck by the fact that Sobolev speaks as though she cannot hear him. He wonders if he should say something like, *Still a great beauty!* out of kindness, but would that just remind her of where her good looks have landed her? And how could she forget her surroundings? Should he say that he does not need to see the infamous Golden Hand, now fallen so low? That might be noble, but he is curious. He rises onto the balls of his feet to see inside. There she is, a small woman with keen blue eyes and a long face, her hair streaked with gray, her mouth crumpled slightly as though she is missing teeth. She meets his gaze with some look not altogether human, then returns to picking at the fabric of her skirt. She wears an iron collar and is chained about her ankles and wrists, and this is her only adornment. "Is she always alone?"

"I doubt it," says Sobolev. "That's what goes for beauty around here, and with the guards—well, you know. Had enough?"

"Yes," he says. "For now."

Outside, Sobolev says, "I should go there more often."

"But why?"

"Because it makes me feel lucky."

Over dinner, the governor asks him about his day, his impressions of the prisoners, his thoughts: his thoughts present themselves as a series of photographs that he views, one by one, until he reaches something worth remarking on.

"I saw a man chained to a wheelbarrow." This is the writer speaking. "He says he sleeps like that, eats like that. To be chained to a wheelbarrow," this is the doctor speaking, "causes certain muscles to atrophy."

"I imagine it does," says the governor.

The obvious moment for this punishment to be explained passes in silence.

"But why chain men to wheelbarrows?" he asks.

"Because the wheelbarrows are inexpensive."

Although this must be a joke, he cannot find the correct laugh for it—even faked—and he nods.

"These men chained to wheelbarrows would strangle you, strangle me, swim back to the mainland, rape and pillage their way through Siberia, tramp on to Moscow or Saint Petersburg, commit all sorts of malfeasance."

"But to chain them to a wheelbarrow—"

"Do you have a sister?"

He nods.

"Then you should understand. This is the duty of the governing forces in Sakhalin: to isolate the criminal element. To contain them with whatever resources we have."

He imagines convicts chained to oxen and small trees, bottles of vodka and prostitutes, as such are the resources on Sakhalin.

"It is to keep the sisters of this world safe. We are responsible for all innocents." The governor's face is perfectly composed in an attitude of patient tolerance.

He nods the nod of the patiently tolerated, and cuts another piece of the large and overcooked and oversalted cutlet. He's known a lot of people's sisters in ways that surely remove them from the realm of innocents.

"Doctor," says the governor, "is Sakhalin what you had hoped for?"

The stench of the prison enters his memory, replaced by the dog's tail thumping on the wooden boards of the verandah. "I wished to execute a census," he replies. He manages a smile. "And there are plenty of people for me to count."

Which is as good a reason as any, and what else could he possibly say? That he has come because there is something intriguing about the ends of the earth, because he was feeling stagnant? What good reason could there be for the journey across Siberia—seven weeks of bouncing along the muddy ruts of the Kozulka, the limited pleasure of a few well-traveled prostitutes, endless bowls of duck skilly reflecting his reluctant face—and on to Sakhalin? He has offered one reason: to complete a census for his medical thesis in place of a dissertation. And people have offered reasons back: to gather material for his stories, to escape a broken heart, to kill himself, since surely the tuberculosis will finish him off, because he is in thrall to the beliefs of Tolstoy, because he is no longer in thrall to the beliefs of Tolstoy. To this he adds Kolia's death.

"Do you know of Przhevalsky?" asks the governor.

"The explorer?" he says. "Yes, of course. I admire him. After his death, I wrote a piece about him for the *New Times*. We need more men like that, like Henry Morton Stanley, like Przhevalsky. These should be our heroes."

"Yes. Przhevalsky." The governor swats at a mosquito tempted by the flushed skin above his collar. "I too am an admirer. Out across Mongolia he went, on his horse, alone. And he returned—which is the mark of a truly skilled explorer. Anyone can go, but not anyone can come back—can bring back these bits of unknown worlds, these things that we paper our minds with, as people here paper their cabins with the labels peeled from bottles and sweet jars." The governor's thoughts turn inward. "But it seems that even the unknown is populated. Like here, there was the possibility of great wealth. But how to get at it, eh? How to settle it with these bands of marauding savages . . . marauding?" The governor pinches the top of his nose, perhaps to unblock the sinuses. "Przhevalsky meant to exterminate them all, all the Mongols."

"An extreme policy," he says.

"Most are," the governor agrees.

"What is the policy on the natives here?"

"Ah, we each are left to make our own. But if you have an anthropological bent, you should speak to our Major Botkin."

"Is he," he says, swallowing a well-chewed piece of meat with aid of wine, "an anthropologist?"

"Of course not," says the governor, "he's a major."

Major Petr Vasilievich Botkin lives five miles from the governor's house, not a difficult walk, but the governor is aware of some delivery being made in that general direction, and so it is arranged that he ride with a settled exile who is bringing a sack of flour, some planks, and two boxes of nails to the major's neighbor. As he makes his way north, sitting stiffly on the hard bench seat beside the driver, rocked and tossed as the wheels bounce into the hard ruts, he sees, wading through the underbrush, a group of Gilyak headed in the opposite direction. It is as if he is rolling on to the future and they—two men, an elderly woman wrapped in a carpet, two younger women, three small children of indeterminate sex, and two thin yet happy dogs—are moving further into the past.

"Why don't they walk on the road?" he asks.

"They never walk on the road," the driver answers. "They never had roads before and they see no need for them now."

Soon the cart draws to a halt and the driver points and says, "The major lives there."

He thanks the driver for his time and company—which was calming in its lack of conversation—and gives him some kopecks. As he makes his way to the house, a backward glance reveals the driver biting the coin and finding it acceptable.

The major is waiting for him on the doorstep, plainly sizing him up, and so he returns the favor. Major Botkin is a lean man with coiled energy and darting gray eyes. The major nods agreeably as he makes his way to him and clears his throat as prelude to something.

"I've been waiting for you to pay me a visit," says the major. "I've been saying, 'Where has the good doctor been this day?' But I knew, eventually, you'd find your way here. And look where your census has taken you!"

"Petr Vasilievich," he declares, surprising himself with the miracle of having recalled the major's name, "I've been told I could count on your hospitality." Although no one said anything to support or refute this. "I was hoping to learn something of the Gilyak. I've heard you're the local expert."

"I have my eyes open. And if your eyes are open, you see the Gilyak. And if you see the Gilyak, you notice them." The major looks purposefully one way, then turns and does the same in the opposite direction to illustrate, one assumes, his superior gifts of observation.

"To look around will be a privilege. I've done a little reading," he says. "It seems their population is dwindling."

"How can that be? One sees them everywhere," says the major.

"It does seem that way. But fifty years ago"—he produces his notebook from his pocket—"there were over three thousand, according to," he consults his notes, "Boshnyak. Fifteen years later, Mitzul says there are half as many. And now the governor tells me there are three hundred and twenty."

"And all of them living upwind of me!" says the major. "Have you been to one of their villages? The reek of it—split fish lying in the sun, to dry, of course, but the smell of it! And you know they don't wash, never! Who knows what soap and water would reveal? A complexion light as mine, maybe. And they live with their dogs, for their dogs. As dogs." Here the major laughs heartily. "And it's time for lunch!"

To underscore this shift, the major pounds him on his right shoulder and he lets forth a dry cough.

"So, good friend, lunch first, and then I'll take you to their village. Although it's more of a—I don't know—reminds me of nothing so much as a bunch of peasants gathered around waiting for a train. Only there's not a train. And they're not waiting. Ha!"

He tries to think of some response, watching a convict limp down the street, his fetters clinking. "Maybe they are," he says finally.

"They're what?" says the major.

"Waiting," he replies.

"Ah!" says the major. Initial concern is replaced by a wide smile, the planes of his face wrinkle happily. "A joke! And for lunch I imagine you want nothing but caviar and champagne! But there's none to be had, so we'll make do. Make do. There is—will be—fresh fish and," the major leans in, although what he has to say is no secret and is predictable as wind and prisoners on this island, "vodka!"

"Count me there," he says, and realizes that he is *there,* has been, since he reached this island, and somehow *here* is far from him. He is idling in *there.*

The major is talking with such enthusiasm about G———, has been for the last hour, that he is convinced it is the only novel the major has ever read. And somehow the conversation has been continuing with great enthusiasm—energy!—although he himself has never read G———. Finally, there is a lull, during which even the major is out of words to bring to the book. "More vodka?"

He smiles and indicates about an inch worth with his thumb and forefinger, a suggestion he knows will be ignored. He says, "I saw a woman among the Gilyak. She had a mark around her mouth—black—like a monstrous smile. At first I thought I was mistaken. It could be charcoal. As you say, these people do not wash, but there was something about it."

"Ainu," said the major. "A different tribe than the Gilyak. And that grotesque smile was permanent. The Ainu tattoo all their women, and it's always the same: a black clown smile." The vodka splashes into the glass.

"Do the Ainu and the Gilyak intermarry?"

"They don't marry at all, even among themselves. That Ainu you saw was most likely traded to the Gilyak for a dog or some vodka. That's the true sign of the savage." The major nods and corks his vodka. "That treatment—to treat women like that, like animals, as though they have no need of tenderness."

Tenderness? Is this the vodka talking?

"As if a woman could be—" The major screws up his mouth so that it disappears beneath his mustache. "Well, traded! They think of women as slaves!"

"One might say much the same of Strindberg," he replies. Strindberg? Is *this* the vodka talking?

"Not the same at all!" says the major.

Who knows nothing of Strindberg, other than the fact that the holder of such a name must be from some civilized tribe.

"What womenfolk need is kindness," says the major.

"Petr Vasilievich, do you find women so simple?"

"Knowledge about women comes with knowledge of women, and I know you for a bachelor," says the major.

Here, he can only smile: he knows much of women, and this is precisely what has kept him from marrying.

After lunch, the two men saunter into the street. At first the blast of cold air feels cruel, but soon is bracing—something to argue with the vodka and his postprandial stupor.

"Just a little look," says Botkin. "Well, that's about all you can take, for there's not much to look at."

The Gilyak encampment is a mere mile or two down the road—enough movement to help him understand the influence of the vodka, enough fresh air to make him regret drinking as much as he has. He excuses himself for a moment and finds a convenient place to urinate. As he empties, he thinks it's some essential part of self puddling into that hard ground and knows he hasn't had this thought since he was a child. He buttons up his pants and sees the major ahead, his walk almost a march—although unsteady—as though Botkin is parodying marching or, perhaps, civilization.

"Where are you?" Botkin calls out, apparently having forgotten. And then the major searches through his coat. He watches, amused. Does the major think he has misplaced his guest, put him in a pocket? But no. A flask is produced, and the major invites him to this new toxin, although, upon drinking it, it seems much the same as the previous.

"We're close now," says Botkin. "Can you smell it?"

A deep inhalation introduces the scent of rotting fish. "I smell the fish," he says.

"Then you smell the camp." Botkin wrinkles his nose. His eyes turn introspective. "But many things smell like fish."

Is this the same major with tender words for women? Or is it he himself whose mind drifts easily to the carnal?

And then, to his right and in front of him, he sees the dogs. There are six, some skinny—maybe the presence of worms— and others thick-furred and strong. These dogs are baring their teeth, although not growling. Their tails wag cautiously. He wonders if these dogs—with their lips pulled back and teeth on display—are smiling. He wants to ask, because such knowledge would be useful. Instead, he says, "Do they bite?"

"I'm sure they do," says Botkin. "They're dogs!"

But now there is a Gilyak man approaching. His face is intelligent, inquiring. He sees the man's eyes go to the major's belt and notices, with this Gilyak, that the major is carrying a pistol. The Gilyak man is nodding and speaking in gentle tones and Botkin is following and suddenly he realizes that the Gilyak is speaking Russian.

"Ask him what you want," says Botkin. "Go into any house. This is the summer yurt, on the stilts. In the winter, they dig pits, like shallow graves, and build low roofs, to keep out of the wind. They wear no sleeping garments, just these same rough pants. And the women too. Go on. Ask him. Ask him anything."

"What do you eat?" he says.

"They eat," says Botkin, "anything they can. They eat blubber that to smell it would make you ill. They eat all kinds of fat, but are still thin because of the cold and because that is all they eat."

He looks to the Gilyak man, who nods his head slant-wise—like a Russian—in agreement.

"What do they do for employment?"

"Some trapping," says Botkin. "They have long traded with the Japs. Sometimes they carry the mail for us. And now they will, on occasion, work as overseer in the mines. Sometimes a prisoner escapes and we need a tracker. Across the taiga they go with their dogs."

He looks to the man, who offers no protest.

"Look," says Botkin. "Walk around, no one minds." The major gives the Gilyak man a few coins. "No one minds," the major repeats. Botkin takes a swig from his flask, extends it.

Against his better judgment, he drinks, stops, drinks more, hands it back. Botkin is wandering off. Perhaps he is meant to be alone with this Gilyak. It is probably better, without the major answering questions that might have different answers if a Gilyak were given a chance to respond.

The major gave coins. He too produces a handful of small pieces and gives them to the Gilyak. "Can I see your house?" he says.

There is a moment of understanding that he feels his simple request has not merited. "Wait here short time," says the man.

He waits. He wonders if some sort of sweeping and tidying is happening—or if some tea is being prepared—and looks across the camp, where Gilyak tribe members in stiff wind, having escaped the billowing smoke of their yurts, are smoking pipes. Yes, they could be waiting for a train. A child—he thinks it's a girl—stands before him and stares into his face. This is a game. He will not look away first. He will not smile. They look and look and look until the Gilyak man returns.

"The house is now ready," the man says. Together the two look at a house at the edge of the camp.

He is unsteady—as unsteady as the major—and he realizes this as he makes the last rungs of the ladder. His feet still know where to place themselves, but what to do with one's hands? He grabs the doorframe, bracing himself, and places one clumsy foot carefully on the poorly spaced floorboards, and then the other. His boots are dusty except for a series of droplet marks showing cleaner leather on the left one, and he wonders if he has urinated on it.

"Everything good?" the Gilyak man calls up.

"Yes," he responds, happy not to have fallen backward. But he is looking at the mattress—straw covered with rags—and the girl sitting there. She meets his gaze frankly. He realizes the meaning of the coins. Her hair is neatly arranged, and she is wearing an elaborate embroidered coat that is faded and much repaired, but tells the story of an earlier Gilyak era where such attire was created and required. She is calm under his scrutiny. He hears her expel some air through her nose—cautious disdain—and wonders how old she is. There is something about those large, dark eyes that challenges him.

"Do you speak Russian?" he asks her.

She continues to look at him, untucks her legs from beneath her, and extends them forward, crossing her legs at the ankle.

"Is this your home?"

More silence. If she is apprehensive, she does not show it. He thinks she might be fifteen, but he has trouble figuring out these Asiatics who stay youthful for years, turn skeletal overnight, and live in that animated, fleshless state until they die.

"I didn't mean to purchase you," he says. He doubts she understands. He takes some steps around the yurt, sees a cooking pot and picks it up—there is some strong animal smell that he thinks is blubber—and sets it down. "Do you live here?" he asks.

And then she speaks, something short, polite, not gentle.

On an old packing crate, there are a few folded garments. These are of no interest, but he's still keeping up some pretense of seeing this genuine Gilyak dwelling. He doesn't know what else to do. "I am a doctor," he says, to banish silence from the room. She moves her position on the mattress, shifting back to sitting on her feet. "I am here to conduct a census." He picks up a mirror, tarnished, and, to his eye, Russian. He wonders how old it is. She watches him fixedly while he handles this precious object, and he sets it back down. "Is that man your father?" he asks. He's really not interested in the answer, but he thinks the girl might understand this word. "Your father," he repeats. "Is he your father? Father? Father."

The girl watches.

"Father," he says. He stands with his shoulders squared, and brings his hands to his hips in fists. This is a manly stance. "Fa-ther," he says. He will teach her. "Faa-theer."

And then she barks. She barks like a dog, barks at him. She's barking, now on all fours. Bark. Bark. Bark. And shaking her head at him. Bark. Bark. Bark. She barks and barks and barks as he escapes the yurt, backward, quickly down the ladder. And when his feet are on the ground, she is silent. He looks up the road and sees the major, a small, unsteady, diminishing figure. The Gilyak man is approaching him, concern on his face. He manages a big, false smile for this Gilyak man. All is well. He shows his teeth, his head bobbing. He smiles and nods.

He imagines this man talking to his daughter, asking her, "Do they bite?"

There is to be a flogging, and he has been invited. He wonders in what capacity he has earned this invitation, and wonders who else has been included. What is his response? The man says no.

The doctor says yes. And the writer? Well, yes, of course. The man has been outvoted and he will attend.

He has been told to present himself at the overseer's lodge, which he knows is somewhere up the street from the governor's house. He has given himself twenty minutes to get there. The sky is dark, promising rain, and the wind unusually still. He stops a girl rushing in the opposite direction, carrying a bundle of laundry, and asks her where the overseer's lodge is.

"There, your honor, there!" she says, and points—indicating north and everything northward—with her chin, her arms embracing the sheets and clothing. "It's right there," she says. "It's where everyone is headed."

This additional information awakens him to the fact that most people are walking in the same direction as he, and several, as he watches, enter the darkened doorway of a building he'd assumed was a barracks. He follows at the same pace as the others, perhaps a little slower, and enters the lodge with a feeling of trepidation. Major Botkin is there, but not in charge. The major is attending as a spectator. He wonders who would choose to be at such a thing, and realizes that he has made such a choice. He steps back to remove himself from Botkin's line of vision but is too late. He nods in acknowledgment. This is enough. He does not need to stand by the major to think of how easily he becomes that man, how little separates their two ways of being.

"Seeing all the sights, your honor," comes a voice. It's Sobolev.

"Sometimes," he says, having forgotten now why he's come, "we see things to make sense of them."

"Well," says Sobolev, "good luck to you with that."

"What brings you here?" he asks.

"You, always making it sound as though I have a choice

in these matters." Sobolev waves a sheaf of pages at him. "This is some minor task of paperwork, for which they think I am well suited, because of the elegance and precision of my handwriting." Sobolev raises his eyebrows ironically to drive home the joke.

He would like a drink now, to reach into his coat pocket and produce a flask, to share a jolt with his friend the forger, but he has not allowed himself the luxury of traveling with such a thing. He would be drunk all the time. One month on Sakhalin has taught him that; two months to go keeps him in check.

"Father Vasiliev is here," says Sobolev. "Would you like to meet him?"

"Do you think I need a priest?"

Sobolev smiles. "Maybe not just yet, but some day," he says nodding, "some day you will call for the priest, and I will too, but right now it is only because he is an interesting man, a bit like you, educated. Kind. But not as much fun."

Father Vasiliev stands by the door. This Vasiliev reaches into his pocket and produces a watch, which is consulted before returning it. Vasiliev's hand returns to the same pocket and produces a handkerchief to mop his brow. The handkerchief goes back into the pocket. Again the priest reaches into the same pocket. Will the priest produce a rabbit, he wonders? But the priest has merely brought out some beads, which are squeezed anxiously, then returned.

He approaches the priest, unsure of what to say, but the priest sees him and nods in acknowledgment, and it is as though they have known each other before. "You are the doctor with the census," says the priest. "I am Fedor Alexevich Vasiliev. Call me Fedor. There is no room for titles here. Most people will say, 'no room for titles in this godforsaken place,' but I won't willingly admit that. Not yet. But ask me again after we witness this flogging."

A few comments are exchanged about the weather, the status of the census, the duties of the priest. He likes this man who is probably about thirty, the same age as he, but carries himself as someone older. "Are floggings always well attended?" he asks.

"Yes. This is what happens when there are no plays, no music. We have a very high birthrate, and everyone shows up for a flogging. Of course, I would like to reduce this cohort by one—me—but sometimes these poor chaps look for a priest, want my blessing. And other times they spit at me." The priest lifts his hands. "Either way, I feel I'm helping."

"What is this man's crime?" he asks.

The priest moves his head from side to side, thinking. "Well, I suppose they would call it escape. He did escape. But he and his companions came upon an Ainu village. You might think they'd not want to linger, but they found time to murder the men and rape the women. And then murder the women. The children they strung up from the beams of the main dwelling. The sight of this still burns in my memory, and I have seen much and live with the thought that if I have not yet seen all, then some horror might be waiting for me. They killed one of the soldiers sent to bring them in. This man who you will see flogged today was meant to be hanged with the others, but he says he didn't kill anyone. Maybe it would have been better for him to be hanged, because now he is sentenced to ninety lashings as well as being chained to the wheelbarrow."

"Wouldn't he choose to be alive?" he says.

"Probably," says the priest. "But now that he will be lashed in this way and chained to a barrow, he will kill someone. He will. The moment they remove his fetters, he will earn them back. And then he will be unfit for God. But now, if he were—as he's said—innocent of murder, and hanged, he would be guilty only of escape. God would take him in."

"Isn't there repentance and forgiveness?"

"I have witnessed that a few times," says the priest. "But genuine repentance—the real agony of one coming to terms with the wrongs one has committed—seems the stuff of novels on Sakhalin. God may be everywhere, but here he seems to be wearing a disguise and is hard to recognize."

A rattle of chains at the far end of the room draws everyone's attention. The prisoner enters—a smallish man with a straggling beard and small black eyes. He is clearly terrified and looks with plain horror at the sloping board—attendants are checking manacles and ankle straps—that is there to accommodate him. "Come on, then," says a guard. "We haven't got all day." The prisoner's shirt is removed, and he is told to lie facedown on the board. A guard tugs the prisoner's trousers down to his knees. His wrists and ankles are fixed in place. The guard with the whip, a single strap that terminates in three sharp-looking thongs, says, "Brace up!" and the man does. The whip is flung with precision. The prisoner emits some sort of panicked cry, more of a squeal. The overseer says, "O-one!" in a controlled way, as though he is saving his energy in order to make it all the way to ninety. After the first five lashes, the guard needs a break. The prisoner is already seized by uncontrolled tremors.

"How long will this take?" he asks the priest.

"Hours," says the priest.

He thinks he will leave, but then forces himself to stay, as if witnessing this display and assigning it the appropriate degree of horror will somehow restore a small measure of humanity.

The last two months of his time on Sakhalin, he will rise at five in the morning and not sleep until late into the night. He will record the lives of as many of the people as he can manage in this short, arctic summer, as though preserving some facts on paper recognizes their devalued existence. He will look at the questionnaires filled out by Russians, Tatars, Chinese, Mongols, Gypsies and wonder at the falsehood of paper: he feels as if he is a conjurer attempting to steal souls. As he's sailing to Hong Kong, he'll imagine what it would be like to dump the forms overboard, to see them buoyed up by the waves, sucked down to the bottom. The urge to do this, to cleanse his mind of Sakhalin, will be so strong that he will have to struggle not to succumb to it.

Twelve years later, in Badenweiler, Germany, he is completing the last movement of his long involvement with tuberculosis. He thinks, "I am not indigenous," although he also felt alien in Yalta. His thoughts will return to Sakhalin. He will remember the ship that brought him there and the one that carried him away. In his memory, he sees 10,000 sheets of paper—his census—floating on the waves, and feels the satisfaction of having tossed them all, although he knows them to be locked up in a trunk in his Yalta home. His wife, an actress, is fussing, talking to doctors, rushing here and there with a creased brow. This is a different room in a new hotel—they had to leave the last one, as his coughing was keeping up the other guests—and Olga has yet to figure out the staff. She catches him watching her and comes to sit beside him, looking very composed, but no one ever looks that calm, and he knows she's playing the part: the wife who holds together in the face of adversity.

"I told the maid she had to stop that child from banging on the piano," she says.

He'd found the inexpert "banging" a kind of comfort, the tortured nocturnes in the glare of day a sort of insane serenade for the nearly dead, but clearly it has been working on Olga's nerves.

"What will you write next?" she asks. She's pretending he has a future. She bends to hear, as his voice is soft.

"A play," he says.

The characters are led by an explorer into the Arctic. He sees these hoary men, beards dripping with icicles, on the prow of a ship. They don't know where they're going, because explorers never do.

"What is the subject of this play?" she asks, the picture of a person with rapt curiosity. He prefers the face of exaggerated calm.

"Explorers," he says. He sees the thoughts play across her face. First, concern. If the play is about explorers, then there will not be a part for her. Second, she remembers he is dying.

He will never write this play. Even in his mind, the explorers are stuck in the ice, incapable of movement.

"Like Przhevalsky?"

He nods. He thinks of his explorers, looking out across the ice, with the glacial corridors creating a music of buffeting winds and hissing snow. He thinks of the winds of Sakhalin: he was there, although in the summer, all those years ago. But it is easy to imagine that place in winter. He sees the Gilyak standing in a group, waiting for the Russians to wipe them out, and the Ainu women with their tattooed faces—clown smiles, to keep them looking cheerful. And there are the men chained to wheelbarrows. He thinks of the priest who, he heard later, took a Gilyak woman as his common-law wife and disappeared into the margins of Siberia. Or Japan. His explorers are going somewhere cold, because consumptives love the winter and most often die in the spring. His explorers are looking for the eternal winter, and they will find it and bring him there.

He whispers, "Sakhalin."

Olga adjusts her mask. The initial concern (are disconnected words a prelude to the death rattle?) is replaced with a cavalier, conversational expression and posture. "Sakhalin," she says, "how grim. What will you have your characters do? Steal things? Murder people? Flog people? Be flogged? Hanged? Escape? Be apprehended? Be flogged again?"

She has read his book on Sakhalin.

"I suppose a lot could happen on Sakhalin. There's a lot of action. But what would the people talk about?" She shrugs. She's forgetting to act. For the first time in days, Olga is actually being Olga. "Honestly, Antoshka. Sakhalin? What kind of play would this be?"

He takes a moment to respond. He remembers the buzz of flies lifting off the drying fish at the Gilyak compound, Botkin's weaving march, the "O-one" of the man's flogging, the priest lifting his hands. He remembers how he found it difficult to sleep with the knowledge that when he exited his room, there would be no city, and he could walk into a seemingly conjured blankness if he strayed from the main road. There is a soft knock at the door. He remembers Sobolev the forger's large hands. The doctor stands casting his shadow. He remembers the smiling dogs. Olga politely waves the doctor away. He remembers the nailed picture of Pishchikov's wife. Olga looks at him, her aggravation its own kind of beauty. "This play—"

"A comedy," he says. For what else is there?

Acknowledgments

This book was a bit of an undertaking and although I'm glad to be standing back on solid land I do appreciate the journey. I had some help

I would like to thank Cathy Ciepela for suggesting, over the rim of a martini glass, that I check out what Chekhov had to say about Przhevalsky. Without her, I wouldn't have known about Chekhov's interest in explorers. At the time, I thought I was done with the book and sort of wanted to kill her, but now that it's finished, thanks! "On Sakhalin" would not look the way it does without the input of Katia Kapovich, who gave it a Russian read (a truly terrifying experience for me) and changed all the names of the minor characters—and a few other things—nudging it toward authenticity. To my dad, Dr. Jerry Murray, who, learning that I was writing a book about exploreres, gamely produced his undergraduate thesis on Hanno, having no idea whether it would be useful or not. It was. He also checked the accents for the Greek. And thanks to Arthur Kinney for his close read of "Full Circle Thrice" and for being the sort of man who knows that Dampier would not have frequented a pub but rather an alehouse.

And to my intrepid agent, Esmond Harmsworth, and my trusty editor, Elisabeth Schmitz, for their support and faith in my work. Also, thanks to Jessica Monahan for her comments and the copy editor, who drew the short straw on this one (how difficult could a collection of short stories be?) and, on top of everything else, fact checked the lot. And to my husband, John Hennessy, who is my first reader. And to my son, Nicholas Hennessy, who drew the image for the people on the stairs when we couldn't secure the rights for the photograph.